THE LAND OF LIMPING LAW
THE COMPLETE CASES OF
CALHOUN, VOLUME 1

THE LAND OF LIMPING LAW

THE COMPLETE CASES OF CALHOUN, VOLUME 1

EDWARD PARRISH WARE

INTRODUCTION BY
ROBERT SAMPSON

ILLUSTRATED BY
F.M. FOLLETT

COVER BY
LEJAREN HILLER

POPULAR PUBLICATIONS · 2021

TABLE OF CONTENTS

INTRODUCTION BY
ROBERT SAMPSON

WEST OF THE Mississippi lie the Sunken Lands of northern Arkansas—a swampy tangle of mud, snakes, vines matting together a density of bushes and trees. Here channels of black water wind. Mosquitoes cloud. There are shanties by carpets of lily pads and shabby boats. The sun is heavy and the humidity strangles.

Over the Sunken Lands hovers the thick stench of vegetation decaying in heat. Through the tangle prowl quaint old swamp rats, inseparable from their rifles. And here slink thieves, murderers, and such blood-soaked riff-raff as add violence to a frontier environment.

The scene is ferocious. And through it moves Ranger Jack Calhoun, Chief Inspector of the U.S. Rangers, his beat the Sunken Lands. Calhoun's official title varies, but he, himself, does not change. He is the lead character in Edward Parrish Ware's short story series that was published in *Flynn's Weekly* and *Flynn's Detective Fiction Weekly* from about 1926 to about 1935.

The stories are in that most simple of forms—the tale of the single good man against the forces of lawlessness. Packs of human vermin, in this case. Out into the wilderness.

Ranger Calhoun paddles. His mission is simple: Bring in those killers.

Since their condition on return is specified, Calhoun brings them in dead, often as not. He wears a pair of .45 revolvers and carries a rifle. Since these are stories of danger and violent action, his weapons grow white-hot through the chapters.

At the series' beginning, the action is not so lethal. In "One Good Man" (September 18, 1926), Calhoun goes after a pack of thieves who fled into the swamp. Sheriff Lundsford, the resident thick-head, red-necked, blow hard, collects a posse and paddles fiercely off in the wrong direction.

Calhoun reasons out where the quarry is, then slips down on them by night. He slugs them down, one by one, shooting only once. Then brings the whole batch back to the glory of the U.S. Rangers.

You expect this sort of competence from Calhoun, who once remarks that he is "hard-boiled without much conscience."

That isn't Calhoun's real opinion of himself. It's something Edward Ware read in *Black Mask* and thought it would be nice added to Calhoun's character. For Calhoun is tough but not hard-boiled. Not really. He is too sympathetic to young love and feminine feelings to be without conscience. On the whole, he's a competent professional of the type described as "bad news."

In "The Negative Clue" (November 20, 1926), he Sherlocks around the swamp, pondering why Old Razorback, who has been arrested for a double murder, didn't just throw the bodies into the mud. Why did he try and bury them?

Because he didn't do it, obviously.

If that story is run-of-the-mill, "The Panther" (July 9, 1927) is hard-nosed, unblushing suspense. It moves at an unrelenting pace—no introspection, no psychological finesse, no complex character building.

Just a continuous pressure of danger, fear, and physical violence.

That infamous outlaw, The Panther, is running amok in The Devil's Bowl region. Calhoun is ordered to bring him in. And The Panther's gang, too, while you're at it. Thereafter, Calhoun:

—finds a wounded man, almost dead, marooned on a mud island in the swamp.

—is fired on by an ambusher with a rifle.

—disguises himself as a swamp rat and bluffs his way into The Panther's camp.

—is interviewed by the tough leader, who conceals himself in shadow, only his white hands showing in the lamp light.

—discovers an imprisoned woman.

—gun fights his way free.

—returns with a horde of Rangers for a brutal fire-fight and slaughter of the outlaws.

—discovers that the man he saved on the mud island was actually The Panther, displaced of command by the more bloody faction of his outlaws.

—allows The Panther and his sweetheart to escape, since they assure him that they have reformed.

Although faint elements of mystery occur, this is basically an old-fashioned adventure story. In another climate, Hopalong Cassidy could have handled the same assignment in the same way and with equal gusto.

"The Grave on Number 10" (August 10, 1929, *Detective Fiction Weekly*) tells how an old drunk sees a night murder and burial out on a mud island. He blabs about this at all the bars, ends up in that same grave. Calhoun, full of intuition, locates the grave and uncovers a clever identity switch and a second murder.

From mid-1929 on, the stories cease their effete posturing and hunker down to straight blood and violence. "The Red Record" (September 14, 1929) suggests that Dunn had been mightily impressed by Hammett's "The Gutting of Couffignal" (*Black Mask*, December 1925). The Jungle Butcher, a crazy outlaw, has declared war on the Arkansas river counties. He is methodically murdering and burning his way along the Mississippi.

The first part of this story sounds as if it were rewritten from a Western Story novel. It is full of horses, six-guns, posses. Horsemen gun down the only witness. In an old, board hotel, Calhoun walks into a gun trap. Pistol battle in the halls. A henchman grips his bullet-smashed arm. From a horse-drawn cab, a treacherous shot. Then the mysterious girl is whirled away.

So far, this is another job for Hopalong Cassidy. Now, however, the story veers toward the Mississippi. Trailing the girl, Calhoun comes to a wharf, is attacked by a gang. He battles free. Escapes in a boat. Is alone on the River.

Almost drowns.

Blunders into the Headquarters of The Jungle Butcher by luck. Is captured. Tied up.

The Butcher announces that he will attack and destroy Barfield's Point. After that, he will amputate Calhoun's hands and nail them above his door.

Down the river they swoop, about 150 men on a couple of riverboats.

At Barfield's Point, they rage ashore.

It's like old days at Northfield, Minnesota. The Rangers are waiting there, a rifle in every window.

Massacre.

While the streets fill up with smoking brass, Calhoun saws loose his bonds on broken window glass. Grabbing up a gun, he cleans up on those of the gang surviving the ambush. He captures The Butcher and the story ends with the banners of Good floating high.

As the 1930s progressed, the Calhoun stories gradually shortened. Stripped-down plots packed in ever more action. In "Calhoun's Way" (January 18, 1930), the sheriff suspects a meek bookkeeper of robbing a bank. But Calhoun grows a set of whiskers and runs down the real robber, just as he's sailing off for a new and merry life.

"Satan's Sink-Hole" (August 25, 1934) redoes the opening of "The Panther," although in summary. A masked man has marooned this poor naked fellow on a mud island. "Sign these papers or die." But Calhoun has been investigating back at the poor guy's cabin. Through the swamp he comes, just in time to gun down the leering fiend and save valuable timber rights.

Now the stories are published less frequently and are more familiar. They melt into the great pulp magazine sound. Violence haunts Calhoun. Everywhere danger lurks. Let his attention wander and his skull is slammed.

Searching the swamp for missing men, he finds a dead man peacefully leaning against a tree. ("Killer in the Cane," January 19, 1935.) Immediately Calhoun is slugged, pitched into a bottomless bog. Using his belt, tie, and a helpful tree branch, he barely escapes. Is immediately recaptured and imprisoned in a shanty. There a smart city gangster has terrorized a girl and her father into hiding him out. He is running a buried treasure racket, luring fools into the swamp and killing them for their money.

The girl frees Calhoun. But they are trapped in the cabin. The gangster has set fire to the place and lurks outside, his weapon cocked. While the murderer gloats, Calhoun slips through the roof and kills him with a single, long-range pistol shot.

Down into black swamp water the blood runs. Over the corpse, Calhoun stands, tanned face expressionless. In the silence, a fish splashes. Circular rings spread silently across polished water. Another cartridge, another death, another triumph for Inspector of U.S. Rangers, Jack Calhoun.

It grows dark. Over the body, Calhoun stands motionless. He will not move until the next story. He stands immobile, without feeling, lifeless as the corpse at his feet. In 1926, he was a vigorous, if shallow figure. In 1935, he is an efficient killer, one among many in the bloody pulps. Here he will stand, unchanging, waiting, until Edward Parrish Ware feeds another sheet of paper into the typewriter and the story begins again.

— Robert Sampson

CALHOUN PLUGS A HOLE

*It Was Easy Enough To Understand
One-Shot's Version Of The Killing, But
The Evidence Offered Better Proof*

1

JACK CALHOUN, UNITED STATES Ranger stationed at
Hell Hole, glanced at the little tin clock on its wall bracket,
noted that it lacked fifteen minutes of midnight, estimated
with an appraising eye that the oil in the lamp would last
another hour, and settled to his book again.

When Hell Hole was not extremely noisy it was very
quiet, and since Hubbard Wheeler, ranger chief, had ruled
that Jeptha Cluggage's saloon must close at ten each night,
the community usually settled down at that hour. When
Calhoun glanced at the clock, the night was so still the
bullfrog chorus in the placid St. Francis sounded as though
it might be in the room with him.

He read on. Presently the lamp wick flared a smoky warning, and he closed his book regretfully. Again he glanced
at the clock. Half past twelve! How that three-quarters of
an hour had flown!

B-o-o-o-m-m-m-m!

Calhoun sat motionless while one might have drawn
a deep breath, then sprang to his feet, automatically
slipped his six-gun out of its holster, tried the hammer,
and dropped it loosely back again. Then he snatched his
hat from the table, extinguished the light with a breath,
and slipped silently out of doors.

Hell Hole's quiet had been shattered by a pistol shot,

As Potter placed a lamp on the counter, the
ranger approached a window behind it

muffled and prolonged, and the ranger knew from past
experience that trouble was afoot. A faint moon shim-
mered in the river at his back, and dimly lighted the big
clearing around the edges of which the villagers' stilt cabins
stood. Not a light showed anywhere, and nothing moved
in the big circle.

Calhoun's eyes sought the squat, log saloon at the
extreme north end of the place, and found it dark. The trad-
ing post, in the center of the clearing, came next, and as his
glance touched the front a faint light flickered in its cavern-
ous interior and, simultaneous with its appearance, an eerie
wail, a woman's cry of horror, sent him racing forward. He
vaulted to the high veranda and plunged against the door,
to find it unyielding.

Again came the scream, and Calhoun leaped to a
window, cleared the glass from the frame with a sweep of
his booted foot, and stepped inside. The big room, redolent
of groceries, hides, and other odorous merchandise usually
to be found in a swamp general store, was dark except for

a yellow flame flickering in the west end. He made out the form of a young woman in nightdress, her tumbled hair framing a white, frightened face. It was Mary Enloe, the trader's daughter, and only kin.

"Mary!" he called sharply. "It's Calhoun! What's happened?"

The girl gave a low wail, and came toward him, her candle causing weird shadows to trail over the floor.

"It's pappy!" she gasped. "He's—he's dead!"

Calhoun snatched the candle from her hand and went swiftly to the back of the room, almost stumbling over the body of a man who lay upon the floor. He bent down, peered critically at the blood-stained, bearded face of Seth Enloe, noted the big, round hole in the center of his forehead, then turned in time to drive back the crowd of half dressed natives who at that moment surged into the store.

"Stay where you are—all of you!" he ordered sharply. "Potter," he added, picking out a lank trapper who combined undertaking with his other duties, "light the lamps, and bring one here."

Potter hastened to obey, while a woman from the crowd led Mary Enloe into her room at the back.

A man pushed through the throng at the door, and came to Calhoun's side—a tall, blond giant. He spoke quietly, but with suppressed excitement.

"I'd like to go inside," he said. "Mary will be wantin' of me."

It was Len Barrett, the freighter, and Mary Enlow's lover, Calhoun bade him go ahead.

Potter placed a lamp on the counter, and the ranger

approached an open window behind it; a hinged affair, opening inward.

"No taint of burned powder here," he reflected, sniffing the air. Then his glance sought and found the trader's strong box, a steel chest such as express companies use, which stood on the floor behind the counter about five feet east of the window. The lid was up, and the box seemingly empty. A second glance disclosed a bright object on the bottom, and he withdrew a large, new chisel from it. He held it in his hand for a moment, then dropped it back. Something on the counter in front of the box then attracted him, and he noted a short crowbar lying there. Like the chisel, it had been taken from the stock.

Something else drew his attention. In the southwest corner of the room the trader had been wont to stack dry hides, awaiting removal to his warehouse. The stack, he noted, now lay in a tumbled heap on the floor.

"Is—is Seth daid?" came a question from the crowd.

"Yes!" Calhoun replied. "Clear out, all of you! You can do no good here, and you may do harm. Potter, you and One-shot Hendricks remain. You will be needed. Cluggage," he went on, addressing the tall, black-coated saloon-keeper, who stood near, "you are familiar with telegraph instruments. Go to my cabin and notify Captain Wheeler, at Oak Donnick. He'll send word on to the county seat."

Cluggage hurried out, and the rest of the crowd followed more slowly. They were loath to go, but in the year since Calhoun had come among them they had learned that he expected his orders to be obeyed—and that trouble always came to those who showed an inclination to argue or dispute.

The ranger then made a thorough examination of the corpse. Seth Enloe had risen from his bed and gone into the store from his room in the south side of the building, not taking time to dress. He carried a lighted candle and, ten feet inside the room, had dropped dead from a bullet wound, the missile passing clear through his head. In all likelihood he had not seen his slayer, as he would have been in darkness.

"Take him into his room," Calhoun bade the two who had remained. "Then tell Mary to come here."

As soon as they had passed out with their burden, he seized the lamp, closely scanned the floor beneath the window, the adjacent counter, then held the light outside the window and examined the ground below. When he turned to Mary Enloe, who came in directly, his face wore a grim expression.

"A few questions, Mary," he said gently.

"Sit down."

He placed a chair for her, then sat on an edge of the counter.

"It's necessary, or I should not do this," he went on. "But you are brave, I know, and it will soon be over."

"I'm ready to answer," came the low-voiced reply.

"The pistol shot awoke you?"

"Yes," she replied.

"How long after that before you entered the store?"

"I went into pappy's room, as soon as I heard th' shot, and saw that he was not in bed. Then I noticed th' do' into th' sto' was open, an' I went in. Th' place was dark, and I went back and lit a candle. Then I saw pappy on th' flo', an' knew he was dead. I screamed, and sort of lost my senses, an' th' next thing I knew you-all was callin' to me."

"You saw nobody when you came in?"

"Nobody."

"Did you hear any sound—like, maybe, a man would make climbing through a window?"

"I didn't hear a thing," was the positive answer.

"How about the window—was it closed when your father went to bed?" Calhoun changed the direction of his queries.

"Yes. I closed it, as usual, and put th' peg in th' hole in th' sash, to keep it from swinging back on its hinges."

"Are you sure?"

"Yes. I remember, because the string the peg hangs by when th' window is open, broke, and I aimed to fix it with another, come mornin'."

Calhoun nodded. "It is certain, then, that the window was closed," he conceded. "Take a look at those hides in the corner."

The girl did so, then exclaimed:

"Why—they're all-scattered! They wasn't thataway when we closed up!"

"I thought not," Calhoun commented. "Now, how much money was in the strong box?"

The girl considered that for a moment, then replied.

"About two thousand dollars. Pappy had it on hand to buy hides with. There's always a bunch comes in late in th' spring."

"I want you to be very certain of your next answer, Mary," Calhoun cautioned. "It means a lot. Did your father have any enemies that you know of?"

"He was a friend to everybody," she answered, a sob in her voice. "If there was a single man that wasn't a friend to him he didn't know it! Of course, there's them as pappy beat out in business, but they'd hardly do him dirt!"

"That is all," Calhoun told her. "I want to get all the information possible, so as to be ready for Lundsford when he comes in. You may go back to your room now, and it will be best not to open the store or allow anybody to enter it until after the sheriff gets here. You'll understand why later, and I am going to expect you to obey to the letter."

"I will!" Mary assured him. "Do you think that whoever it was that killed pappy done it because he was an enemy? It looks to me like he just wanted the money."

"You may be right," was the ranger's reply as he dismissed her.

After the girl retired, Calhoun secured a hammer, broke up a packing case and nailed strips over the window he had wrecked. Then he made a minute examination of the section where the tragedy had been enacted—particularly in the vicinity of the window, after which he passed out by a rear door. Going to the north side of the big building he examined the sod beneath the window through which the killer must have leaped, searching about carefully by the light of a candle. The ground there was torn up, as Calhoun had expected it would be. He glanced toward the near-by forest, mentally estimating the time it would take an agile man to reach cover after dropping to the ground.

"He was safely hid before I was outside of my cabin," was the conclusion.

The houses which circled the big clearing all showed lights, and here and there small groups were congregated.

Calhoun passed inside his own shack, replenished the oil in the lamp, and sat in thought until daybreak. At last he stretched himself, got up and set about getting breakfast, a queer gleam in his eyes.

"You may come when you will, Mr. Sheriff Lundsford," he said under his breath. "I'm ready for you!"

2

A GLANCE OVER Hell Hole settlement would give one no idea of its importance. A big log store building at the foot of Lake St. Francis, where the river leaves it on its southward trend, set in a clearing surrounded by enormous cypress trees; a score of stilt cabins scattered in careless lack of design on both sides of the store and in the edge of the clearing; one log building, housing Cluggage's saloon; the St. Francis, wide, sluggish and crystal clear, circling it close up on the east—such is the physical aspect of the Hole. Its importance begins to emerge only when its reason for existing becomes apparent, and its remoteness from civilization is taken into account.

Cultivation on the outer rim of the Sunken Land country, in Arkansas, in driving the game animals toward the heart of the swamp, automatically vanquished the trappers and hunters—the native dwellers. They withdrew into the bottom of the great bowl, to continue their hereditary pursuit. Civilization could not crowd them there; they were secure, bulwarked by many miles of low ground cut by sloughs and bayous and the many-channeled St. Francis, hidden behind an almost impenetrable wall of trees.

Seth Enloe saw his big chance when the natives began to migrate, and established a trading-post at the foot of St, Francis Lake, and thenceforth there was no need for the swampers to make the thirty mile trip to Marked Tree. He was fair in his dealings, and it was not long before he controlled the entire take of the trappers of the district and, in addition, sold them their supplies.

Merchants in Marked Tree, who had enjoyed that lucrative business in the past, sought in every way to regain it, but Enloe's position was secure; none could dislodge him. A costly effort to compete with him on his own ground had proven financially disastrous, and Jeptha Cluggage, who had sponsored the rival store, thereafter set up his saloon. That was a part of the swamp trade Seth did not want. He had come to stay, and he throve mightily.

Respect for law, never very pronounced in the swamper at best, was altogether lacking in the settlement. Men quarreled, fought, killed, and went about their business undisturbed. When a man was slain no coroner was notified, nor was the sheriff at Jonesboro informed. The corpse was buried, and that ended it.

When the news reached the ears of authority the sheriff, accompanied by a squad of heavily armed and nervously alert deputies, visited the place and made a great show of taking charge. The natives did not invite him, and there was never a welcome for him. His life, and the lives of his associates, were safe only so long as they contented themselves with making a big stir—and doing nothing.

After a time—a few days or a week at longest—the law party would depart, wisely shaking their heads and promising much. Nobody was fooled by such activities, and nobody was alarmed. Furthermore, no offender ever was taken downriver by the sheriff to answer for his crime.

Then Hubbard Wheeler and his rangers were sent into

Sunken Land country to establish governmental authority there. Within a short time offenses against the government were few and far between—inevitable capture and
punishment awaited the man who made illicit whisky, stole
government timber, disturbed the colonists the land office
was instrumental in locating inside the swamp, or, in short,
ran counter to the Federal laws.

State and county offenses, however, were different. The
rangers never interfered in local matters, though they were
at all times available should they be appealed to by the
county. That seldom occurred, and usually resulted unsat-
isfactorily. In time Wheeler and his men came to realize
that local officers were concerned mostly in administering
their offices in the populous centers. The denizens of the
waste lands could take care of themselves.

When Calhoun was sent to Enloe's Settlement—a
designation long since lost in the fitter one of Hell Hole—
relations between government officers and local authorities
were in that condition characterized by the word strained.
They continued so. Calhoun's growing popularity with the
natives, hard won and jealously cultivated, was a thorn in
Sheriff Lundsford's side, and he had consistently ignored
the ranger's well-meant offers of assistance when necessity
called him into the settlement.

Finally Lundsford complained to Wheeler at Headquarters House on Oak Donnick, twenty miles from Hell
Hole, that his man Calhoun was interfering. Wheeler,
knowing the circumstances, instructed the ranger to have
as few contacts with the sheriff as was possible. There the
matter rested, or seemed to rest.

But Calhoun was laying for Lundsford, awaiting his

chance. In the death of Enloe it looked as though the opportunity was at hand. There was no animosity on the ranger's part. He was determined to bring about a better state of affairs in Hell Hole, and only by downing Lundsford could the thing be accomplished.

It was in the mid-afternoon of the day of the killing that the put-put-put of a motor boat told the ranger that Lundsford had come, and he went to the landing while the officers—half a dozen of them—disembarked.

"Well, Cal!" the sheriff called, with attempted jocularity, "your fellow citizens have been cutting up rough again, it seems!"

Calhoun nodded a greeting to the deputies, then turned to Lundsford. "Somebody has killed a mighty good man," he said. "And it's up to you to make him pay for it. Seth Enloe was a valuable citizen."

Lundsford grunted an unintelligible reply and walked off toward the trading-post, where he was admitted by Mary Enloe. Calhoun followed the party inside.

3

THE SHERIFF, POMPOUS in his high-roller hat and black frock coat, strolled about the store, particularly that part where the killing had occurred, asking questions all the while.

Mary Enloe's story was a repetition of the one she told Calhoun. She could add nothing to it.

"Hum! I see! Yes, it's perfectly clear!" Lundsford declared after he had viewed the body. "Plain case of theft, turned into murder because of interruption and threatened capture. No doubt about it. Well, we'll do the best we can." He turned to Calhoun, who had been a silent observer. "What you got to say, Cal? You was first on the scene. Notice anything worth mentioning?"

"Nothing that you can't see for yourself, if you'll look," was the reply. "Except that Enloe's body lay on the floor, where I afterward made that chalk mark you have doubtless observed, everything is just as it was when I entered."

"Humph! Thought you'd 'a' laid the killer by the heels long before now," Lundsford commented sneeringly. "Can't expect us poor, untaught hounds to pick up a cold trail when you couldn't follow it hot!"

"I haven't said I didn't follow it," Calhoun reminded him quietly. "Time was when I would have hurried to you with my tips, but since you have requested Wheeler to stop me from 'interfering' that has changed. I saw that you were notified immediately, and that's as far as I will go—with you."

Lundsford shot him a malignant glare. "Aim to hold back your tips, and try to show somebody up, huh?" he grated.

"I am going to try to plug the hole your dodging of the issue leaves open for criminals to escape through," Calhoun said, looking at him levelly. "This store—the entire settlement, for that matter—is on Government ground, and Seth Enloe was a duly acting postmaster for the district. It won't take much stretching to make this a Government case. There are leads enough here, if you'll take the trouble to look for them—two, in particular, that ought to nail your man for you. Good hunting to you!"

With that he turned on his heel and walked out.

Half an hour later Lundsford appeared in the ranger's cabin.

"We've decided to stay on for awhile, Cal," he said. "May be something doing round here pretty soon. Guess we'll have to put up with you, if you ain't got any objections."

Calhoun waved his hand toward the bunks which lined two sides of the cabin. The post had been fitted out to accommodate reenforcements should they be needed.

"Plenty of bunks," he replied. "You can rustle blankets from the store, and grub too. I suppose Mary will get somebody to open up at once, seeing that it's the only Store here. Maybe she will run the business until she can sell out."

"Sure," the sheriff agreed. "I told her to go ahead, and she's got that chap Barrett to help her. Feller that done

Seth's freighting down to the Tree. Guess they'll make it all right."

The deputies came in, and half an hour later they had secured bedding and provisions, to be quartered on Calhoun until further notice.

They had hardly got settled when the ranger, looking out across the clearing, saw One-Shot Hendricks coming toward the cabin. The bearded swamper was accompanied by four others, and presently they stepped inside.

"Sheriff," One-Shot began, "us folks is int'rusted in findin' out who done kilt Seth—an' we thinks we knows."

Calhoun pricked up his ears. For the first time within his knowledge the citizens of Hell Hole were putting in with the law. In the background he listened attentively and wonderingly.

"How's that, Hendricks? Think you know, eh?" Lundsford was surprised, too—and patently pleased. "All right! You name him and we'll take him! Who do you accuse?"

"We ain't accusin' of nobody," One-Shot stated, "but we thinks Len Barrett done it!"

"Len is the chap you spoke of, Lundsford—the freighter," Calhoun said quietly. "Engaged to marry Mary Enloe, report has it, and has it correctly I believe."

"Len is the one we suspects!" Gabe Halton, a lank, ague-ridden native, declared. "We want him took down to th' county seat an' locked up fur it, too!"

"Let's don't be too fast!" Lundsford ordered. "What makes you think Len Barrett did it?" he asked One-Shot.

"It's like this: Seth war a keen minded man, an' he made a heap of money, fust and last. Some says a hundred thousand dollars wouldn't cover it. I don't know about that, but

I do know that he went to Jonesboro five year ago an' had his will drawed up by a lawyer thar. He left everything to his gal, Mary, an' in th' will he app'inted two Jonesboro men as guardeens, and had th' will read so Mary couldn't handle th' prop'ty ontel she war twenty-fo' year old.

"Now Mary begun pesterin' her pap to move outten th' swamp, atter he had made what she said war a-plenty of money to live in a better place, but Seth wouldn't hear to it. Then she wanted to marry up with Len an' go out with him. Asked her pap to give them a lot of money to git started with, an' Seth wouldn't hear to that.

"Now, here's what makes us suspeecious of Len: Mary Enloe come twenty-fo' a month ago, an', in case Seth died then, she could do as she pleased with th' prop'ty. Then somebody up an' kilt Seth. If them sarcumstances don't p'int straight to skullduggery, then I don't know a skunk-hide frum a bed-quilt, an' all th' rest of us don't neither!"

"One-Shot has said it!" Gabe declared. "And we stands behind it!"

"Looks bad, I'll say!" Lundsford agreed. "Len Barrett would profit through the girl!"

"Len war here las' night," One-Shot urged. "And, fuddermo', he war at th' sto' ontel late bedtime. Then he went to his cabin an' war seed to leave it right atterwards, goin' towards th' sto'—an' sneakin' along! It wa'n't mo' than a hour later that Seth war kilt. When Len come a-runnin' from his cabin, atter th' killin', he war full dressed—an' he war th' only man amongst us that was!"

Lundsford leaped to his feet. "By George!" he exclaimed, "I believe you fellows have got the right of it! Yes, I believe there's evidence enough—"

He stopped short and eyed the natives.

"Say," he began, "what about taking Len out of here? How are the rest of the folks going to act—"

"They ain't goin' to do nothin'," One-Shot said aggressively. "Len's guilty, an' we-all aim to see that he gits punished fur it! We-all will help you!"

"That offer ought to be enough to tell you that there's something dead up the creek, Lundsford," Calhoun spoke up, scorn edging his voice. "Take my advice and pass it up!"

"You keep your trap closed!" Lundsford snapped. "I can run this without your help!"

"Go ahead!" Cal bade him. "But you'll need my help before you get Len Barrett out of here—and don't make a mistake about that!"

"Where is Len?" Lundsford demanded.

"Over in his cabin!" said Gabe.

"Then we'll go get him!"

Calhoun followed the crowd across the clearing to the cabin occupied by the young freighter. He meant to be present all the way.

Lundsford called a halt directly in front of the house, the door of which was closed.

4

"HEY, BARRETT!" SHERIFF Lundsford bellowed. "Come out here!"

The door opened a crack, and a calm voice inquired:

"What you-all want with me?"

"Come out!" Lundsford told him. "Else we'll come after you!"

Crack!

A puff of smoke and flame spouted from the doorway, and Lundsford heard a bullet sing past his head. He ran for cover, followed by his deputies and the natives. Calhoun alone stood his ground.

"Come an' git me, you damn skunks!" Barrett yelled after the departing ones. "You may do it—but I'll sink lead in the next man that tries!"

"Barrett!"

Calhoun's voice was crisp and clear. He waited.

"Well, Mr. Calhoun, what do you-all want?"

"I want to talk with you, inside your cabin, and I promise not to attempt to arrest you. I'll leave my gun here on the ground, if you say so."

There was a moment's silence. Then the door opened a bit wider. "I know you-all, Mr. Calhoun, an' you can come in," Barrett told him. "But if anybody else tries it he gits kilt—an' I mean it!"

"You are accused by One-Shot and a few others of killing Seth Enloe," Calhoun informed the freighter, when he
stood inside. "You didn't do it, of course. Still, there's no
use resisting the law. At best you can't be tried until the fall
term of court, and that's nearly six months away. Before
that time I'll have the goods on the real murderer. I won't
promise, understand, but I'm thinking you won't even have
to leave with Lundsford. You may, though. Will you go?"

"Good God, Mr. Calhoun!" Barrett cried. "Who
done laid that charge ag'in' me? Who besides that dawg,
One-Shot—"

"Never mind!" Calhoun broke in. "They mean to arrest
you, and if you resist and kill somebody you'll have to
answer to a charge of murder that can be proven. Lundsford is an officer, after all. Go quietly, and I'll give you my
word no harm shall come to you. Resist and there's no telling what may happen."

There was a long silence, during which Len considered
the matter. "I see what you mean," he said at length. "If I go
now I'll not be hurt. If I resist I'll have to do some killin',
an' then I'll git hanged certain. Well, tell 'em that I want to
see Mary first, then I'll say what I'll do!"

"Fair enough!" Calhoun approved. "I'll send Mary over."

He sought Lundsford, and found him behind a cabin
about a hundred yards away. "I'll hand your man over to
you," he said, "on two conditions. One is that you let him
alone until he's ready, and the other is that you do not
attempt to take him out of here to-night. What say?"

"I say it seems like you are taking a mighty high hand—"

"You want your man, don't you?" Calhoun snapped.

"Of course I do!" Lundsford declared.

"That's the only way you can get him—alive!"

"Well, have it your way," Lundsford agreed. "Anything to avoid bloodshed. But tell Barrett that I won't take any fooling!"

Half an hour later Calhoun, accompanied by Len and Mary, left the freighter's cabin and approached the ranger station. Len was dressed for a journey, and Mary, red-eyed from weeping, clung to his arm.

"Here's your man, Lundsford," Calhoun called, stopping outside. "You can keep him in my place—and you needn't put the irons on him. He'll stand hitched! Come, Mary!"

He led the girl away and sat on the veranda of the store talking to her until nightfall. Then he sought One-Shot Hendricks in his cabin.

"Lundsford wants to see you, and Gabe, and a few other of the prominent citizens—Jep Cluggage and Hugh Soule, among them," he informed the swamper, with a pointed emphasis on the word "prominent." "Let 'em know about it, and all of you come to my cabin in half an hour."

"What's it about?" One-Shot desired to know.

"About the charge against Len, of course," Calhoun replied. "You be there—understand?"

Next he visited a number of the other cabins in rapid succession, his movements masked by darkness. In each of the places visited he spoke a few words to the head of the family. Before the specified half hour was up he was again at his own Cabin.

"Lundsford," he informed the officer, "a committee will call here very shortly, thinking you summoned it. I did—in your name. When the members arrive I shall seat them together on that bench against the north wall," he indicated the spot, "and I want you and your men to occupy chairs in an opposite corner—you may thank me for that precaution later. Anyhow, that is what I want you to do."

"What's going on?" Lundsford demanded, beginning to bristle. "What's the meaning of this?"

"You'll know pretty quick now," Cal replied. "Here comes the committee."

One-Shot and the others filed in. All those named by the ranger were present, mystified but obedient.

"Sit on that bench, all of you!" Calhoun ordered.

They glanced inquiringly at Lundsford. "I thought the sheriff was running things over here," Cluggage said grumblingly.

"Me too!" declared One-Shot.

"Give Cal time, men! Give him time," Lundsford joked. "He's giving a little party to celebrate his birthday—"

"And the rest of the guests are outside!" Cal finished grimly. "Take a look out the window—but don't open the door! It would not be healthy!"

Lundsford and One-Shot peered outside, then the latter turned a puzzled face to Cal. "There's a lot of men out there—all with rifles!" he said uneasily.

"Yes—two dozen citizens, in a circle about the place," the ranger replied, addressing all. "They are from the decent element here—an element not represented in this room. They're there to see that no man leaves here until I give the word. Their orders are to kill any man who tries to cross the sill—and you can bet they'll do it!"

"What in hell—!"

"Shut up and sit down!" Calhoun turned on the sheriff, eyes blazing a warning. "From this minute on I'm running things here! The man who speaks out in this meeting will regret it the next instant! I'm not fooling, and anybody who thinks I am can try me!"

Lundsford subsided, and silence reigned in the room. There was a look in Calhoun's eyes, and a set to his jaw, that nobody but a fool would misconstrue. He stood in the center of the floor, the group of swampers directly in front of him, the officers on his left. Len Barrett, a dazed look on his face, sat alone on a bunk.

5

"**LUNDSFORD, PROMPTED BY** One-Shot Hendricks and others, arrested Len Barrett for the murder of Seth Enloe," Calhoun began slowly. "He had it pointed out to him that Len would benefit by Seth's death, through the daughter whom he means to marry. That supplied a motive. Where Lundsford made a mistake was in not considering the others who would profit by Seth Enloe's removal.

"There are others—former traders whom Seth's success put out of business. Three or four live in this district—any one of whom would welcome a chance to grab the big profits Seth has been making. I don't mean that all of those men are alike in wanting to get that profit through Seth's death, but I am saying that at least one of them felt that way about it. Remember that! I'm going to prove it to you pretty soon!

"In the meantime I'm going to describe to you just what occurred in the trading-post last night—move by move, act by act.

"A man—a money-loving creature without a conscience—one well enough known in the settlement to mix with the crowd at Seth's store at closing time, crept behind a stack of hides in the room when nobody was looking that way. He was a patient man, and he stayed there for nearly two hours after the place was closed. Then he crept out—brushing the pile of hides as he did so and scattering them over the floor. They made no noise to speak of, and after a bit he felt his way in the darkness to the window in the north wall.

"He was thoroughly familiar with the interior of the store, and could move about in the dark at will. Arrived at the window he withdrew the wooden peg which held it shut and opened it, thus preparing a way for a hasty exit. That done, he went to the cutlery case, got a big chisel out of stock, procured a small crowbar, and returned to the strong-box near the window. He placed the crowbar on the counter, inserted the chisel in the crevice between the lid of the chest and the front side, and pried up the lid at that corner. When he could get the point of the crowbar into the crevice he did so, and then laid the chisel on the counter. Working with the crowbar, having plenty of leverage, he cautiously exerted pressure, a little bit at a time, until the lock snapped. Then he placed the crowbar on the counter, raised the lid and took out two thousand dollars in bills. The theft was an accomplished fact.

"Now, if theft had been his only motive he would have dropped out that open window, and Seth would have known nothing about the burglary until morning. Did he do so? You all know that he did not.

"Here is what he did. He picked up the chisel again, crouched in the dark at the west end of the chest and below the window, then, with a large caliber pistol in his right hand, his eyes glued to the door through which he expected his victim to enter, he began pounding on the edge of the box with the chisel. Why? The purpose is obvious. He wanted to awaken Seth Enloe, and entice him into the room. He succeeded.

"Seth heard the noise, got up and investigated. Doubtless he had done the like before. Certainly he did not anticipate personal danger, for he was unarmed. In the hand which should have held a gun he carried a lighted candle—and by that light the man in the darkness could see him clearly enough to send a bullet through his brain. When Seth fell the murderer leaped through the window and disappeared in the woods. That is what happened."

Calhoun paused and glanced at the faces of those about him. They were pale and drawn, all of them, and the interest of his hearers was so intent they scarcely breathed.

"How do you figger all that, Cal?"

It was Lundsford who broke the silence.

"The scattered hides revealed the hiding place," the ranger replied, "and the fact that the window was opened from the inside indicated also that the thief had hidden inside. As for the rest, the crowbar would have been found on the floor had Seth interrupted the man at work. The chisel was the first tool used, yet I found it in the box, which showed that he had used it after the lid was up.

"What possible use could he have put it to? I read the answer on the edge near the handle. Numerous newly-made nicks in the steel. On the edge of the box nearest the window were small particles of bright metal, showing conclusively that he had pounded on the box with the chisel. Why? He wanted to make a noise, of course.

"Now, I'm going back to the moment when the killer crossed from the hide pile to the window. It's a hinged window, like all the rest in the settlement, and is held shut by means of a small peg placed in a hole in the frame back of the sash. All of you have such fasteners. When the window is open the peg hangs idle by means of a bit of string attached to a nail in the frame, one end of the peg being notched to keep the string from slipping. The killer removed the peg and was surprised to find that it was not attached to the frame. Mary Enloe had broken the string when she closed the window that night.

"He stood there for a second, the peg in his hand. He didn't want to drop it on the floor—it might make a bit of noise, and he wasn't ready for noise yet. The counter was some distance away, and there was no handy place to lay it. What did he do? Why he did the most natural thing in the world—what nine hundred and ninety-nine men out of a thousand would do!"

Calhoun paused, eyelids narrow, facing the group on the bench.

"What are pockets for, men?" he asked them. "He dropped the little peg into his coat pocket—and I'm betting that, like most men, he forgot the thing. It's in his pocket yet—"

Jeptha Cluggage's white face seemed to leap in front of the ranger's vision, excluding all others. His right hand swept toward his coat pocket—stopped. But he was too late—Calhoun had seen. He finished the downward sweep of his hand, touched his hip and swung his gun up.

Calhoun's gun crashed into the silence, vomiting smoke and flame, and Cluggage, his weapon useless in a palsied hand, tumbled to the floor—a hole in the center of his forehead.

"Up high with 'em, One-Shot!" The ranger's sharp call

broke the spell, and there was sudden movement in the room.

One-Shot stared through the smoke at the speaker, his eyes wide with terror and his hands above his head.

Calhoun strode to the man on the floor, drew a small wooden jeg from his pocket—a peg tied at one end with a bit of broken string.

"There's your killer, Lundsford," he said quietly. "One-Shot was his accomplice; His part to stir up feeling against Len, and cause you to arrest him. The law must have a victim—and Cluggage meant it to have Len." He paused, then looked the open-mouthed sheriff in the eyes. "This thing I hold in my hand, this little peg, is that plug I spoke to you about—and if it doesn't fit the hole I miss my guess."

It did.

Lundsford's popularity with the voters was not strong enough to withstand the assaults of ridicule and blame arising out of the Hell Hole case, and the new sheriff, finding the hole plugged up, kept it that way. Strangely enough, it was Ranger Calhoun's influence with the natives of the swamp lands that carried the successful candidate to victory, and Hell Hole, because of that same ranger, makes him welcome when he comes.

CALHOUN USES HIS HEAD

The Sheriff Was Stumped And The Coroner Was Mystified. But Calhoun Thought The Death Through And Proved His Theory

1

JACK CALHOUN, UNITED STATES Ranger, stationed at Hell Hole, removed his high-top laced boots, and substituted a pair of light gaiters. That done, he took two long buckskin thongs from a cupboard, and looped the end of one of them about his left ankle, folding his trouser leg snugly above his shoe top, and winding the thong around it, securing it in a knot just below the knee.

The right leg was treated similarly. It was a trick he had learned from the natives of the swamp lands, and experience had demonstrated its usefulness.

From the bottom of the same cupboard he took a pair of rubber boots, knee-length type, and tossed them on the floor beside his blanket roll, camp kit, and knapsack.

Selecting a rifle from the rack which formed a part of the ranger station's armament, he filled the magazine and slipped the arm into its waterproof case. His revolvers next underwent careful scrutiny, and later were also encased in waterproof holsters.

"Rain, and then more rain!" he exclaimed disgustedly, going to the door of the cabin and looking out toward the swollen St. Francis. "And the river already on the rise! Another twenty-four hours of this, and there won't be a patch of ground big enough to start a supper fire on in the whole Sunken Land country!"

He closed the door and walked over to a table which supported, among a clutter of odds and ends, a telegraph instrument. Digging it out, he got headquarters, at Oak Donnick, and sent a message to Hub Wheeler, his chief, twenty miles down the river.

"Off on four-day trip. Brush Lake section. Lot of fresh-cut logs drifting down on rise. Timber thieves working. Instructions?"

Such was the message.

"None. O.K." was Wheeler's answer.

Calhoun, slicker-clad, lugged his pack down to the river and dumped it in the bow of his dugout, stepped into the stem, and swung its nose upstream. He stood, wielding a long-handled paddle, his round-brimmed Stetson pulled low in an effort to shield his eyes against the hard-driven spring downpour.

"Hell Hole," he apostrophized, looking back at the cluster of stilt cabins that constituted the settlement, farthest outpost of the ranger organization, "you lack a lot of being tamed yet, though you're showing faint signs of dawning civilization. Hope you behave while I'm gone!"

In the heart of the great swamp which covers a corner of northeast Arkansas, far removed from anything even approaching effective supervision by law, Hell Hole was at best a wild, ungovernable spot in a well-nigh impenetrable hinterland which only the government could hope to conquer and reclaim.

No local authority availed there. In a measure, the presence of Calhoun, with the strength of the Federal government and Wheeler's efficient organization of hard-bitten battlers behind him, served to curb the tendencies of the

Tolbert's big frame was easily recognizable,
paddling the leading boat

lawless element at the Hole. Thefts of government timber, blockading, interference with government projects, and other offenses strictly Federal in their character, were reduced to what might be termed a minimum. State laws, however, might as well not have been.

"Except where major crimes are involved—murder, for instance—keep your hands off. Enforce Federal law. Let the State take care of its own."

Such were Wheeler's orders to his men, and they were obeyed.

The St. Francis was rising rapidly, the ranger realized when he passed the mouth of Little Caney, a tributary, and noted the immense volume of water the slough was bringing in.

Soon the parent stream would spread over its low, marshy shores—dangerous, then, to boatmen, and destructive to such settlers as had attempted to reclaim bits of interior lowland.

He glanced down at his taped trouser legs, and was glad he had taken the precaution those buckskin thongs represented. With the river rising and spreading out, a spill would be dangerous at best; with boots on, or with trousers flapping about his legs, absorbing water and weighting him down, drowning would probably result.

The light shoes and the buckskin ties were in the way of being life-preservers. Thus prepared, one could the more easily fight the current.

The St. Francis wound snakily through heavily timbered virgin country, with here and there a stilt cabin visible in its brushy setting. The downpour increased.

At noon the ranger went ashore, followed a dim footpath through the tangle, and ate dinner at the cabin of a native, Heck Tolbert, questioning him as to the state of the sloughs and bayous farther inland.

"Risin' fast," was the information. "Big rise, shore. Hope it don't come afore Greene Garner draps by an' takes my winter catch of hides often my hands. He's a leetle slow, this trip, account of so much water. Be along soon, though, I reckon."

Tolbert reckoned correctly. Just as Calhoun finished eating and lifted a live coal from the hearth to the bowl of his pipe, a hail outside announced the arrival of Garner, the hide buyer.

"Bring 'em out, Tolbert!" came the call. "I'll count 'em up, make an offer, and pick 'em up on the down trip!"

"Come in an' eat a snack, first!" the big trapper invited.

"This here law officer has left a few bites, an' you-all air shore welcome!"

Calhoun laughed, and got up to shake hands with a short, slim man of middle age, who showed up in the door.

"You must have been close behind me, Garner," he commented. "I beached here about half an hour ago."

"No. I've been up Little Caney, looking over the hide situation. Had to make a trip overland from the slough to Dave Suttler's place, and I'm not much of a hoofer—particularly when all the little creeks are running water. These trappers that live back from the river are nuisances."

He pointed to his gaitered feet and taped legs. The shoes were sodden, and the trousers, soaked to the calves.

"I carry a pair of rubber boots in my boat," Calhoun told him. "When I have to make a trip overland, through marshy ground, I put 'em on. Why don't you?"

"Usually do," Garner replied, "But I snagged my 'snag-proof' boots, last time up, and forgot to lay in a pair. Now I'm paying for it."

"Hayden keeps 'em, up at Deep Landing," Tolbert volunteered. "You can git a pair when you git thar."

"Reckon I will," the hide buyer told him. "And pay Hayden's price, which is half again as much as I'd have to pay in Marked Tree. Trouble is, I won't get to Hayden's for two days yet; too many side trips to make."

He laughed, and dismissed the subject of boots.

Calhoun departed, leaving the hide man eating fried catfish, and drinking hot coffee in the native cabin.

2

TEN DAYS LATER Calhoun stood on the doorsill of the ranger station, and looked out at the receding St. Francis. His trip up river had lasted four fruitless days spent in an almost continuous downpour.

If timber thieves were operating, as it seemed they were, their camp lay far interior, along some slough which the high water prevented him from investigating. However, the river was falling, the flood was over, and he could soon take up the search again.

A number of dugouts, moving in a group toward the landing at Hell Hole, and coming from up the river, attracted his attention, and the ranger walked over to the bank, eager for news of the upper country.

Heck Tolbert's big frame, topped by his mop of gray-streaked hair and tangle of beard, was easily recognizable at a distance; he paddled the leading boat—and towed an apparently empty one behind. The other boatmen were natives from the vicinity of Hayden's store, near the foot of Brush Lake.

The boats put in, and Calhoun noted that a strip of tarpaulin was spread over the towed dugout.

"Found a dead man floatin' above th' mouth of Little Caney," Tolbert announced gravely, as he stepped ashore.

"Been dead some time, probably back in th' brush; an' come out when th' water drapped."

"Know him?" Calhoun demanded, eying the covered boat.

"Well," Tolbert stated, "kain't say as I do. Pretty bad swole up. From his clothes, and such, I take him to be Garner, th' hide buyer. Him as war at my place th' day you-all war thar.

"He went on up river, sayin' he had to make a long trip up Black Bayou, an' would be on th' down trip in about a week.

"He didn't come, as fur as I knows, an' I reckoned he war helt up by th' high water. Take a look. You-all ought to reckernize him."

"It's Garner, right enough," Calhoun declared, spreading the tarpaulin back over the boat after a long look at the gruesome object it contained. "His clothes, for one thing. Another, he has on a pair of brand new rubber boots. Remember him saying he meant to buy a pair?"

"I do, now you mention it," Tolbert replied.

"Who found him?"

"I did," Pegleg Davis, a fisherman, spoke up. "Me and Davy Little war s'archin' fur some traps th' rise ketched, an' he come a floatin' in from th' timber. He come kind of slow like, lookin' like a log which war only showin' a leetle ways. 'Is it a log, or ain't it?' thinks I. Then I tuk a look, an' knowed it wa'n't no log."

"I knowed it wa'n't, too," Davy Little testified.

"Thar wa'n't a better swimmer, ner a better boatman on th' St. Francis than Greene," Ezra Pauley asserted. "Reckon it war th' rubber boots as got him. No man could handle hisself in th' high water, once them boots filled up. An' they'd dang soon fill, after he spilled."

"Pretty nigh as soon as he struck water," Tolbert agreed.

"Careless, him havin' boots on," commented another.

"He probably came to the river after a hike overland," Calhoun surmised, "and neglected to change back to his shoes. Had he done so, being a good swimmer, as he undoubtedly was, he could have made it to a tree, or some other place of safety, after he capsized.

"Those boots, though— Poor devil! I advised him to get a pair—and he did, just in time to die by them!"

Calhoun ordered the body removed to a vacant shack near by, one used in season to tar nets in; then reported by telegraph to Wheeler.

"Seems to be plain case of accidental drowning," he wired. "Garner had rubber boots on, capsized, couldn't swim with them hampering him."

"Will send undertaker from Marked Tree. Hold body for him. Anything suspicious?" came Wheeler's reply.

"Not a thing."

"So-long."

The ranger returned to the cabin in which the corpse lay, locked the door, and put the key in his pocket. Then he dismissed the party that had come down river, after taking the statements in writing of the two who had made the discovery.

"The coroner may come up with Spence, the undertaker, though I don't think it likely," he told them. "If he should do so, however, he may want you fellows. I'll send you word."

Spence came up next morning, and Coroner Steve Barrett came along.

"Reckon everything is all regular, Cal," said the latter, when the ranger had made his statement. "Spence wanted company, though, and I might as well have a look."

"Sure."

Calhoun led the way to the shack.

"He's been in the water too long to be recognizable," Barrett remarked, standing by the long table on which the body lay. "Looks a lot too big for Greene, but the swollen condition may account for that."

"That wouldn't affect his height," Calhoun reminded him. "Garner was about five feet eight, I'd judge."

The tape seemed to verify the supposition that the body the river had given up was that of the hide buyer. It measured a fraction under five feet eight inches. Later on a search of the clothing revealed further corroborative evidence.

A silver watch, well known as Garner's property; a pocketknife, readily identified by Spence, who was well acquainted with him, and a revolver, all tallied out. The remnants of clothing were like the various articles of apparel the hide buyer was known to have worn on the trip.

"Any money in the pockets?" Calhoun asked, eying the contents of the clothing which lay in a sodden jumble on a chair.

"None, except a few dollars in silver," the coroner returned.

"Wasn't he likely to have had considerable cash, out on the spring buying trip?" queried the ranger.

"Well, yes," Spence replied. "Sometimes, though, he paid in checks."

"Look for check books," Cal requested.

The inner pocket of the coat was found to hold one such book, and the ranger examined it.

"Queer," he commented, tossing the book onto the chair. "There are only half a dozen blanks in it. Such a trip as he was on would have required considerable outlay, and in numerous separate payments. Just the one book?"

"That's all," Barrett said. "Does seem queer."

"Damned queer," Calhoun agreed, with emphasis. "No money, and only a few blank checks—yet he was out to buy furs, and a lot of 'em."

"He may have already bought—"

"No. That wasn't his way," Spence interrupted. "Greene always made the trip upriver in his dugout, routing out the trappers and notifying them when he'd return with his barge. That was done in order to save time on the down trip; the sellers would have their furs out to the river bank.

"He kept his barge at Billing's Point, at the head of Brush Lake, and he certainly would not pay for hides until they were delivered on that barge. He usually carried plenty of cash with him from Marked Tree, because lots of the natives won't have anything to do with checks.

"I'd say that Greene probably had as much as three or four thousand dollars with him, in bills of all denominations, when he left for this trip. The roll might have dropped out of his pocket, after he fell into the river. Probably did."

"Might have been stolen, after the body was found," Barrett suggested.

"Davis and Little do not strike me as being the type of men who would rob a dead man," Calhoun objected. "I've been up here over a year, and there are, in my opinion, no better citizens than they in the section. They've had charge of the body since they found it, and I believe they did not search it. Still, the possibility is worth considering."

"I have never heard of anybody being held up and robbed in this section, either," Barrett commented. "Garner certainly never was bothered while alive, and he has traded around these parts for the past fifteen years. On second thought, I don't believe anybody would rob his dead body. More likely he lost the money out of his pocket when he spilled."

"Would a man be likely to carry as much as three or four thousand dollars so insecurely that it would fall out of his pocket easily?" Calhoun asked quietly.

"Well, you never can tell," Spence replied. "Greene was a careless sort, in some things. Witness him having boots on."

3

"BY GEORGE!" BARRETT exclaimed. "Let's get those boots off. He may have put his roll down in a bootleg. That would be a handy and a safe place for it."

It was necessary to literally cut the boots away, so badly swollen were the legs and feet of the corpse.

"No money here," Calhoun stated, after a thorough examination of the remnants. "And that settles it," he went on. "No matter what your official verdict is, Barrett, this case is going to be investigated. Garner carried money, that is certain.

"The fact can easily be determined beyond doubt, by inquiring at the bank he did business with in Marked Tree. He had not yet begun buying.

"Nobody has seen anything of the barge he kept at Billing's Point. I'll find out whether it ever left there. There is a faint chance, I'll admit, that he may have lost the money—but his roll was too big to be carried carelessly. I take it Garner was not exactly a fool."

"Well," Barrett replied, "I guess I might as well impanel a jury, then report my findings to Lundsford. If the sheriff thinks it's worth while—"

"Do so," Cal interrupted, shortly. "Do your part, and let Lundsford alone for his. I'll take charge of the clothing, and these articles taken from the body. They will be safe with me, and available when they are wanted.

"As for the body, it should be taken down to Marked Tree for an autopsy. Find out if there are any marks on it that might have caused death. Sometimes these accidental drownings turn out to be actual murders. Not likely, in this case—but enough has developed here to warrant every care being taken.

"I'll give Lundsford every assistance I can, when he gets up here—if he isn't too proud to accept aid. He usually is. He'll want to talk with every person known to have had contact with Garner in this section. I'll see that they are present. Guess that's all."

He left for his own quarters, carrying the personal belongings of Garner in a bundle. After storing them in a cupboard, and snapping the padlock, he filled a pipe and sat down, his brows knitted in thought.

An hour later he again called headquarters.

"Send man to Marked Tree," he requested of Wheeler. "Find out how much money Garner carried. What denominations, if known. Have him get pair of snagged boots belonging to Garner, if possible. Send him up here with them soon as can."

After that he settled down to wait.

In the afternoon of the following day, Ranger Murdock came upriver from Marked Tree. He brought a wrapped bundle, and a sealed envelope, which he turned over to Calhoun.

"Found the boots at Garner's house," he said, indicating the bundle. "The letter is from the City Bank, where the hide man did business."

Calhoun was already reading the letter, and consulting some figures it contained. While he was doing so, a call came from Wheeler.

"Lundsford will arrive to-morrow," the message ran. "Requests that you get witnesses for him. Any developments?"

"None positive," Calhoun replied. "Am off for Brush Lake. Am keeping Murdock."

A bit later, leaving Murdock in charge, he set out upstream, paddling swiftly.

SHERIFF LUNDSFORD ARRIVED at noon the next day, escorted by the squad of armed deputies that accompanied him on his rare trips into the Sunken Lands. He was in high ill humor to begin with; and the information that Calhoun was away after witnesses, and the time of his return uncertain, did nothing to assuage it.

About three o'clock Calhoun returned, bringing several swamp men with him—among others, Heck Tolbert, Pegleg Davis, Davy Little, and a native called Beeswax Brown. The latter lived several miles distant from the St. Francis, on the banks of Black Bayou.

Oscar Hayden, keeper of the store at Brush Lake, was also among those present. The latter had given Calhoun considerable trouble, when he first took over the district, in the matter of selling blockade whisky over the bar which was an adjunct of his general store, and was at the moment under indictment for selling illicit liquor.

His bearded face was heavily sullen when he stepped out of his dugout at Hell's Hole landing, and his small blue eyes smoldered with resentment he lost no time in voicing.

"I ain't got much stomach for this thing, Lundsford!" he

exclaimed, walking over to where the sheriff sat before the door of the ranger station. "I don't like bein' called away from my business, for just nothin' at all—somebody's damn fool idea that Greene Garner was dealt foul with! Whar did you-all get such a fool notion?"

"Ask Calhoun!" Lundsford snapped. "He's responsible for it! And keep a civil tongue in your head when you talk to me! I ain't any more pleased at having to waste my time than you are!"

"The Government will take over this matter any time you see fit to lay down on it, Lundsford," Calhoun said quietly.

Lundsford shot him a baleful glance, then proceeded to ask questions.

"I'll look into it, since I'm here," he replied. "First, what makes you think Garner might have been killed?"

"I have not said that I thought he might have been killed," Calhoun replied. "I say there is a strong probability of his having been robbed. When be left Marked Tree, *en route* upriver to buy furs, he carried four thousand dollars in bills, in denominations ranging from one dollar to fifty dollars.

"When his body was recovered, he had exactly three dollars and fifty cents in his pockets. He had bought no furs; he met death before he had completed his trip to the head of Brush Lake, where he keeps a barge; and the barge, with its two rowers, is still there. Where is the money?"

"Who found the body?" Lundsford demanded.

Pegleg Davis and Davy Little stepped forward.

"Did you search Greene when you found him?"

"Never touched him, more than to fasten a line on him

so we could tow him ashore," Davis answered, his face
showing anger. "And th' man that accuses me of robbin'
a dead body is due to have trouble, sudden an' complete!"

"Nobody accuses you," Lundsford reminded him. "What
did you do with the body?"

"We towed it ashore close to Heck Tolbert's place,
an' Davy went and fetched him down. Heck had a extry
dugout; so we loaded Greene in it an' brung him down here.
That's all I know."

Davy Little nodded in corroboration of his partner's
statement.

"Did you touch the body, Heck?" Lundsford asked.

"Not except when I holped lif' him into th' dugout," the
trapper replied.

"When did you see Greene last, alive?"

"About two weeks ago," Tolbert answered. "Th' day
Calhoun was at my place, goin' upriver, an' et dinner. Greene
come by to notify me to git my furs ready. Calhoun seed
him thar."

"What about it, Cal?" Lundsford queried, turning to
the ranger.

"Greene came to Heck's cabin just as I was on the point
of leaving. He had been inland, up little Caney, and his
shoes were soaked from wading. Said he had snagged his
boots on a previous trip, and had forgotten to get a new
pair. He had no boots with him that trip."

"Hadn't, eh?" Lundsford showed interest in that statement. "Where did he get the ones that caused him to
drown?"

"I sold 'em to him," Hayden said. "He come up to my

place about three days after he'd been to Heck's, and bought th' pair of shoes he had on when he got drowned."

"Did he say where he was going from there?"

"Up Black Bayou," came the answer. "He run past the bayou, an' come to git th' boots. Said th' water was gittin' too high, an' he'd need 'em."

"Was he alone when he came to your store?"

"Yes."

"Was that the last time you saw him?"

"Shore."

4

"ANYBODY ELSE HERE who saw Greene, either before he went to Hayden's or after?" Lundsford asked, addressing the crowd which had augmented in numbers since the inquiry began. Fully fifty natives were then grouped around.

"Several saw him before he went to Hayden's," Calhoun answered. "I talked with a number of them on my trip up after witnesses. None of them had anything unusual to offer. I'd like to ask a question of one of those who had contact with him, and whom I brought along."

"Go ahead," Lundsford permitted, openly bored with the whole proceeding.

"Beeswax Brown lives ten miles up Black Bayou," Calhoun stated. "He, among others, was called on by Garner, and all agree to what I'm going to have Brown tell you." He turned to the man in question. "When did you see Garner? Remember the date?"

"He war at my place six days afore the day he was found drownded," was the answer.

Calhoun addressed Lundsford. "That would be three days after I saw him at Heck's." He turned again to Brown.

"Did Greene have boots on when you saw him?"

"He did not."

"All who saw him on that trip up the bayou are agreed

that Garner had no boots," Cal informed the listening crowd. "Did he remark about the lack of boots?" he asked Brown.

"Yeah. Said he meant to git a pair when he got up to Hayden's."

"That's all," said Calhoun.

"Well, what about it?" Lundsford demanded. "What's that prove?"

"To my mind, it proves that Hayden is wrong in his statement that Garner bought the boots prior to his trip up Black Bayou."

"Well, what if he was? Can't a man be mistaken about a little thing like that, and still be honest in it?"

"No doubt," Cal told him. "I think, though, that the date of the purchase of the boots is not a small thing."

"Nothing is small, to hear you tell it!" Lundsford snapped, getting up. "Here's what I find: Greene was fool enough to wear rubber boots in his boat during high water time, capsized, and was drowned. His roll fell out of his pocket when he hit the water, and is somewhere down in the mud right now.

"I'm sorry to put all you fellows to unnecessary bother, and wouldn't have done it if I'd been let alone. Of course, when an investigation is demanded, I ain't got any choice.

"Not that I don't want to make all necessary investigations. I certainly do want to do my duty to the fullest. But sometimes outside interference puts us all to a lot of bother. You men can go on back to your homes and business. This case is closed."

"Wait!"

Calhoun spoke quietly, but there was authority in that one word.

"Well, what do you want now?" Lundsford demanded.

"I want to finish what you have begun," Cal told him.

He nodded toward Murdock, who stood near.

"If any of you men want to try to leave here before I give you permission to do so, try it," he told the crowd. "Lundsford has washed his hands of this matter—but the Government has not.

"If you want to know my authority for making this a government case, I'll just remind you that the St. Francis River is wholly within the province of the United States Reclamation Service—and a floater found in its waters is government business. Now, from this moment on, I'm conducting this investigation."

Lundsford, quick to see the point Calhoun had made, sat down again, a scowl upon his face. To do him justice, he was so sure that there was nothing underhanded about the death of the hide buyer, he actually believed the investigation to be a waste of time.

"It's up to you, Cal," he said. "I'm done."

"Hayden," the ranger began, "says that Garner bought a pair of boots from him before he went up Black Bayou. Half a dozen men who saw him on that trip assert that he had no boots. Therefore I believe that he had none. You say the point is unimportant—and I'm going to prove that it is most vital."

"You aim to make me out a liar?" the storekeeper demanded, belligerently.

"Speak when you're spoken to!" Cal snapped, turning squarely upon him. "I'm going to let you prove yourself a liar. Who was with you when Greene came into the store and bought the boots?"

"Nobody," was the sullen answer. "I was alone that day."

"Do you carry a full line of shoes and boots?"

"Of course I do!"

"Have any trouble fitting Greene?"

"No. He fitted himself."

Calhoun again addressed the sheriff.

"I verified the statement—in advance—that Hayden has just made. Remember it. He carries a full line."

He motioned to Murdock, who entered the cabin and returned with a bundle which he placed in Cal's hands.

"Here is the pair of boots Greene owned before he bought those from Hayden," Cal informed the crowd, which sensing that something unusual was about to break, gathered closely around. "See where he snagged this one?" He held up a boot, pointing to the snagged place.

"Them's Greene's, all right," Beeswax testified audibly. "He snagged that one th' last time he war up th' bayou."

"Quite right," Calhoun said. "This pair of boots belonged to Garner—*and they are the last boots he ever purchased!*"

The statement was received by the crowd in silence, with here and there a sound of nervously shuffling feet. Calhoun paused long enough for the full meaning of his declaration to sink in, then went on talking.

"Two men had planned to rob Greene Garner when he came up on the spring buying trip. One of those men planned to get out of the country where he could have a better chance to ply his former trade of dealer in moonshine whisky—and he needed some ready cash. He had a partner who lived downstream in the direction Greene would come when he entered the swamp. They planned it together.

"The one thing that troubled them was this: how to dispose of the hide buyer's body? They would have to kill him, because both were well known to him. Then they conceived the idea of drowning him.

"Everything was right for it, the spring rise was on. But—Garner was known to be an expert swimmer, and a man who knew how to handle a dugout. Would acquaintances question the probability of such a man drowning accidentally?

"Then one of those men heard Garner say, in the presence of a witness, that he had no boots with him, but would get a pair from Hayden. That gave the idea. Garner would not be likely to drown, in case of a spill, if he wore his light shoes and his trousers taped.

"But in case he happened to have neglected to take those precautions—had rubber boots on instead, no one would even inquire past the fact that his body had been so found. Any swamp man knows how difficult it is to swim with rubber boots on, and how impossible it would be to reach a point of safety when the river was out of banks and running swift.

"Every swamp man knows, also, how prone lots of us are to take chances. Greene was known to be a chance taker. What is more natural than that he should neglect to change to his shoes after returning from a tramp overland?

"Such was the reasoning of the man who conceived the boot idea—and his partner saw the point. They knew where Greene was going, and they laid for him at a lonely place near the mouth of Black Bayou. When he came up to them, knowing them and thinking nothing of their being on the river, they robbed him; and later drowned him by holding him under water until life was extinct."

5

"HOW IN HELL do you know all that?" Lundsford demanded, impressed in spite of his skepticism.

"I'll get to that directly," Calhoun told him. "After life had left Greene one of the men produced a pair of rubber boots which he had brought along for the purpose; they stripped the dead man's shoes off and placed the boots upon him. Then they threw him into the slough, and sank his dugout. That is what happened to Greene Garner."

The crowd, more restless now than ever before, suddenly broke out with questions.

"Who saw all that?"

"How do you know it?"

"Prove what you say! You're accusin' some of us of bein' killers an' thieves!"

Calhoun knew that he was not dealing with children or cowards. He knew that he had to make his words good. He took out his wallet, drew forth four five-dollar bills, and held them up.

"See these bills, men?" he called.

The crowd became silent while each man looked.

"Garner had them when he came up here—and I got them in change for a twenty, from Oscar Hayden, when I went upriver last." He took an envelope from his pocket. "The cashier of the City Bank, Greene's banking place, not only knew how much money the hide buyer had when he left—but had a record of the numbers on each bill.

"Greene, as is well known, handled a great deal of money through the bank, and for Greene's protection, the cashier always kept the numbers of the bills he drew out when going where there might be danger of robbery. I got these bills—"

He broke off, snatching his revolver from its holster, and covering Hayden who, white-faced and staring-eyed, had slipped his right hand beneath his coat.

"Hands where I can see 'em!"

The storekeeper complied, and the next instant Murdock snapped a pair of handcuffs on his wrists.

The crowd was milling about excitedly by now, almost concealing one of their number who had begun to edge his way toward the river. One man saw him, however.

"Come back, Tolbert!" Calhoun called, and swung his gun on the trapper. "I want you!"

A minute later he also was in irons.

"What the hell do you mean?" Hayden bellowed, recovering his presence of mind. "What—"

"You carry a full line of boots, Hayden—yet Greene Garner came in person to your store, purchased a pair *two sizes too big!*"

The crowd seemed yet uncomprehending. They looked inquiringly at the ranger. He picked up the old boots that had belonged to Garner.

"Greene was a small man, with small feet," he explained. "These boots I hold in my hand are number sevens. The ones he had on when found were number nines.

"Would he have tried to walk in such boots? Furthermore, had he done so, could he not easily have kicked them off in the water?"

Then they understood. With a growl of fury they turned upon Hayden.

"It was Heck planned it all!" the storekeeper cried, his face livid with fear. "I wouldn't 'a' done it, if—"

Then Lundsford and his deputies came to life. They perceived the danger in the threatening attitude of the enraged swamp men, and acted promptly.

"Hands off, men!" the sheriff shouted. "I don't want to hurt anybody, but the law is going to take its course with these men, if we have to shoot up all the rest of you!"

That crowd was made up of men who had known the hide buyer for many years, and had liked him. Now that the truth was known, they thirsted for vengeance.

Yet they knew that not only was Lundsford in earnest; but there would be an aftermath, should they succeed in routing the sheriff, in the shape of Hub Wheeler and his fighting machine. They drew off sullenly, beaten.

Meanwhile, Calhoun and Murdock had hustled their prisoners inside the cabin.

"If you'd kept yo' mouth shet," Tolbert blazed, shaking his manacled hands at Hayden, "nobody ever would 'a' knowed—"

"You're wrong there, Heck," Lundsford interrupted, stepping inside. "There wasn't a chance for you, once that bloodhound, Calhoun, got his nose to the trail! How did you figure it all out, Cal?" he asked, reluctant admiration in his voice.

"It was all simple enough, once my suspicions were aroused," Calhoun replied. "Greene's money being gone seemed queer, but that alone would not have caused me to investigate. I would have assumed that he lost it when he fell out of his boat, and let it go at that. But I couldn't overlook the mute evidence of those boots.

"Ever try to walk in boots that were too large? It can't be done, with any good effect. Blisters and callouses will appear like magic. Garner was an old timer. As well think he'd buy a pair of boots too big, as that he'd put out upriver in carpetslippers. I knew that he did not buy those boots.

"Hayden lied. Why? He was interested in covering up the facts. Furthermore, he was fixing to leave the swamp—skip his bond in that Federal charge, and was the most likely suspect.

"I suspected Tolbert, of course, but had nothing on him. He would have been trapped when he attempted to get rid of his share of the loot, of course; but it never entered the mind of either crook that a record of the numbers had been kept. Doubt if they ever heard of such a thing before."

"Too big!" exclaimed Lundsford. "Well, who'd have thought that a little thing like that would be the means of putting a rope around the necks of a pair of crooks! If those boots had been the right size—"

"Something else would have been overlooked," Calhoun interrupted, positively. "There always is a clew. That's why the average crook is caught before he gets started good—he tackles something that's too big for him, to begin with."

THE UNMARKED SNOW

*The White Blanket Was Undisturbed, Save
By His Own Footprints, And Calhoun
Felt The Force Of Its Argument*

1

JACK CALHOUN, UNITED STATES Ranger stationed at Hell Hole, in the Sunken Land district of Arkansas, was far afield, on foot, and the January snowstorm was rapidly blotting out landmarks. Moreover, the all-day fall had spread a four-inch white fluff on the ground, and the going was anything but easy.

"I won't make it to King John's cabin to-night," he concluded, as he came out of a cypress brake that spread over the vicinity of Long Pond, and headed northwest across a maple flat. "No other cabin for more miles than I can handily cover, so here goes for camp and supper, I'm hungry and I'm tired."

He shook the snow from a huckleberry bush, lodged his rifle and pack in its branches, and twenty minutes later was devouring hot supper before a roaring fire.

Darkness closed in, and he occupied himself in constructing a brush shelter for the night; scraped the snow from beneath it, banked his fire and turned in. Tired though he was, he lay in his blankets and considered the matter which had brought him so far from his cabin at Hell Hole.

Timber thieves—the bane of the rangers' existence—were at the bottom of it. Winter is their time for operating; then the ground is hard, and logging easily carried on. Wherever maple trees grow in profusion, there might thieves be expected. A single tree, of the superfine quality growing in the Sunken Lands, would often net its purloiner five hundred dollars—delivered at certain points on the Mississippi River. Many fine logs did find their way along lonely bayous and creeks to a juncture with the Big River, in spite of all the rangers could do to protect government property. But the activities of Calhoun and his mates had lately discouraged the practice greatly, and it was a cruising trip, in search of illicit timber operations, upon which Cal then was.

So far, he had seen nothing suspicious. Two days before, he had beached his bateau at the foot of Swan Lake, where the St. Francis River leaves it, and had struck off overland in a westerly direction. He spent the first night at a deserted cabin and calculated to reach King John's place for the next. The snowfall prevented.

King John was an Englishman. More than that no man knew. He had come to the Sunken Lands five years before, built a cabin on the east shore of Coon Creek, in the most isolated spot he could find, and there had taken up his abode. His nearest neighbor was twelve miles distant. Once every three months he made a trip to Marked Tree, fifty miles below, asked for and received a letter at the local post office, and then invariably proceeded to the village bank. It was supposed that he made a deposit while there each time, but nobody knew it for certain.

King John, after his trips to the bank, would proceed to McFall's saloon, purchase as many cases of Scotch whisky as he could carry up river in his bateau and depart.

The Englishman, though always polite, was coldly

Calhoun succeeded in raising the whining animal with him

so, and did not appear to desire friends. It was an Irish
tie-cutter who, learning that his name was John Harrogate,
dubbed him "King" John, and the nickname stuck. No one
thereafter called him anything else.

Calhoun had visited the Englishman's cabin on three
occasions while cruising, and had been made welcome for
the night. Being an excellent cribbage player, Cal was more
than welcome, for King John loved the game, and there
were none about who knew even the rudiments of it, save
the ranger and one other.

Gaston Le Foie, the French trapper, whose cabin stood
on the same bank of Coon Creek as King John's, twelve
miles to the northeast, was the one other man in the
swamp who could play cribbage. For that reason, more
than because of any desire for the Frenchman's society,

King John frequently entertained him in his cabin. Other than he, the Englishman had no near-cronies.

"I'd rather be sitting across the table from John, right now," Calhoun reflected drowsily, "than be in my present location—but it can't be helped when the snow drives."

He fell asleep. Inured to hardship, he awoke only once, and that at two o'clock in the morning. He noted that the snow had ceased falling, and stars were out; then knew nothing more until day broke.

Cal made a cup of coffee, but deferred breakfast until he should reach the Englishman's place. At eight o'clock he struck Coon Creek, followed its course two miles, and reached the southern edge of the small clearing which the cabin centered. There he paused and called a loud greeting.

Two gaunt hounds answered, coming through the six-inch snow in great leaps. They recognized the ranger, however, and turned back toward the house, allowing him to overtake them.

Again Calhoun hailed the house, but got no answer. His glance sought the top of the stick-and-mud chimney visible above the east end of the roof.

"Hump!" he mentally exclaimed. "John is lying abed late. No fire. I say, Royalty, show yourself!" he raised his voice jocularly.

The hounds leaped to the veranda in front of the cabin— five feet above ground, stilted like the main house—ran to the closed door, scratched against it and raised their voices in solemn howls.

"Queer," thought Cal, as he pounded on the door and got no answer. "John must be inside. If he were out, the dogs would be with him."

The one window giving onto the veranda—a glass-less opening, fitted with a hinged shatter—was securely fastened from within, as was the door itself. Calhoun walked to the edge of the veranda and surveyed the white expanse of snow which sparkled in the sunlight.

"If he isn't inside, he left here before two o'clock this morning, when the snow ceased, because mine are the only tracks out there—except the dogs'. Maybe he went out the back door."

The ranger circled the house, trying the window on the east without being able to open it, and found the back door fastened from within. Moreover, not a track, save those made by the dogs, lay in the snow anywhere about the place. No one had entered or left the cabin since about midnight the night before; that Calhoun knew, because no snow fell after two o'clock. It would have required two hours of snowfall to completely wipe out a man's tracks.

2

HAVING TRIED THE doors and windows without success, the ranger now sought a crack through which he might gain a view of the interior. He was uneasy, but hesitated to break the Englishman's door down when there might be no real reason for doing so. After all, a man's house is his castle—even though it be a log hut in the middle of a forest. After a moment's search, he found a chink-hole between the logs of the east wall, and applied his eyes.

The window holes, being shuttered, all was dark within. He could at first make out nothing. Presently, however, his eyes became accustomed to the obscurity, and various objects began showing dimly in the light which sifted in through holes in the chinking. A fire smoldered on the hearth, giving no light, barely discernible beneath the ashes.

"It would be a grand fire that would last from twelve o'clock at night until nine in the morning—on an open hearth!" Cal exclaimed. "John is inside—and here goes!"

He found an ax sticking in the bole of a tree at the back of the cabin and, without hesitation now, smashed the shutter off the veranda window. Stepping inside, he halted abruptly, leaning against the window sill and allowing his eyes to rove over the room.

King John lay stretched upon the floor beside a table

in the room's center. He was dead. The light from the window at Cal's back streamed across his face—the wide, staring eyes, the partly opened lips. Calhoun knew, without moving from his position against the wall, that the Englishman was lifeless.

After a moment's observation, he crossed and knelt beside the body, laying a hand upon the face.

He came to his feet instantly—alert, his eyes searching every dark corner of the room. Darting to the bunks, of which there were two, he threw the covers off, then peered beneath. A lean-to at the back served as a kitchen, the only other room in the structure. He entered, gun in hand. A search revealed no one.

"Queer—damned queer!" muttered the ranger, returning to the front room. "Nobody here—yet John Harrogate has been dead not more than an hour! His face and hands still have warmth—and the blood from the hole in his chest is not yet dry!"

He lifted his glance—then leaped backward into the lean-to.

"The loft!" he exclaimed softly, pushing the door almost to. "He could have potted me from there, easy as not!"

For that the man who had killed King John was hiding in that loft, was a firm conviction in Calhoun's mind.

Where else could he be? No one had left the cabin since twelve o'clock, yet the Englishman had been killed not more than an hour before. The murderer was, therefore, still in the house. The loft of the main room, reached by ladder in the northwest corner where a square hole in the ceiling gave into it, was the only place he could possibly hide.

Then it occurred to Cal that a man would be a fool to

so trap himself. He had only to wait below, out of range of that manhole in the ceiling, and take his man when he came down. The killer would, eventually, have to leave his hiding place—that, of course, was certain.

But why hide there in the first place? Would not the killer know it for the trap it was? If disturbed by Cal's approach, why had he not potted him when he came up?

Calhoun began to reflect a bit. Had he been too hasty in assuming that murder had been done? Might not King John—

"He isn't the kind to kill himself!" Cal rejected the thought almost before it was formed. "Those cold-blooded English don't pull such stunts. Yet—"

That blanket of snow about the cabin, undisturbed by human feet save his own, spread itself before his eyes, and he felt the force of its argument.

"I'll wait a bit," was his conclusion.

Drawing a chair to the door, he sat down just within the lean-to.

"He can't shoot me from here," he thought, "if he really is in the loft—and, sooner or later, he'll move a bit. Those loft boards are loose, just laid on the rafters, and if he moves they'll betray him. Yes, I'll wait."

He dared not climb up and investigate the loft. In case a murderer were hiding there, to thrust his head through that manhole would mean instant death. Calhoun was no fool.

He sat motionless in the chair while an hour dragged slowly by. During that time he did not allow himself to speculate upon what had happened: speculation induces reverie, and Cal's senses were strained to catch the slightest creak of a board, an unguarded movement from above.

He heard nothing, save the occasional effort of a dog to enter through the window, the wrecked shutter of which the ranger had pulled to before crossing the room.

"Maybe I'm mistaken, after all," he thought. "John might have had news from abroad—bad news; such news as rendered him no longer desirous of living. Maybe he drank too much of the Scotch, got maudlin over his outcast condition. Yet, I can't get rid of the feeling which first assailed me—that I was in the presence of a murdered man. Why, I was as certain of it as one may well be of anything."

A dog whined at the broken shutter, and the ranger straightened suddenly. A moment later he dashed across the room, opened the window and permitted the dog to enter. Closing the shutter, the room was again in gloom.

Keeping close to the west wall, Calhoun then slipped softly to the ladder leading to the loft and mounted it, pausing before his head reached the dangerous opening.

"Here, Buck!" he called softly, snapping his fingers to the hound. "Come, boy! Come!"

The hound hesitated, looking up at him questioningly. He sat on his haunches, lifted his gaunt muzzle up and howled long and dolefully.

Calhoun dropped to the floor, seized the dog by the collar and dragged him to the ladder.

Better to sacrifice you, old fellow, than get plugged myself," he thought. "For, after all, a dog is only a dog."

The hound held back, but Calhoun succeeded in mounting halfway up the ladder and in raising the whining animal with him. Then with an upward swing, he elevated Buck through the manhole. And with gun drawn, he hung there—waiting.

The dog howled again, then sat at the edge of the hole, looking down with mournful eyes at the man on the ladder.

"Sic him, Buck!" Cal urged. "Find him, boy!"

The hound turned and went pattering across the attic boards, then he came to the manhole again and sat on his haunches.

It was enough. Calhoun was now convinced that no one was in the loft. Had there been, Buck would either have been shot or would have bayed at him. He climbed up, and searched the dark place.

It was empty.

He lifted Buck through the hole, dropped him to the floor and followed.

"Suicide," he muttered, looking down at the clean-shaven, finely chiseled face of the dead man. "Wonder what terrible thing happened to cause you to do it, John? I wonder!"

Buck trotted into the lean-to, barked a time or two, then stood in the door looking at Cal.

"Poor devil is hungry," he thought.

He admitted the other hound, then searched the cupboard. A platter of fried rabbit was disclosed, and he fed the animals. While they were eating, he reentered the front room, threw on some dry kindling and wood and soon had a fire going on the hearth. Then he opened the windows, flooding the place with light.

Hunger gnawed at him, but he could not partake of food until he had looked over the things in the room—to read, if possible, the record of what had occurred. Then breakfast.

Beneath the table, which was near the center of the room and about six feet from the fireplace, lay a revolver.

The ranger broke it open and noted that one chamber only had been fired. Next he examined the wound in Harrogate's breast.

"Clothing burned, flesh scorched and powder-marked," he reflected. "Muzzle must have been almost in contact with his body."

That was a strong argument in favor of the suicide theory—but by no means conclusive.

3

"**I CAN'T GET** rid of that first impression," Cal muttered.

"The impression that John Harrogate had been murdered. Guess I'm foolish, considering there is no one in the house who could have done it—and no one could have left the house after it was done. Snow would have caused a trail a blind man could follow. No, I guess, after all, he got tired of life, and ended it."

The next thing to catch and hold his glance was an empty quart bottle which stood upon the table in front of which the dead man lay, his outstretched left hand almost touching the mud of the hearth. A chair was drawn up at the west end of the table, one at the south side, and one was overturned at the east end—evidently that in which King John had last sat.

Calhoun took the bottle up, noting that it had once held Scotch whisky, but was now empty except for a few drops. Three or four drinking glasses wore also there—as they usually were, Cal remembered. A bit of foil, and a fresh seal, patently torn from the cork of the bottle, attracted him. They lay on the table.

"Hum! That seal was recently removed," was Cal's thought. "John was tidiness itself, and would never have allowed it to lie there long—nor the empty bottle to be in evidence. Now it stands to reason that he did not drink the entire contents of that quart of Scotch at a single sitting—alone. He must have had company. Ah, the cribbage board!"

It was on the table, together with a deck of cards.

"He might have played 'dummy'—no! I've often heard him declare his aversion to dummy cribbage! Somebody played cribbage with him last night, or this morning!"

His thought immediately clove to the only person who could have played cribbage with King John—save himself.

Gass Le Foie!

But what of that? Gaston Le Foie occasionally played cribbage there. He might have visited the cabin the night before; that would account for the cribbage layout, and for the empty bottle.

"He'd have no reason to kill John," Cal considered. "And, for that matter, Le Foie could no more have left this place without leaving a trail than could any one else. He hasn't wings—and only a bird could have crossed that snow and no one be the wiser."

He searched the dead man's pockets, but found only some small change, a pocketknife, and other articles which meant nothing whatsoever.

"I wonder if he deposited his money at the bank in Marked Tree?" The ranger knew of those quarterly trips to the post office. He straightway began searching for a checkbook. Every possible place where one might have been was examined, and no blank checks were found. No deposit book, or slips, were turned up. "He cashed those checks," Cal decided, "and kept the money by him. Yet—no money is here, except a few bits of silver."

He turned to a calendar on the wall, noting that the date was January the tenth. Harrogate was due to receive his usual remittance a few days previously. That he had made the customary trip, the amount of whisky on hand, and the condition of the larder, attested.

"I don't have any idea how much money he got through the mails," Cal acknowledged. "But it must have been a fair sum. He lived off it, and he lived very well indeed. None here, however. Wonder if he and the Frenchman gambled? That might account for it—Gass might have won."

There was nothing else to be determined from the contents of the main room, and Cal entered the kitchen, let the hounds out the back door, and took up the search there. The Englishman might have hidden his money in a can of beans, coffee, or whatnot.

On the shelf in front of the cupboard lay a square of bacon from which several slices had been cut. Calhoun counted them.

"Eight!" he exclaimed. "John must have had an appetite! And eggs! Six, all broken in a bowl, ready for the skillet!"

He grew thoughtful. No man, no matter how healthy, would consume eight thick slices of bacon and six eggs at breakfast—or any other meal.

Also, if John contemplated killing himself that morning, would he have bothered about getting breakfast? Hardly, Cal thought. Yet he had meant to cook breakfast, for the cook-stove held live coals.

"Everything points to the fact that King John had a guest last night, and also this morning. He was in the act of preparing food for himself and the visitor—but, hell! Where is that visitor? He is not here, and, unless he had feet like a dog, he hasn't left!"

Another thing struck Cal as being against any one's leaving the cabin. The doors and windows were secured from the inside. The front and back doors alike were equipped with bars, one end bolted through a board at the center of the door, the other free to be raised and dropped into a wooden catch on the jamb. Both doors had been barred from the inside.

He made a close examination of the kitchen door and came to the conclusion that it would be impossible for any one to raise or lower the bar from the outside. There were no cracks between the boards except those which were tightly battened. The front door was precisely the same.

But was it the same?

Cal was standing before the closed front door, and his eyes caught a pencil of light. Investigation showed that it came through a nail hole in the door, about as high up as his chin. Another moment, and he had wrenched the bar from the door and was examining the inside of it. He gave a long, low whistle.

The nail which had been driven through the door-board, had also penetrated the bar about one-eighth of an inch— enough to hold it up and prevent it from interfering with the opening and closing of the door.

"Once outside, the nail was withdrawn—and the bar dropped down into the catch! That's as plain as can be! King John wouldn't have done that—bar himself from his own house! No—the man who killed him drove that nail! I may be a fool, but nothing can convince me now that John Harrogate took his own life!"

Then the impossibility of the murderer's being able to get away without leaving tracks in the snow smote him, and he sat down to think.

"It couldn't be done—tracks would show, in spite of anything. And nothing bigger than a dog has crossed the snow from here, and that's certain."

He left the veranda and crossed the clearing, the dogs following. A complete circle of the place failed to disclose a trail of any kind except those of animals. Along the creek bank were coon, squirrel and dog tracks, where they had gone down to the water to drink, but no human footprints were there.

"Nothing for it, I guess, but to get to a settlement and notify the sheriff and coroner," he decided, reentering the cabin. "King John killed himself—the untracked snow proves it beyond doubt."

The admission came reluctantly—the act was so out of character with the man. Circumstances, however, forced the conclusion upon the ranger.

He cooked a bit of breakfast, then set out along Coon Creek for the settlement at Swan Lake. It was a twenty-mile trip, and the nearest place where a telegraph instrument could be had—one maintained by the rangers.

At two o'clock that afternoon he was hailing Gaston Le Foie out of his cabin—the only habitation he had struck so far. The Frenchman was a short, slender man of about forty, who trapped the Coon Creek country for a living. Like Harrogate, he dwelt alone.

"When did you last see King John?" Calhoun asked, greetings over.

"Las' night," was the unhesitating answer. "We play creebbige, aft' supper, an' Jean he dreenk too much. So I leave early—mebbe nine o'clock. Snow she come down hard, like ze old woman she picking her geese in ze sky. Jean fine mans, but dreenk too much ze Scotch."

"John's drinking days are over," Cal said abruptly. "He is dead."

He watched the effect of the announcement upon the Frenchman. His words seemed to make no serious impression.

"Dead drunk, you mean?" Le Foie queried with a grin. "Jean ver' near zat when I leave heem las' night!"

"I mean," the ranger said slowly and impressively, "that John Harrogate has passed out—dead, with a bullet through his heart. He must have shot himself last night, or some time this morning."

"I—I no beleeve!"

Le Foie's face was a picture of astonishment and incredulity.

"It is true."

"But las' night I play creebbige wit' heem!" he cried in protest. "He not seek, not sad—nothin' lak eet! He ver' happy! For why he keel himself?"

"That will probably never be known," Cal replied. "I want you to make a trip to the settlement and get Hobbs, the storekeeper, to send out two messages which I will write. I don't like to leave the corpse lying there alone, and will get back before night."

"Mak' ze messages!" Le Foie exclaimed. "I tak' heem een! Poor Keeng Jean—my ver' good frien'! An' I play creebbige wit' heem only las' night!"

Calhoun wrote two messages. One was a brief report to Hubbard Wheeler, ranger chief, at headquarters on Oak Donnick. The other was to Sheriff Lundsford, at the county seat. He watched the Frenchman's bateau paddled speedily downstream toward Swan Lake, until a bend in the creek hid him from view, then turned back on the long hike to King John's cabin.

4

WHEN, AT NOON two days later, Sheriff Lundsford and
Coroner Steve Barrett, accompanied by two deputies and
piloted by Gaston Le Foie, reached King John's cabin, they
found Calhoun still there. He had not been alone, since
the news, spread by Le Foie on his trip out, had caused a
number of natives to forsake their trap lines and hasten
to the scene. Several of them had remained to keep the
ranger company.

Any one who had noticed Calhoun two days previously,
marked his restless bearing and his disturbed countenance,
would have been surprised at the change in him now. His
face no longer depicted puzzlement, and he was again his
usual calm, unruffled self.

"Well, Cal, what have you dug up this time?" Lundsford
called, stepping out of his motor boat.

"That's for you to determine, Mr. Sheriff," the ranger
replied. "There's a dead man here, and common sense seems
to admit of no other theory but suicide. Still, that theory is
so at variance with the known character of John Harrogate,
it's hard to credit."

The party started up from the creek bank, such as had
come in bateaux and dugouts carrying their oars. At least,
all were, with one exception. Le Foie left his in his boat.

"Forgetting your paddles, ain't you, Gass?" Calhoun

queried. Stooping, he caught up the two eight-foot paddles and handed them to their owner. "Careless, Gass," he remarked. "A real riverman never leaves his paddles in his boat."

The Frenchman shot the speaker a sharp glance, then laughed.

"Ver' much oblige', my frien'," he said. "You theenk for me. That is well, for since I fin' out my good frien', Keeng Jean, dead, I no have ze heart for theenk!"

The crowd had gone on, and Calhoun and Le Foie followed them into the cabin. There the ranger pointed out the matters which had caught his attention on the day of the discovery—the evident preparation for breakfast for two, the manner in which the bar on the front door could have been dropped from the outside, and like details.

"The fact remains, though, that no one was hiding in the cabin, and there were no human tracks in the snow," Lundsford commented. "You are not going to affirm that it would be possible for a man to walk across the clearing without leaving tracks?"

"I'm not affirming anything." Cal replied. "I'm just giving you the history of the case as I know it."

Lundsford looked at the young man keenly. Time was when he would have made very light of him—scoffed at his theories and derided his suspicions. But that time had passed. On more than one occasion the ranger had proved himself to be remarkably able in solving the most difficult cases. Lundsford had been shown up on several investigations, and he had resolved to be more attentive to Calhoun's words and views in the future.

"If you know anything else, Cal, spring it!" he exclaimed.

At that moment Barrett finished his examination.

"Shot through the heart with a forty-five caliber revolver," he asserted. "Died instantly. Condition of clothing, and the flesh about the wound, shows that the muzzle of the gun was almost against his chest when discharged. Suicide, in my opinion."

"That, together with the untracked condition of the snow in the clearing about the cabin when Calhoun made the discovery, is, to my mind, conclusive," Lundsford proclaimed to the gathering. "Unless a man had wings, he could not have departed from here without leaving tracks. That is certain. Has anybody here anything to say in opposition to the conclusion that Harrogate took his own life?"

His eyes sought Calhoun's face, as though he expected contradiction from that quarter.

"There is one thing I discovered after returning here from Le Foie's place," Cal spoke up after a moment, "which struck me as odd—and later on as peculiarly significant." He pointed to a corner of the room where Harrogate's two eight-foot-paddles reposed. "I noticed that those paddles are each about four inches shorter than they should be—than they were, in fact, when I saw them last."

Lundsford looked at him in astonishment mixed with impatience.

"Well, what of it?" he demanded. "Are you serious? This is no time for funny stuff. Cal, I want to remind you!"

"I was never more serious in my life," the ranger assured him soberly. "Each of John's paddles has had four inches sawed off the handle end—and recently. The night of the—" he hesitated briefly—"suicide. I found a bit of fresh sawdust in the kitchen. Discovered, too, that John's hammer is missing."

"Well, what of that?" Lundsford wanted to know. "What if all his tools are missing—what has that to do with it?"

"There is something else odd—and enlightening, if one chooses to view it so," Calhoun continued, paying no attention to Lundsford's irritation. "If Barrett will observe closely, he will see that John has no belt on. That would not be so odd, except for the fact that I found the buckle in the ashes of the fireplace. Now, why would John burn his belt?"

"I don't know—and I don't care!" Lundsford rasped. "But since you have begun it, suppose you tell us what significance it has!"

"It has this significance," Calhoun declared, his voice hardening. "The shortened paddles and the disappearance of John's belt proves that he was murdered—and I am going to show you how. Going to reconstruct the whole thing so you all can see. But first—I'm going to arrest the murderer!"

He wheeled toward the Frenchman, seized his wrists in a steel-like grip, tripped him and left him lying on the floor—handcuffed.

"What—what does this mean?" Lundsford cried, amazed. "Be careful, Calhoun—you want to know what you're doing!"

"I do know!"

"Take dees t'ings off!" howled Le Foie. "Ze man Calhoun ees ze beeg dam' fool! Keeng Jean, he my good frien'! I nevaire harm heem! *Mon Dieu!* He my frien'!"

"Another word, and I'll gag you!" Calhoun admonished sternly. "You are a murderer—the worst of the breed! The

kind who takes advantage of friendship, turning the free-
dom it assures to an infamous end! Shut up, or I'll stuff
your mouth full of rags!"

The Frenchman, cowed by the threat, subsided, glaring
murderously.

5

"**GASTON LE FOIE** came here on the evening before Harrogate's death, to play cribbage. He was in position to know that John had just drawn his remittance, and that there would be plenty to drink in the cabin. I am taking his word for it that John drank heavily, and I am guessing that the latter displayed his money.

"I asked you, in my message, to ascertain the amount John drew at the bank, Lundsford. Did you do so?"

"The amount was fifteen hundred dollars," the sheriff replied. "He receives a like amount every three months from relatives in England—a remittance man, I believe such as he is termed."

"Very well then," Calhoun resumed. "John must have had the entire sum, less maybe a hundred dollars, with him that night. He either told Le Foie about it, or the latter suspected it. At any rate, the Frenchman wanted that money. They played until late, then Harrogate invited his guest to stop for the night; the snow was failing thickly, and travel would be unpleasant. Le Foie accepted.

"When they turned in that night, the Frenchman, in all probability, had only flirted with the notion of robbing John. When they arose, the ground was covered with a six-inch blanket of untrodden snow—and that gave the Frenchman his idea.

"The snow was without tracks, save those of the dogs. It would doubtless remain so for days, because no one would be likely to come near the isolated cabin in such weather. No one would have, in fact, had I not been caught out in it. Now, Le Foie reasoned, if the first comer to that cabin—and Frenchy meant there should be one before the snow melted—should find Harrogate dead, under the conditions which actually existed when he was found, he would look first of all for tracks. There would be none, and the only possible inference would be that the Englishman had killed himself.

"You see, that snow had given Le Foie an idea—an idea which would, worked out, enable him to leave the cabin without making any betraying footprints. It was so easy and simple, the idea!

"Harrogate was in the lean-to preparing breakfast. He had cut the bacon and broken the eggs. His gun was probably under his pillow, or on the mantel. Frenchy got it, called John into the room on some pretext or another, and shot him dead—holding the muzzle against his body, just as John undoubtedly would have done, had he shot himself in that particular place.

"After securing the money, the next thing was the get-away.

"You have noticed the dog tracks out yonder in the clearing. They appear as so many holes in the fluffy snow—small, round holes. One knows that a dog, or deer, or some other long-legged animal made them, because nothing else could have done so. Had the snow been crusted, Gaston's scheme would not have worked. Being fluffy, it did."

He paused a moment, then motioned them out of doors.

Leading the way to a line of tracks in the snow, he got down on his knees and carefully cleared the way to the ground. On the bottom layer of snow was the clear imprint of a dog's foot.

"That was made by a dog—it is obvious," Calhoun pointed out.

Then he led the way to a second line of tracks which led off in a zigzag toward the creek. They appeared to be exactly similar to the tracks he had just uncovered. Carefully, he dug the snow away—and exposed an entirely different result.

That track was merely a deep impression in the lightly frozen earth—a hole, and nothing more.

"What kind of animal made that?" Cal queried, looking at the sheriff.

"Damned if I know!" Lundsford exclaimed. "But I would have sworn that a dog made it, until you exposed it!"

"So I thought!" the ranger declared, getting up. "And so I would have continued to think, had I not noticed that Harrogate's paddles were too short."

"I don't get it yet!" Barrett declared. "Tell us the rest of it!"

"That's easy," Calhoun said, once more in the cabin. "Le Foie had his paddles in the cabin—he doesn't forget 'em often—and he made a pair of stilts out of them— using blocks cut from the handles of Harrogate's, and the latter's belt for the straps. That's how it was done. The stilts merely made holes in the deep snow, precisely like those a dog's legs would make. He even walked in a zigzag toward the creek, as a dog would do in marking the same course. Simple? Yes—very."

"Eet ees ze big lie!" shouted the Frenchman. "I nevaire done eet! I nevaire harm my frien'!"

Calhoun laughed, and pulled a hammer out of his hip pocket.

"John's hammer," he said. "Frenchy needed it to work the bar on the door, and he needed it to tear up his stilts when he got to the creek. Here's the rest of the evidence."

He tossed two round, four-inch lengths of wood on the table. Each was equipped with a short length of leather—the stirrup-leather, in fine.

"He had to get rid of those things, so he dropped 'em in the water along with the hammer, trusting to the creek to keep his secret. It would have done so, had I not suspected foul play. It took me three hours, and got me a fine wetting in cold water, to find 'em, but, once convinced that they existed, I kept at it until I got every last one of 'em."

He picked up the Frenchman's paddles.

"See the nail holes in each?" he queried, pointing them out. "There is where the blocks were attached to the staffs. Now observe the smaller holes in each, about five inches above the larger. There is where the stirrup-leathers were attached. Watch!"

He picked up a block, laid it against the staff of an oar, the hole in the end of the block corresponding with the hole in the paddle, then he stretched the leather up.

That action spelled doom for Gaston De Foie—for the thing fitted the marks on his paddle beyond possibility of doubt!

CALHOUN'S DEPUTIES

*"You Can Best Settle The Homesteaders
By Wiping Out The Redeyes, Root And
Branch," Tersely Ran Cal's Orders*

1
____

SATURDAY NIGHT IN Marked Tree, back in the '90s, was a night to make the timid shudder and hide indoors. Even the bold were wont to walk in wariness, ready to draw and shoot it out, or duck into the nearest cover if the odds appeared too great.

Perhaps some of the qualities of its sinister founder entered into the village's early development, for, be it known, Marked Tree was, in its beginning, a rendezvous for John A. Murel and his band. At any rate, the place continued, long after death laid the outlaw by the heels and his organization was destroyed, a worthy monument to Murel.

The vast Sunken Land district also contributed much to Marked Tree's lawless state. Inhabited only by hunters and trappers, the great swamp, at the southern edge of which the village stood, was a tangled, impregnable wilderness—a tribute to nature in a most destructive mood; a stronghold for men who were, in large measure, too primitive to comprehend the reason for statute law, much less live according to it. The denizens of the swamp had their own code, and it a simple one:

Live as the spirit moves you to live, and circumstances permit. If your conduct offends a neighbor, let the neighbor come out like a man and give battle. The long-barreled rifle and the bowie knife rules in the Sunken Lands.

In course of time the Government decided to reclaim a few of its three millions of acres of waste, and the job of taming the land was assigned to Hubbard Wheeler and his rangers. It was a gigantic task, and necessarily slow. Yet it progressed. Bit by bit portions of the wilderness were brought into at least partial subjection. It was Wheeler's mission to eventually carry the law to the farthest reaches.

On the heels of Wheeler came homesteaderers. Government opened certain tracts to those who were hardy enough to enter upon them and help in winning the land.

It was the coming of some of those homesteaders that precipitated trouble on a Saturday night in July, just after the flood had receded, and the country, delivered from complete inundation, seemed, about to settle back into its accustomed routine.

The coming of the railroad, a few years previous to that memorable night, did much to improve Marked Tree—but it could not take it off its stilts; that could be done by drainage and reclamation only. The entire village sat high above the ground, on pilings, and the sidewalks, built of rough boards, were elevated accordingly. Two general stores, a restaurant and hotel, a hardware store, barber shop, and other minor enterprises composed the business section of the town.

Also, there were five saloons, all flourishing. Each saloon ran gambling games openly, with dance halls in connection.

A lone marshal and a justice of the peace administered what law there was in the place. The county sheriff lived at the far end of the district; he seldom appeared there, and deputies came and went. Mostly "went."

They halted by thrusting their paddles down into the bayou's bed

Such was Marked Tree in the '90s.

Late in the afternoon, on that Saturday in July, Marked Tree began to exhibit signs of great activity. Gradually the sidewalks became more populous, the saloons more energetically engaged. Where the increase in population came from was not evident to one lacking intimate knowledge of the country. To one in the know it was not a secret.

The swampers were gathering from up and down the St. Francis River, for their usual Saturday night and Sunday carousal. They would continue to drift in during the night and the following morning, each new arrival dry, and eager to become wet. After that—well, left come what might, so it be exciting enough.

Excitement, to the swamper, meant something more than games of sport. It meant dangerous indulgences, such as shooting promiscuously at windows, lights—anything, in fine, which happened to challenge his inflamed mind. Often, it is true, Marked Tree's Saturday nights passed without mortal casualties—but more often not.

Along the walk which spanned the north side of Main Street, upon which all five saloons fronted, two men walked in the early dusk. They were not dressed in the mode of the swampers or the citizens. Booted, clad in brown duck britches and blouses, wearing round-brimmed felt hats, these men would have impressed the sober observer very favorably indeed. Both were six feet tall, lithe and muscular, keen of face and eye, and neat as pins in attire.

They were, in fine, Rangers Tom Murdock and Jerry Sanes, sent down from headquarters at Oak Donnick, twenty miles up the St. Francis, by Wheeler that Saturday. Upon their shoulders rested the dangerous responsibility of preserving the peace in Marked Tree.

"A fine night in prospect, Tom," quoth Sanes, cocking an eye comically toward the sky, which was just beginning to disclose a few faint stars.

"Yeah."

They walked on a few paces, courteously sidestepping two natives who, arm in arm, were reeling westward along the walk—and occupying it entirely.

"Saw Brome Crowder put in to the landing this afternoon." Sanes went on, as they stood beside the railing of the walk, looking off toward the river. "Tobe Shotwell and Frank Parnell came along just ahead of him."

He paused then, eying his partner expectantly.

"News for news," Tom spoke up with a grin. "Hez Calloway and Oscar Bell delighted my vision as I came up the walk to meet you. I haven't seen any more members of the Redeye factions to-day—but it's a bet, since some are here, the rest of the two gangs will be here, too."

"Yeah, and if they do gather, and Red Ellif drops in—what?"

"There will be hell."

"Bucktail Lake has a large sprinkling of representatives among those present tonight," Sanes went on, "exclusive of its two Redeye factions. This appears to be their night."

"And they'll all side either with Red Ellif and his gang, or Brome Crowder and his thugs," Murdock predicted. "Make no doubt of that. Well," he went on resignedly, "if Wheeler just won't spare a few more of the boys on these Saturday nights, we'll have to do the best we can alone. Here's hoping for a fairly quiet evening."

"Yeah."

Neither had the least idea that his hope would materialize. They were wise to the psychology of crowds, and the crowd then gathering resembled, to their thoughtful eyes, a great, black cloud in the sky. A cloud with a hint of vivid and destructive lightning to come.

Presently it came. Several flashes, followed by sharp, startling thunder.

"Some of the boys are getting restive," Tom remarked, straightening away from the rail.

"Yeah. Better move down that way, I reckon. Somehow, Tom, I have a feeling—"

"So have I," Tom interrupted. "I'd give a month's pay if Jack Calhoun would happen in right now."

"We're thinking the same thing," Jerry told him. "I'd give something myself for a sight of the inspector's homely mug."

2

"YE-E-E-O-O-OW!" CAME A shrill yell from far down the walk, where a knot of men could be discerned in the dusk. "Come one, come all! Wet up! Free beer! Free as long as th' kag lasts!"

"Wow! Wow! Wow! Free to who, Brome?" came a high-keyed question.

Silence; then after a moment:

"Free to eve'body—but th' mangy Ellif ki-yutes!"

"Ha, ha, ha! Ho, ho, ho! Ye-e-e-o-o-w! That's th' talk, Brome! None of th' cussed Ellifs kin wet their snoots frum this here kag!"

Pop! Top! Pop! Flash! Flash! Flash!

More thunder and more lightning. Men began to leave the vicinity of the crowd at lively gaits; others pressed in; all milled around, laughing, shouting, cursing—hurling challenge after challenge at the, as yet, silent Ellif crowd.

"Better scatter 'em?" queried Sanes.

"Ours but to do, and try," paraphrased Murdock, hunching his powerful shoulders forward and heading down the walk. Sanes kept close at his side. Each man's service revolver was tied down—the flaps of the holsters open.

Red Ellif, leader of one faction of the peculiarly colored breed of swampers commonly called "Redeyes," dwelt upon the north side of Bucktail Lake; with him lived half a dozen of his kin—kin both in blood and spirit.

Brome Crowder, leader of a second division of Redeyes, lived on the south side of the lake, along with a number of his kin. What divided the factions, in the beginning, no man knew—or, at least, would tell. That they were divided all the country had cause to know.

A Redeye could be distinguished at a glance, because of a certain red tinge in the whites of his eyes and pupils, which resembled small, red berries—dogwood berries, perhaps. Also, the Redeye was characterized by skin much darker than the so-called white native—a skin of singular transparency, underlaid with pink. Long, straight, black hair gave rise to the conjecture that blood of the North American Indian flowed in their veins, but definite evidence of their origin never has been adduced.

Suffice to say that all Redeyes were bad—root and branch. They are now almost extinct—and nobody has put on mourning or sent flowers.

The shouts of insult and defiance continued to emanate from the crowd on the walk—increasing in volume and in color.

"Ain't they no Ellifs here?"

That call was often sounded. No replies came.

"Wonder what's keeping the Ellifs quiet?" Tom speculated, as they neared the Crowder faction. "They're not usually so timid and retiring."

"Hump. I reckon it's because Red ain't here—they lack their leader. Lord!" Sanes ejaculated fervently. "I hope he's broke a leg or something, and can't come! Otherwise this night is going to breed evil in great, smoky gobs!"

They paused at the rim of the crowd. In the center, occupying the sidewalk, Brome Crowder, looking more like a great black bear than anything else to which he might be compared, sat on a stool. On a box beside him was a half barrel of beer with a faucet in the bung. In the hands of the crowd were tin cups which were continually being filled from the barrel. The crowd numbered half a dozen Redeyes and perhaps thirty swampers not so distinguished. All drank.

Brome looked up and saw the rangers.

"We done moved th' saloon outdoors," he called, leering drunkenly. "Got any objections?"

Murdock shook his head. "Not if you don't create too much disturbance," he replied. "Have all the fun you like—but stop at fun."

The words were spoken quietly, and had no element of threat in them. Just a bit of well-meant advice. Everybody within hearing, however, understood that Murdock meant what he said. The rangers were not given to bullying, neither were they given to overlooking disobedience of orders. Some one laughed good-naturedly.

"We ain't aimin' to harm nobody, ranger!" came a voice from the crowd.

Murdock looked around and picked out the speaker. It was "Foxtail" Beeler—so called because his headgear, no matter what the material or shape, invariably had a fox's tail hanging in the back—a trapper from the Bucktail Lake region. He was not a Redeye, but was known to side with Brome Crowder. A fair enough man, as swampers go, was Foxtail; one with a bit of humor about him, as was evidenced by the fun-lines around his mouth and the droll look in his eyes. The ranger addressed him.

"Of course, not," he said. "You boys are just in town for a little celebration—fun, and such. Nobody objects to that. Still, you never can tell when something may happen to turn farce into tragedy. Let's be careful, boys," he went on, speaking to all, "and go home to-morrow night without anybody having to pay the fiddler any harder coin than maybe a busted head."

Pop! Pop! Pop! Flash! Flash! Flash!

More thunder and more lightning. This time from a point two hundred feet down the walk.

"Ye-e-e-o-o-ow-w-w-w-w! Who-o-o-p-p-p-e-e-e-e! Gether round, folkses! Free beer down here, too! Come and wet up!"

Another saloon had been moved outside. A second group of men were gathered around another leader who personally superintended the dispensation of drinks.

That leader was a tall, raw-boned man who looked as much like a big brown bear as Crowder resembled a big black one.

"Who you aimin' for to drink yore beer, Red?" came a jeering voice.

"Anybody whichsoever—savin' an' exceptin' them Crowder polecats!"

Red Ellif and his crowd had entered upon the scene.

A sudden hush came over the street. Men waited for—most anything. Then:

"You-all talks big, you Red Ellif!" Brome shouted, leaping on top of his barrel of beer.

"I acts jest as big as I talks, you Brome Crowder!"

Red Ellif could be seen above the heads of his hench-men, standing on his keg.

"Get down, Brome!"

The command came in stern tones. Murdock shouldered his way to Crowder's keg, his gun in hand.

Jerry Sanes, speeding lightly down the walk, waded in and gave Red Ellif the same order.

"Why in hell don't you rangers leave us swamp men to settle our own rackets?" Red demanded, looking down at Jerry.

"Get down—and don't argue!"

Red, looking over the crowd, saw that his enemy had descended, and followed suit.

"Oh, hell!" cried Lem Parkins, a redeyed henchman of Ellif's. "Why'nt we-all settle with them Crowders now—an' if th' rangers git in th' way, why, let 'em!"

A movement down the walk betrayed the fact that the Crowder gang was acting on the same idea—only sooner. They came on in a bunch. Ahead of them, backing up, gun in hand, was Murdock—trying to the last to stop them without bloodshed.

Ellif's bunch stampeded toward their oncoming enemies, just as Sanes, gun drawn, leaped ahead of them menacingly.

"Crowders gather round!" Brome yelled.

"Come on, all you Ellifs!" bleated Red.

"Wait!"

The command came from a lank native who at that instant leaped to the walk from below. Halfway between the two hostile factions, he stood panting; hat gone and face red with effort.

Both factions paused. The man was "Beartrap" Benson, a trapper from the mouth of Bucktail Bayou—known to all, and liked by both gangs.

"This here ain't no time to be fightin' among ourselves!" he declared between gasps. "Know whut's happened? Well, I'll tell you-all whut! Know that land across th' St. Francis, opposite th' mouth of Bucktail? Th' land th' gove'ment done set aside for homestidders? You know it, don't you? Didn't think hit would ever be homestidded, though!"

He paused as for a supreme effort.

"Well—it is goin' to be!" he shouted. "Th' homestidders is come! Ten wagons of 'em! Men-folks and wommern-folks! Cattle and house goods! They's camped this side of Big Openin'—an' you-all, dang you, air here a fightin' mongst yourselves! Shame on all you swamp men—Crowders and Ellifs and all th' rest! Shame!"

A deep silence ensued. Presently Red Ellif called out:

"Brome Crowder, does you-all hear me?"

"I does, Red Ellif!" came the answer.

"Say on!"

"Air you-all willin' to declar' a truce, whilst we joins up an' runs them thieves clean outen th' Sunken Lands?"

"I am!" came the instant response.

Then let's git together an' fix up plans!"

"Whereat are them dam rangers?" somebody yelled.

They were nowhere to be seen. Silently, upon the announcement of Benson's news, they had slipped away.

Through the darkness, Murdock and Sanes were driving their dugouts, racing for Big Opening, three miles above town. Racing on what they knew to be a mission having life or death as an issue.

3

THE HOMESTEADERS HAD come!

Murdock and Sanes both knew what that meant. There were other homesteaders in that part of Arkansas. Some in the Buck Island district, and some at Squatters' Bend. The rangers had aided materially in settling them on their claims, and in maintaining them there. Such was part of their mission.

The Big Opening country, however, had been withheld by the Government until some new ideas in drainage could be tested; now that the test had proven good the land had been opened. Big Opening lay just across the St. Francis, opposite the mouth of Bucktail Bayou, and it had been freely predicted that the Redeyes and their fellow swampers in the Bucktail Lake region would bitterly oppose its occupancy; civilization would be in evidence much too near their stamping grounds. For that reason the homesteaders had gone in quietly.

Could they hold the land?

Undoubtedly they could—with Government aid. But it was desirable, almost imperative, that the occupation take place without a battle between Government forces, homesteaders, and swampers. It was not the Government's policy to shed blood to get its lands reclaimed—but the

Government would brook no armed opposition to its project.

It was unfortunate that the arrival of the homesteaders had been coincident with the Saturday night orgy in Marked Tree. For, fired by liquor, opposition would undoubtedly develop—serious opposition. It is true that Beartrap's announcement had averted a pitched battle between the Redeye factions, but it would have been much better to have them fight among themselves than attack the newcomers.

"Wonder how many fighting men they've got?" Sanes called through the darkness to Murdock, just ahead. "They'll need 'em to-night, or I miss my guess."

"Save your breath—and swing your paddle, Bigboy!" Murdock shouted back. "They won't be long behind us!"

Thereafter nothing but the slight swishing of paddles in water, as the two drove their dugouts against the current, broke the nighttime stillness.

The St. Francis comes into Marked Tree from the north in a sweeping curve. The banks then were timbered for three miles above the town, where the prairie, called Big Opening, began on the west shore. Two miles farther on, Bucktail Bayou enters the river from the east. Fifteen miles up Bucktail Bayou is Bucktail Lake—the region of the Redeyes.

North of Bucktail Bayou is Cypress Bog. It extends up the country for ten miles, and runs back parallel with the course of the bayou clear to the lake. South of the bayou is a similar bog, called Beargrass, equally as impassable as the one on the north. The only avenue from the lake country to the outland is the bayou; it is strictly a boatman's country, since to attempt to cross the bogs on foot would mean disaster, sure and swift.

East of the lake lies more bog, clear to the Mississippi, with bits of high ground here and there upon which the natives' cabins stand. The country immediately adjacent to the lake is also high, affording fairly substantial foundations for dwellings.

The country is, or was at the time, a trappers' and hunters' paradise.

Before the two rangers reached the location of the homesteaders the lights of their camp fires, shining ruddily against the sky, betrayed their presence. They pushed on, eager to reach the place and set about organizing the best resistance possible under the circumstances. Presently they rounded a bend and the encampment lay exposed.

It was strung out along the west bank for several hundred yards—each wagon group with its individual cooking fire. The odor of broiling meat and steaming coffee filled the air, and from the sounds which reached the rangers' ears, all were merry.

Murdock, in the lead, nosed his boat ashore and stepped out, Sanes hurrying after. They proceeded at once to the nearest fire, around which were gathered a number of persons. A man past middle age, two young men, a middle-aged woman, evidently the mother of the young men, and two girls in their teens—trim and pretty.

On hearing the newcomers approaching the elder man looked up and spoke cheerily:

"Welcome, strangers! You're just in time for a snack!"

"Thank you," Murdock returned, "but I'm afraid we

won't have time. You won't either. You know, of course, that there is opposition to you folks coming into this country?"

The elderly man nodded. "We do," he replied.

"Well, you are about to be visited by a band of men who are not only hostile to you at best, but are now pretty well liquored up. They are armed, and mean to run you out. What are you going to do about it?"

"Maybe I can answer that, Tom," said a quiet voice in the shadow of a covered wagon.

Murdock wheeled at the words, and saw a tall, lithe, homely man—young like himself and dressed as he was— who moved toward the fire.

The man was Inspector Jack Calhoun.

The two subordinates snapped their hands upward in salute.

"Who is starting the trouble?" Calhoun inquired, stopping beside the fire and looking with approval at the two tall figures before him.

"The Redeyes," Sanes told him. Then he sketched what was afoot.

Calhoun's face grew grim. "I picked Saturday night on which to pilot these folks in here," he said. "Knew nearly everybody from the district would be hitting it up at Marked Tree. It leaked out, of course—now we'll have work to do."

He fell silent, eyes upon the fire, considering.

"Reckon we better get ready to fight?" asked one of the young men.

Calhoun nodded. "How many?" he asked of Murdock.

"About fifteen Redeyes in town, and they'll be joined

by fully as many of the other swampers from this district," was the answer.

"There are fifteen men of a fighting age in this company," Cal said, evidently thinking aloud. "We make three more. Eighteen all told."

He turned to the elderly man and spoke swiftly.

"Get word to all the men," he ordered. "Also bid your women and children get under cover. Have your men come to me here, bringing their arms and plenty of ammunition. Step lively!"

Graves, the head of the family group at the fire, faded away, followed by his sons.

"Down at the bend, yonder," Cal went on, speaking to his men, "is the logical place at which to intercept the swampers. They'll have to reach here by river—and we'll have the advantage. Each of you will head a group which will act under orders from you. I'll do the talking. Maybe we can avoid serious trouble—but I doubt it. At first sound of gun fire from the attackers turn your men loose—and let them shoot to kill. We can't be squeamish with women and children in danger."

Murdock and Sanes nodded, signifying their complete understanding of what they were to do.

Men came running to the fire, rifles in hand. They were excited, but one and all eager to do whatever might be asked of them.

The two Misses Graves, assisted by Mrs. Graves, busied themselves among the women and children, hurrying them to safety behind the wagons.

"You will be out of range here," Murdock assured one of the girls, Nina by name, as he went among the gathering, offering advice and reassurance. "It is only in case some of them should succeed in getting by us that you would be in danger. They won't get by."

The young woman, her face prettier than before under the emotion of the moment, gave him a quick smile. "We are not afraid," she assured him. "We rather expected trouble."

"There won't be much—right now," Tom replied, feasting his eyes on—according to his fine judgment—the prettiest woman in the swamp country. "We will probably have a parley, and the Redeyes and their gang, knowing themselves at a disadvantage, will drop back down river—to hatch further devilry at their leisure."

A hail from Calhoun brought the big ranger to quick attention, and he hurried off down the river bank with the rest of the party.

Tom's prediction as to the outcome of the impending encounter was purposely optimistic. Sober, the swampers would have acted pretty much as he told the girl they would. But they were not sober.

Calhoun left one party, under Sanes, just beyond the reach of the firelight, cautioning them to take cover in the flags which grew there. A second group, under Murdock, was posted a hundred yards farther down. He continued on with his contingent.

"Mind," he cautioned them all, as he placed each man in advantageous cover, "no shooting until I give the word. Then shoot straight."

Having everything to his liking, the inspector crouched on the ground back of a convenient log, and waited.

4

HE HAD NOT long to wait. The swampers came silently, two
to a dugout. They glided up the stream like so many shadow
boats, about thirty strong. These men were taking what
they believed to be a justifiable course—the only one open
to them if they would preserve the land from invasion. It
never occurred to a single one there that the Sunken Lands
was a part of the province of the United States Government. They had, for the most part, been born and reared
in the swamp; many had never been farther into the world
than Marked Tree. The country was ideal for their needs:
they could hunt, fish, trap—make a living. Moreover, they
could do it in a leisurely fashion. Their fathers and grandfa-
thers had done so before them. Should not they be allowed
to retain their birthright?

Now "furriners" were coming in, bent upon hogging
their lands. They would build levees, dig drainage ditches,
cut the timber—destroy the land, in fine. The swampers
took no account of the fact that the land would be the
better for the levees and the ditches; that corn and hay and
fruit would replace the forest trees, and that sheep and hogs
and cattle would appear magically in the place of bear and
deer and turkey. Those things were outside of their ken.
Besides, if people wanted to till the soil, raise cattle, and
the like, let them find other places to do it in. No swamper

wanted to do those things. He had what he wanted—and, come what might, he meant to keep it.

Calhoun had all that in mind while he waited for them to arrive. In his heart was a feeling of strong sympathy for the misguided natives. He could and did get their viewpoint, and, wrong though it was, he could understand that they might think it right.

But—there were women and children to protect, and, above all, the dominion of the Government to uphold. He hoped that there would be no need for bloodshed, and if it should be necessary, was heartily glad it would be the worthless Redeye contingent, and their ilk, who would get the bullets.

The boats came on. Picking out the burly form of Brome Crowder in the leading dugout, and that of Red Ellif, a close second, Cal suddenly stood up behind his log.

"Crowder!" he called, his voice startling the men.

Brome suddenly backpaddled.

"Whut you want?" he cried. "Who air you?"

"I'm Jack Calhoun, and well known to you," came the reply. "I want you to go back down river, and take your gang with you!"

There was silence for a moment.

"The hell you say!" Red Ellif bawled. "Who air you-all to give orders to we'uns? We ain't goin' nowhar, ceptin' whar we wants to go! Push on, Brome!"

"Yeah! Tell th' damned ranger somethin', Red!" Hez Calloway applauded, standing tipsily in his boat and waving his paddle.

"Push on, men!" shouted Crowder.

Shouts and yells of approval came from the entire band.

"Better stop, before it's too late!" Cal warned, his voice losing the friendly note it had held. "The first man across the point opposite me will get lead—and that goes! "

"We-all eats lead!" shouted Jess Lukens, one of the Crowder gang. "We loves it—and loves it hot!"

He leaped to his feet, snatched a gun from his belt and-fired straight at Cal.

The ranger, however, had anticipated the shot. It passed harmlessly over his head as he crouched behind the log—and the next instant Lukens pitched forward over the gunwale of his dugout, shot dead by Cal's unerring aim.

What happened directly thereafter cannot be adequately described. Hell on a busy night might compare with it. The river suddenly leaped into flames, as the swampers, sobering now, got into action. The leading boats tried valiantly to run past the point opposite Cal and gain the bank beyond. One succeeded, but was sunk by a withering fire from Murdock and his men.

From farther up the shore Sanes and his contingent swept the river with a hail of lead. Boats, shot through, sank, and there was a wild scramble on the part of the occupants to reach the cover of the opposite bank.

Calhoun, searching in the gloom—there was moonlight enough to make objects distinct on the river—for Ellif and Crowder, caught a glimpse of the latter as he headed his boat toward the bank almost at his feet. The big swamper held his revolver ready for deadly use, while his eyes searched the fringe of grass for the ranger.

Taking careful aim, Cal sent a slug through the Redeye's right shoulder, sending him down in the boat, his gun into the river.

"Put back, men!" Crowder shouted. "They's too many for us—got all the edge! Git away, all that kin!"

His own paddler swept his boat around and headed downstream.

Ellif, sitting calmly in the bow of his dugout, his smoking gun useless in his hand, since his ammunition had been exhausted, looked up toward the spot where he fancied Calhoun to be, and called, with venom in his voice:

"Frum now on, Calhoun, it's war 'twixt you an' me! Many's th' time I could a potted you in th' swamp, an' didn't do it! From now on, look out!"

Cal answered nothing. The firing had ceased, and the last of the native dugouts was dropping down river. Ellif, unhurried, as though well assured that the ranger would not shoot him from behind, followed into the darkness.

Then Calhoun set about learning the extent of the casualties on his side of the river.

"They got one of the young chaps—Tim Graves," Murdock told him when he reached that group. "Two more slightly wounded. I—I kind of hate to tell his women folks about it—the Graveses, I mean. They'll likely take it hard—"

"Any other injuries?" Cal interrupted.

"None here."

Sanes's group, being farthest away, had not been touched. One man in Cal's party had a drilled shoulder.

Later three bodies were recovered from the river. Jess Lukens, Oscar Bell, both Redeyes, and a swamper named Cole.

How many were injured on the other side could not be learned at the moment, but there were several as Cal knew.

When the three rangers returned to the Graves's camp-fire, they found three weeping women there—and the still form of young Tim Graves on a blanket beside them.

"Bert, the other boy, saw the man that shot Tim," old man Graves informed Cal. "A big man with reddish hair. He had on a red flannel shirt, and was in one of the leading dugouts."

Cal nodded. Red Ellif," he said. "No other would fit that description."

"Are you going to arrest him?"

The question came from Nina, who turned a tear-stained face upon Cal.

The inspector shook his head negatively. "We are going in after him," he assured her. "But he'll never be brought out of the lake region alive."

Then—then what will you do?"

"We'll bring him dead," Cal answered shortly, and turned to other camps, leaving the Graves family alone with their dead.

5

MORNING FOUND THE homesteaders on the march—and Calhoun, in charge of locating them, with probably the biggest problem he had ever tackled in his life, on hand.

That the previous night's affair would have a terrible aftermath he well knew. Blood had been shed, and that would call for more blood. The Redeyes had lost at least two of their number, and they would be hot for retaliation. So would all the swampers of the Bucktail Lake region.

No need to attempt to smooth matters over now. The struggle was on, its end shrouded in a blood-mist which might already be envisioned. That Wheeler's force was large enough and efficient enough to win out over all odds was true. That Wheeler would not pit his men in warfare against the swampers, if there was any possible way to avoid it, was likewise true. Yet the homesteaders must be located, and they must be protected. The Government had invited them in, and the Government would not shirk its responsibility.

Calling Langs to him, just before the ox-drawn train reached the heart of the Big Opening country where it was to stop permanently, Calhoun ordered:

"Report to Wheeler. Tell him all that has occurred, and say to him that I think great trouble is coming. Get his orders."

Sanes saluted and departed on the ten-mile hike to Oak Donnick.

A halt was made, and Calhoun told the men of the party just what they might expect.

"You probably won't be bothered for some time," he said, in summing up. "The natives will likely allow you time to get settled partly, then, when your fears have presumably become lulled, they'll strike—and strike hard. Now, go ahead with your settling. You will be guarded by me and my men, and when danger threatens, you will not have to meet it alone. Ranger Murdock is permanently assigned to your party, and Ranger Sanes will remain when he returns to-night. Heed the advice of Murdock and Sanes as you would mine. They know the country, the natives, and are well equipped to act as your advisers. I will see you again soon."

With that he departed.

His dugout had been hidden at a point a short distance above the mouth of Bucktail Bayou, on the west shore of the St. Francis, when he had left the river to go afoot to meet the homesteaders. Shortly after regaining it, he paddled across the river and headed into the bayou.

Calhoun had some thinking to do. Moreover, there were plans to form. He wanted solitude, and the opportunity to make some unobserved investigations in the Redeye region. He had to make those observations on the quiet, for to be caught in that district now would mean instant death.

It was Calhoun's habit to use his head in the way nature meant heads to be used: To think with. Using his head had made him the most efficient of all Wheeler's host—had, in fact, elevated him from the ranks to the post of Chief

Inspector of Rangers. By continuing to use his head he could maintain his position, justify his promotion, and, in fine, make good on the job.

The job. That always came first in Jack Calhoun's interest. Not some future job which might be anticipated, but the very job which then lay under his hand.

The job now under his hand was the settling of the newcomers in safety upon their allotted lands. He must do it.

Cal did not penetrate far into the Redeye country; did not, in fact, enter it. He paddled his dugout up the bayou for a distance of five miles, then slipped into the brush on a bit of high ground, drawing his boat into hiding after him.

There, sitting on a log, his pipe going, he took out his pocket-plat of the district—one he had compiled himself, and could rely upon. Hour after hour passed, pipe after pipe was smoked, while he studied the plat and, at length, began drawing plans on the back of an envelope.

When at last he arose the sun was past the meridian, and he took to his boat, desiring to reach the river before the swampers, their Marked Tree celebration over, might be counted upon to show up in the bayou.

As he dropped downstream toward the St. Francis, the plan he had sketched on paper began to take better form in his mind, and when he went ashore opposite the mouth of Bucktail and rejoined the homesteading party, he was a lot easier in mind than he had been when he left it.

As though nothing out of the ordinary had happened, the homesteaders had set about the first step in making their location a permanent one. Everywhere was activity.

Murdock reported all quiet. No swampers had been sighted.

At dusk Sanes came downriver in a dugout, and gave Cal Wheeler's written orders. They read:

> Settle the homesteaders at all costs. Do so with as little bloodshed as possible. It occurs to me that you can best do that by wiping out the Redeyes, root and branch. They have been troublemakers long enough. Drive them from the swamp, and a great step in the right direction will have been made. You may have twenty men to aid you in that task. They will be along Some time to-night. Report progress.
>
> WHEELER.

"Do those orders suit you?" Sanes queried with a grin.

"Down to the ground!" Calhoun declared, his face lighting up. "He has ordered me to do the very thing I planned this afternoon—the only thing possible, under the circumstances. There's action ahead, lad—and plenty of it."

"Do we get in on it—Tom and me?" asked Sanes eagerly.

But Cal did not hear him. There was a far-away look in his eyes, and the beginning of a grin on his lips. His job had been defined for him—Wheeler had attended to that—and he had anticipated it.

Suddenly his face relaxed, and the grin became a chuckle.

"Tell you what, Jerry," he said, "I need some deputies."

Sanes looked at him in puzzlement.

"Deputies?" he queried. "Haven't you got plenty men? Wheeler is going to send twenty, and there's you and Tom and me—"

"Yeah But I need more—about one hundred more, to be definite. And, by golly, lad, I'm going to have 'em!"

6

BEGINNING TWO DAYS after the fight at Big Opening and continuing over a period of ten days' duration, the denizens of Bucktail Lake region were in a greatly disturbed mental state. The average swamper has all the physical courage usually inherent in primitive people; show him danger that he can comprehend and he will face it without a tremor. It is only when he is confronted with something which threatens in an insidious manner; something he feels means harm to him, but hides the nature of such harm, that he becomes alarmed. The natives of the lake were, if not actually alarmed, perturbed at least.

"I aim to find out jest whut that monkey business means, down below the lake!" Foxtail Beeler declared, on the morning of the tenth day after the battle. "I been down there afore, an' so has Beartrap an' some of th' others; but that dang Calhoun jest grins an' says nothin' at all! By gollies, I'm goin' down an' have it out with him!"

Suiting action to words, Foxtail got into his dugout and paddled off toward the bayou.

"I'm goin' erlong, too!" Beartrap Benson called to him. "I'm aimin' to know th' worst!"

He followed Foxtail. Both paddled in silence, left the lake and proceeded down the bayou toward the river, exchanging no words. Proof positive that they were not in a mental state for conversation.

Two miles below the lake they came to a stretch of straight water, and in the distance, half a mile away, loomed the cause of their uneasiness.

A log raft, twenty feet in width, completely blocked the stream. At that point the bayou was not above a hundred and fifty feet wide, and the raft, directly across it, was anchored securely to the muddy margins at each end.

The raft was not, however, an ordinary one in appearance. A long, low, flat-roofed cabin of logs occupied the center of it. The cabin had no windows, and not a soul was visible as the natives warily approached it. When they had reached a point fifty feet from the strange craft a small, square section of log dropped inward in the wall, and a long-barreled rifle made its appearance in the aperture.

"Halt!" came a sharp command.

Foxtail and Beartrap halted. They came to rest, retarding the further progress of their boats by thrusting their long-handled paddles down into the mud of the bayou's bed.

"Lissen here, you-all!" Foxtail cried. "We wants to know whut this here contraption means! You-all won't let none of us go down th' bayou to th' river, an' there ain't no other way we kin git to town. Th' swamp is on all sides, an' unless we can go in our boats we all air like to starve. Th' store ain't got no more flour, ner meal, an' the likker is jest erbout drunk up. We-all wants to know whut it all means, an' when it's goin' to stop?"

"Fuddermo'," Beartrap added, "we wants to know what right you-all has to plumb seal us up in th' lake country!

Don't you know this here is th' onliest way to and from town? What's th' reason for such tomfoolery?"

There was a long silence, during which the natives began to grow restive. Then a door in the end of the cabin opened and Calhoun stepped out.

"Come down, men," he invited. "I guess the time is ripe for a parley."

He sat on a section of stump on board, while Foxtail and Beartrap anchored and landed.

"Squat," Cal invited.

The two men reclined on their boot-heels.

"First," Calhoun began, "I want to tell you that the homesteaders have come to stay. They are putting up cabins and making themselves comfortable. This raft helped them do that—guaranteeing them against any unfortunate visitations from you lake people. But this was not the reason why the raft was built. It has a much deeper one."

He paused.

"What air that deep reason?" Beartrap inquired, uneasily.

"It is a contraption to catch deputies," Cal told him solemnly.

"A—a which?"

"It's like this: You folks have an element among you that is detrimental to the whole district. The Redeyes. They are murderers and thieves. I have been ordered to rid the country of the tribe, root and branch, and to do it with as little trouble as possible.

"Now, I can take my men—I have twenty inside the cabin—go into the lake region and wipe them off the face of the earth. That, however, is not my way of doing it. Besides having to do a lot of killing among the Redeyes themselves, we'd have to shoot up a lot of more decent folks—you and your kind. I looked for a way in which to accomplish my purpose without all that bloodshed. I have found it."

"You-all air talkin' riddles," Beartrap complained. "Why not come right out an' say what you means?"

"So says I!" Foxtail seconded.

"I am going to do just that," Cal told them. "You fellows will have to admit that I command the situation. Unless by my consent no man, or body of men, can pass down the river to Marked Tree. My twenty crack shots can hold this raft against five times your number. There is no other way in which you can leave the lake region. You are, in fine, bottled up. I am going to keep you bottled up—unless you come to my terms."

Beartrap and Foxtail looked at each other in silence. Each knew that Cal was not exaggerating the situation one particle. He had them, and had them right.

"Looky here, Mr. Calhoun," Beartrap said. "You-all says you air after th' Redeyes. Why does you make th' rest of we'uns suffer? Them Reds is only a small part of th' folks up yonder. They ain't more than fifty, men, wimmen and young uns. Yit you makes about two hundred of th' rest of us pay fur whut they does. It ain't fair!"

"No it ain't!" Foxtail declared.

"Want to know how you can get this blockade removed?" Cal asked.

"We shore do!"

"Bring me the Redeyes—men, women and children," Cal told them calmly. "The Government wants to segregate them where they can be watched. Bring them, to the last one, and I'll open the way. Otherwise this craft will stay right here—and any man who crosses it without my consent will cross it feet foremost. Do you get that?"

Both natives gasped in unison. They were plainly incredulous.

"What's that you-all say fur we-uns to do?" Foxtail demanded, after recovery.

"Get Four fellows together—you regulation natives—round up the Redeyes and bring them to me at the raft," Cal repeated. "Then you can come and go as you will. Otherwise not. I've said enough. You understand what I mean—and that I do mean it. The rest is up to you."

He arose, and the natives got up too.

"We ain't no officers!" Beartrap bleated in tones of injury.

"Whyn't you-all go in an' git them fellers?" Foxtail demanded. "We ain't no rangers!"

"I've explained my position," Cal reminded them. "Bring out the Redeyes—or take the consequences."

He walked indoors.

Beartrap and Foxtail departed as silently as they had come.

7

THREE DAYS LATER a strange procession was afloat on the
waters of Bucktail Bayou. Over one hundred boats headed
downstream, all loaded with human beings. Some of the
occupants bore arms—some did not. Those who did not
were Redeyes.

The Redeyes were sullen. They had realized the useless-
ness of giving battle to five times their number, so had
given up with scarcely a struggle.

"What air they aimin' to do with us?" demanded Brome
Crowder. Suffering from an infection from Cal's bullet,
and consequently not able to resist, he had been moved
bodily out of his cabin.

"Dunno," Beartrap answered. "Calhoun said th'
Gove'ment war goin' to sellerbrate you-all, an' then watch
you. I dunno whut that all means, but I reckons you air
soon goin' to find out."

So they had gone. There was nothing else to do.

One, however, was missing. Red Ellif was not with the
boat crowd.

Foxtail Beeler, too, was absent. He alone of the natives
had refused to act as deputy for Calhoun.

"I ain't goin' to allow no dang upstart ranger to tell me
whut to do!" he declared, and sat in his cabin door, sullenly
watching the exodus. "Don't forgit to tell th' smart Alec

whut Red told you to say!" he reminded Beartrap, an evil glitter in his eyes.

Calhoun saw them coming, and was out in force to meet them.

Sullen and suspicious, the Redeyes came aboard the raft. Brome Crowder, lying on a blanket, addressed the inspector.

"Now you got us—which you wouldn't of got me, hadn't been I'm sufferin' like all gitout—whut you aimin' to do with us?"

"The Government is going to settle the bunch of you in a different location, on lands you may own if you are minded to," Cal told him. "None of you have anything to fear—if you behave yourselves. There is one man to whom such immunity does not apply. That man is Red Ellif. He must answer for the killing of young Graves."

"He ain't here." Beartrap spoke up.

"Where is he?"

"Back in th' swamp, somewhars. 'Lows he ain't comin' out."

"Why didn't you bring him?"

Beartrap shifted uneasily. Finally he spoke up:

"It's thisaway: Red had some daminite which he aimed to blow up th' homestidders with. Now he's somewhar in a cabin east of th' lake, an' he ain't steppin' foot outside of it. Settin' thar with that daminite handy, fusees fixed. He done sent word that he aims to blow th' cabin and hisself an' us plumb to hell, sayin' we don't keep away from him. That's why we didn't go nigh. We done fotched in th' balance, but we don't figger you-all ought to ax us to take chances on gittin' blowed to pieces."

"Quite right, Beartrap," Cal replied. "I shan't ask you. Who is in the cabin with Red?"

"He's thar by hisself."

"Where is Foxtail Beeler?"

"He's a settin' in his cabin at th' lake," was the reply. "He wouldn't have nothin' to do with this matter. 'Lows you can go plumb to hell, fur as he's consarned."

"Hump. So Red won't leave the cabin, and at first sign of hostile men at his place he means to blow everything to splinters?"

"That's whut."

"Well," said Cal, "I reckon we'll have to give Red a chance to use his dynamite. You fellows have done your part—now I'll do mine."

8

FOXTAIL BEELER, SITTING in his cabin alone, grew uneasy. Night was approaching and the Redeye escort had not returned.

What was keeping them?

Many things might. Calhoun might have played some sort of trick on them. Having practically the entire male population of the lake country in a bunch he might have sprung a trap and gathered them all in together.

Foxtail was so constituted as to make it utterly impossible for him to believe that the rangers or anybody else would play fair. He was glad he had not gone.

Two dugouts coming into the lake from the bayou caught his attention, and he eyed their approach with interest. When they were close to his cabin he recognized the paddlers.

Calhoun and Murdock.

He had barely time to speculate as to the nature of their mission when Cal hailed him.

"Stay where you are, Foxtail," he ordered. "We have business with you."

An uneasy look came into Beeler's eyes. He got up and stood aside for his callers to enter.

"Where is Red Ellif?" Calhoun asked, when in the cabin.

"I don't rightly know." Foxtail denied.

A gunny-sack filled with lumpy articles, lying on a table, interested Cal, and he untied the mouth. It contained numerous packages of food, tobacco, and a bottle of white liquor. The inspector turned to the native, his manner stern.

"I knew that somebody would be supplying Red with provisions," he said. "Red can't, or won't, leave the hideout, and he must eat. You were the likely party, to my way of thinking. Now I know you are the source of his grub supply. Where is he?"

Foxtail's eyes shifted, came back to Cal's steady ones, then sought the floor.

"Them's my groceries," he asserted sullenly.

"You're lying, Beeler," Cal told him shortly. "Put the cuffs on him, Murdock," he ordered. "He's dangerous. You are going down river to be tried along with Ellif for complicity in the murder of Tim Graves, Foxtail. You are aiding and abetting a criminal in evading the law. I'll find Red without your help—and you won't get any help from me at your trial. Get that?"

The native's face took on a sudden pallor, and fear showed in the depths of his eyes.

"I didn't have nothin' to do with that killin'," he exclaimed. "If Red done it, he done it by hisself—"

"Yes; but you are helping him now."

Foxtail considered that. Prison frightens a native far more than a threat of death would.

"Red's in the Maunder cabin, east of th' lake," he informed the ranger surlily. "He's by hisself, an' you are right about that grub. It's for him. I don't see how that's goin' to help you, though. Red's a-settin' thar with daminite planted, and he means business."

Cal made no answer. He was consulting his pocket plat. He found the location of the Maunder cabin without difficulty. It lay three miles beyond the east shore of Bucktail Lake, a quarter of a mile back from Little Bucktail Bayou.

"Any kind of a signal, Foxtail, by which to announce your coming?" he queried.

Foxtail made no answer.

"Better come through," Cal advised.

"Else it's Federal prison for you."

"I hoots like a owl," Beeler gave up.

"How many hoots?"

"Three. One when I leaves th'bayou; one when I'm halfway to th'cabin, an'one when I get almost to the door. That lets Red know it's me."

"Shuck out of those clothes!" the inspector ordered.

"What you want with my clothes?"

"I want to wear 'em—particularly that foxtail cap of yours," Cal replied. "We are the same size, and I'm almost as homely as you. In the dark I ought to pass for you. We'll try it, anyhow."

In Beeler's garb, with the decorated cap on his head, Cal might easily have passed for the native in the dusk. He gave orders to Murdock.

"Handcuff him and keep him here until I get back," he told his subordinate. "I will get back, unless Foxtail has lied and misled me. In that case you will know what to do."

Murdock snapped the cuffs on.

"If anything happens to you, inspector," he said soberly, "I'll put a slug into Foxtail where it will make him mighty sick."

"They ain't nothin' goin' to happen, so fur as my part is

concerned," Foxtail declared. "I've told the truth. It's jest like I says."

Cal nodded and took to the water. He knew the exact location of the Maunder cabin, being almost as familiar with the region as the natives themselves. Night had almost come, and when he beached his boat and gave the first owl-call he could scarcely make out the faint trail which led northward over the bit of donnick upon which the cabin stood.

A bit nearer the place he hooted again, then listened.

A loud answer came from out of the gloom ahead.

He went on, and came to the edge of the clearing in which the huddle of logs stood on stilts. There was a light inside.

The gunny-sack of food was on his left shoulder, and he pulled it around so as to partly mask his face. Then he hooted again.

The cabin door opened and Red Ellif loomed large in the lamplit oblong.

"Come erlong, Foxtail!" he called. "I'm hongry as a bear! Whut done kep' you so long?"

The man was not in good temper, and Cal deferred his answer until he had a foot on the door-log. Red stood silent, peering down into the gloom at the bent figure with its load.

Cal stepped up on the log, dropped his sack and leaped. "By God—"

Cal's powerful grip choked back the rest of the oath, and both men went to the floor together.

Red Ellif was a strong man. He had lived hard all his life, and his muscles were like steel. There was one thing against

him, however: He had not the advantage of the fine train-
ing every ranger gets, and that Cal had in the last degree.

Three minutes of terrific struggle—then Cal arose, leaving Ellif in handcuffs on the floor.

"You said it would be me or you," he remarked, looking down upon his silent, glaring prisoner. "Well, Red, it's
you—in big letters. I arrest you for the murder of Timothy
Graves, inciting a riot, and the illegal possession of dynamite. That ought to hold you for awhile!"

The next day Wheeler received the following message:

> With the aid of a hundred native deputies, I have gathered
> the Redeyes in. No bloodshed. I await further orders.
>
> Calhoun.

THE JUNGLE TRAIL

*It Led From The Banks Of The Muddy
Mississippi Deep Within The Sunken
Lands As Far As Lost Lake*

1

MEN WITH FAMILIAR EYES

UNITED STATES RANGER Jack Calhoun was idling in Memphis, having reached the Tennessee city at an early hour in the morning. Substituting for Hubbard Wheeler, chief of the rangers quartered in the Sunken Land region of Arkansas, it had fallen to Cal's lot to take Joe Henchley, convicted for killing a mail messenger, to the Federal prison at Atlanta, and he was now on his way back to headquarters at Oak Donnick.

Wheeler was on an extended vacation, and Calhoun had been summoned from his lonely station at Hell Hole to fill the chief's shoes during his absence. It was no sinecure. Directing the movements of two hundred men in various parts of the swamp country was a man's job, and Cal looked a bit careworn as he sat on the levee below Front Street, watching the muddy Mississippi flow by. In the back of his mind he knew that he was in reality being tested— given a chance to demonstrate his ability to manage men, and otherwise efficiently discharge the duties of a highly important position.

"The responsibility doesn't feaze me a bit," he told himself, eyes ranging downriver where a small stern-wheeler, pushing a wood barge ahead of her, was rounding

the bend. "If I am made assistant to Hub Wheeler, I will
have achieved something worth while—but I will have a
good deal less active work in the swamps. I will direct the
movements of men from headquarters, and they'll get all
the real excitement of the work. That's what sticks in my
craw. I'm still in my twenties, and not yet ready to grow
stiff in a chair."

The stern-wheeler was coming to a landing at the wharf
of a wood yard just below the ranger's position. She was a
disreputable looking boat, of light draft, and on her pilot-
house was painted her name: Panther.

The Panther had many counterparts in the wood trade
on the lower river, was remarkable in no way, so far as could
be determined from her exterior, but the ranger found
himself watching her as intently as though he expected
something unusual to happen.

Nothing out of the ordinary occurred, however. The
Panther made the dock, her lines were taken ashore and
her gangplank lowered. The skipper, a heavily built, bearded
man of forty-odd, crossed the plank, followed by the first
mate and a mud-clerk, the latter with bills in hand.

"Jump to it, men! Get that barge unloaded!" bellowed
the mate, immediately he set foot on the wharf.

Half a dozen men, crew of the barge, began passing four-
foot cordwood overside to an equal number of wood-yard
employees. They worked as though daylight had great value
in their eyes, and were determined to waste none of it.

There were two men, however, who failed to respond
to the order to unload cargo. Woodsmen, by the look of
them, Cal thought, idly following them with his eyes as
they came ashore. One was tall, raw-boned, and walked

"Lord!" thought Cal, "I may have unleashed a bit of red-hot hell"

with a slight limp. The other was smaller, clean-shaved, and much more agile in his bearing. Leaving the barge, they made for the top of the levee and passed within a few feet of where Cal was sitting.

"That short buck has a familiar look," the ranger mused. "I wonder, now, if I haven't seen him before, and lately?"

The two passed on out of sight, and Cal, being out of uniform, attracted their attention no more than any other citizen would have done.

"I know what it is!" the ranger declared, and his face cleared. "That short fellow has that red tinge in his eyes which marks him as a Redeye, probably from the Bucktail Bayou section of the Big Swamp. They all look alike—swarthy, and red of eye. Quite likely I have not seen this particular bird before."

He dismissed the two from his mind, watched the unloading for a short while longer, then returned to the main part of the city. He had six hours to kill—until eight o'clock in the evening. In Court Square Park he sat on a bench, fed nuts to the squirrels, and crackers to the goldfish in the big aquariums. That occupation soon palled, and he began walking about on the grass, hands deep in his pockets, mind grappling with the problem which had been engrossing him for days.

"I reckon, on the whole, if promotion does come my way, I'll grab it," was his final conclusion. "It is a big work, and my part in taming the Sunken Lands will be more import-ant then, even if it does lose in activity. Yes, I'll take—"

His eyes rested at that moment upon the familiar face of Hank Flobert, Deputy United States Marshal from Helena, and the latter saw the ranger at the same instant. They met in the center of the park, and gripped hands.

"What brings you away from Hell Hole?" Flobert, Calhoun's elder by perhaps fifteen years, queried.

"On the return from Atlanta," Cal told him. "Took Henchley down. And you?"

"Sneaker Barbe is my reason for being in Memphis," the deputy explained. "You fellows pinched him in the swamp, complicity in the same thing you took Henchley down for. At his trial he got ten years, then made a break when he was being returned to prison from court. They picked him up here in Memphis day before yesterday, down on the river front. I'm taking him back to-night."

"Then maybe we can kill time together, for I'm waiting for the same train you will take," Cal replied. "I remember Sneaker—a bad sort. One of the worst. Ten years is about twenty too few for him. I was certain, at the time we took Barbe in, that he was the brains of the gang that robbed the mail car and killed Wright. Henchley and Latimer, the others engaged, were mere tools. Couldn't prove it, though, and since Henchley was known to have fired the fatal shot, he got life, and the others a measly ten years. That's the way it goes, though."

"You fellows in the Sunken Lands are getting fine support from the courts, Cal," Flobert argued. "You can't deny that."

"Don't want to deny it," Cal retorted. "We are getting convictions, but we are mighty careful to have the evidence to get 'em with. The Lord knows that convictions, and lots of them, are needed if the Big Swamp is to be made safe for civilized persons. If you don't believe it, I'll give you a job when I get to be chief, and you can find out for yourself," he ended with a grin.

The conversation changed to other topics, and the two officers parted after dining together at seven o'clock. Flobert departed for the county jail with his prisoner, and Cal read the evening paper at his hotel until time to go to the depot.

2

AFTER THE SHOOTING

WHEN FRISCO TRAIN Number Five pulled across the bridge into Arkansas, the smoking car forward was pretty well crowded. Near the front sat Flobert. Sneaker Barbe, in handcuffs and leg-irons, sat in a seat directly facing the deputy. He was an alert, black-eyed man of about Calhoun's build and age. The prisoner grinned evilly up at the tall ranger when he paused for a moment beside Flobert.

"Well, Mr. Ranger," he leered, "you're on hand for the finish, I see! Guess I'm got, and got right, this time!" He ruefully eyed the irons which secured him. "That ought to make you happy."

"I'm very well pleased to see you caught again, Sneaker," Cal replied without the least trace of animosity. "To tell the truth, I think you are a good deal more dangerous than the average crook infesting the swamp. Glad to know we won't have you prowling into mischief again there. Not for ten years to come, at any rate."

Cal gave the man a cigar and, after finishing his own pipe, retired to the chair car directly behind. He liked a pipe of tobacco as well as the next man, but had no desire to be smoke-cured in the fog which thickened the air of the overcrowded car.

"Good luck, Hank," he said, bidding the deputy good-by. "Reckon you don't need me to help get Sneaker back to prison—he looks tame enough now. Be good, Sneaker—and you'll live longer."

One and one-half hours later, train Number Five slowed to a stop where a small logging road crossed the Frisco ten miles from Marked Tree. The stop was a momentary one, but it was long enough to permit two shadowy figures to creep up from the brushy right-of-way and board the forward platform of the smoking car. Crouched in the darkness, they waited until the train was again well under steam, then both stepped inside.

The taller of the two led, the gun in his right hand and the mask over his face leaving no doubt of his character in the minds of the passengers near the door who first caught sight of him.

"All right, Shorty," came in gruff, muffled tones from the tall man. "Get busy!"

The second bandit, who held the muzzle of a forty-five caliber revolver unwaveringly upon Deputy Flobert, now slipped to his side and thrust the gun almost into his face.

"Them keys—quick!" he grated.

"Good boys!" ejaculated Sneaker, his eyes glittering with excitement and relief. "I knew you'd show up! Get these damned irons off me, quick!"

Flobert drew the keys from his pocket and handed them to Shorty. There was nothing else for him to do. That he would be instantly killed, in the event of refusal, could not be doubted.

The tall bandit stood near the front door, menacing the now excited passengers with a pair of guns.

"Keep still and you won't be hurt!" he called out. "Interfere, and I'll kill every man who does! We ain't after you, and you ain't in no danger!"

Partly reassured, the passengers remained in their seats, watching.

Shorty seized the keys, freed Sneaker's hands, then bent down to release his ankles.

That was evidently what Flobert was waiting for. In the cuff of his coatsleeve he carried a derringer, and it was only necessary to move his right hand a distance of about two inches to bring the muzzle of the hidden weapon in contact with the stooping bandit. With a movement indescribably quick, he jammed the derringer against Shorty's chest, just above the heart, and pulled the trigger.

There was a muffled roar, a flash of flame, and Shorty crashed to the floor between the two seats. A hoarse groan broke from his lips—then silence.

Sneaker, at the instant the report sounded, threw himself forward and seized Flobert's gun-arm with his powerful right. The second shot from the derringer also found its mark in Shorty's body.

"Quick!" Barbe yelled to the remaining bandit. "There's a damned ranger in the chair-car!"

The tall bandit leaped forward, swung his gun into Flobert's face and fired.

The deputy was dead before his body fell across that of the man he had slain.

Barbe, snatching the keys from the floor where Shorty had dropped them, made short work of the manacles on his legs. He freed himself just as the train conductor hurried into the smoker from the express car ahead.

"Pull her down!" the tall bandit commanded, the moment the conductor entered. The trainman stared at him for an instant, then reached for the signal-cord. One look into the muzzle of that menacing gun was enough to insure implicit obedience on his part. He signaled, and the train began slowing up instantly.

Barbe was then in the aisle, two guns holding the milling crowd at the far end of the car.

The train slid to a stop, the front door of the car slammed—and Barbe and his companion dropped into the darkness beside the track.

Calhoun, in the chair-car, had known nothing of what was going forward in the smoker until the train began to slow up. At that moment a frightened passenger scurried into the chair-car and cried out the news.

Instantly Cal was on his feet and rushing to the aid of Flobert. Arrived at the door of the smoker, however, he found the opening blocked by human beings—human beings, moreover, who would not move out of the way. In that they were blameless, for to do so meant death.

The train, having made its stop, the bandits no longer a menace, the way was finally opened, and Calhoun found himself beside the men on the floor. One glance told him that Flobert was dead.

"The top of his head shot away!" he ejaculated softly, then stooped and uncovered the face of the man beneath.

He, too, was dead. But it was not that which caused the ranger to straighten and murmur low oaths beneath his breath.

The dead bandit was the Redeye whom Calhoun had seen on the levee at Memphis, not more than eight hours before.

3

ON "THE JUNGLE TRAIL"

"CITY AGAINST GABE Rawlins!"

The clerk of the municipal court of Memphis, morning session, called the case, and a court attendant opened the door of a small anteroom.

"Gabe Rawlins!" he bawled.

The crowd in the court auditorium watched the doorway in idle curiosity. Nobody knew Gabe Rawlins, and apparently no one was particularly interested in the case. Just the normal attitude of habitual court room loafers.

When Rawlins, answering to his name, came through the doorway and shambled to the prisoner's dock, the crowd was even less interested than they had been before. He was as unprepossessing in appearance as a man well could be. Tall, awkward, clad in the roughest and dirtiest of garments, he lacked little of being actually revolting.

A week's growth of sandy beard covered his jaws and chin, and his hair, uncut for a long time, was touseled and matted. Deep-set gray eyes, watery and shifting, gave his face a furtive expression. The fingers of one dirty hand beat a nervous tattoo on the arm of his chair, while his left hand gripped a disreputable slouch hat.

"What's the charge?" demanded the judge, disgust in his tones.

"Vagrancy, your honor," the clerk replied. "Patrolman Clancy made the arrest."

Clancy came forward, bent toward the judge and spoke in low tones. Those sitting near enough to hear, caught the words "suspect," "holdup on Winchester Avenue night before last," and "partly identified by the victim." There was more, but the few fragments were enough to arouse a keener interest in the prisoner upon the part of those who heard. They passed the word to others farther back. There was a distinct stir in the court room.

"Order!" bawled the court officer.

"How do you plead?" the judge demanded. "You are accused of being a vagrant. Guilty or not guilty?"

"I'm not guilty, yer honor," Rawlins muttered, avoiding his questioner's eyes.

"There's plenty of evidence to the contrary," replied the judge later. "Six months in the workhouse! Call the next case."

Rawlins got up wearily, and followed an officer into the anteroom, there to await delivery to the guards of the prison van and subsequent transportation to the work-house on the outskirts of the city.

The few remaining cases disposed of, court was dismissed and the crowd found its way to a vantage point at the rear of the municipal building, where a barred van was backed against the curb. They were still indulging their morbid curiosity.

A door in the wall at the rear of the building opened, and a dozen men, marching two and two, handcuffed in pairs, filed across the walk to the van. One of the pair at the end of the line was Gabe Rawlins.

To the onlookers it seemed that the big vagrant slipped his wrist out of the steel which circled it, but, in reality, the fault was that of the turnkey who had failed to lock the cuff. At any rate, before the guards about the van realized what was happening, Rawlins had yanked himself free and was covering the ground between the van and the near corner of the building with amazing rapidity. Running directly toward the crowd which stood near the mouth of an alley, the escaping man plunged among them, gained the alley and disappeared.

"Let him go!" snapped the head guard. "He'll be picked up before night! A fellow that looks like he does couldn't hide no-how!"

The fleeing vagrant continued along the alley until it intersected a short side street; up the latter he went and gained Main Street. There he slowed down, mixed with the crowd, was carried down the thoroughfare a matter of two blocks, then he drifted along North Winchester toward the river. By devious routes he found his way at length to Skipper's Place, a water front dive of the worst character. Slipping inside, he found a vacant table in a far and dark corner of the saloon, sat down and ordered a mug of beer.

The bartender served him, looked him over curiously, but returned to wait on the rest of his customers without saying anything to the newcomer. Presently a knot of men drifted in, and the place became crowded. The free lunch was generously patronized, and the vagrant, after buying a second mug of beer, fairly gorged himself upon the food.

Among the late arrivals, near the noon hour, were two

men who had been prominent in the foreground of the group in the municipal court room that morning, and afterward among those who saw Rawlins escape. If the vagrant recognized the two, he made no move to leave his position at the table. Never by word or look did he betray the least anxiety over their presence, or interest in them.

After a bit one of the men, a dapper fellow in a derby hat and neat suit of blue, lounged over to the table Rawlins was holding down and took the vacant chair across from him. He said nothing, and drank the beer the bartender served in answer to a nod of the customer's head. That done, he allowed himself to become cognizant of the vagrant.

"Say, Bo, you want to get farther away than this!" he said in low tones, leaning across the table in a careless attitude. "The dicks will pick you up here, just as soon as dark comes and they figure you'll be hanging around some dump like this. I saw your get-away, and been looking in all the joints along the water front for you. Maybe I can help you."

"How?" came the cautious query.

"Follow me," instructed the dapper young man, getting up and leading the way into a back room of the saloon. He continued through a second door and mounted a ladderlike stairway to a small room on the second floor.

"We'll be safe here for awhile at least," he informed Rawlins, locking the door. "Now," he went on, "come clean. Did you pull that Winchester Street stickup?"

Rawlins gave him a startled glance, started to speak, then thought better of it. He merely shook his head in a negative manner.

"All right," the stranger told him. "Have it your own way. I don't give a damn either way—only, if you did, you ought to have a plant somewhere. It'll cost a bit of money to get you out of danger from your friends the bulls. Got any?"

"How much?" Rawlins asked suspiciously.

"Well, a hundred bucks to be split between me and a fellow I'll introduce you to later on-if we come to terms; then another hundred for another party who will take care of you after you are out of town. Understand, that guarantees you, without putting out any more money, in getting safely away from this part of the country. I mean safely, too, when I say it. Does that interest you?"

"Well—yeah," Rawlins answered hesitantly. "Suppose, now, I did pull a certain piece of business over on Winchester," he went on, a smirk on his homely features. "Suppose I have got a plant, and can dig up the money—when do I get action?"

"To-night—after you have produced," was the instant answer.

Rawlins considered the face of the speaker for a long moment, then nodded agreement.

"I can't get to my plant until after dark," he said. "Where can I go until then, and be safe?"

"That's easy," was the reply. "Come along."

They descended the stairway into the saloon's back room, then Rawlins followed his conductor down a dark passage leading off from the room. Presently they descended into a cellar and, with the aid of a pocket lantern, located a trapdoor, after first removing a large packing case which concealed it. The door was an entrance to a subcellar, the latter furnished with chairs, tables and bunks.

"My name is Ray—to you," the young man told his charge. "If you are square, you'll be safe in the timber before daylight. If you ain't square, you'll be safe, too—but in another way." He applied a match to an oil lamp on a table and prepared to leave. "I'll come for you right after night-fall. So long."

The vagrant sat down beside the table on which the light stood, listening to the noise Ray made while replacing the trap and the packing case. Then, when assured that the crook had gone, his face relaxed in a grin.

"Well," he reflected, "if things keep moving as smoothly as they have up to now I'll have a pretty bunch of rogues to show Wheeler when he returns, and no mistake! I've got just one man to fear, so far as any one's recognizing me is concerned, and that one is Sneaker Barbe. If he's domi-ciled where I am about to go—well, it may be 'good-by Calhoun.' But then, chances have to be taken, and if I can get two days' action before he pipes me off it'll be all I want. Anyhow, I'm in for it now, and no mistake. No matter where this jungle trail leads, I've got to follow!"

He filled a pipe and fell into a brown study.

4

A FISH FOR THE NET

CALHOUN HAD DRAWN an avalanche of adverse criticism upon himself the night Flobert was killed. Trainmen and passengers all urged the organization of a posse for immediate pursuit of the escaping bandits, arguing heatedly that to remain inactive was little short of criminal.

"We are in the midst of a wilderness," the ranger had pointed out. "Moreover a wilderness made almost impassable by bottomless bogs, innumerable sloughs and bayous. The bandits know exactly where they are going, and how to get there with all speed. To search for them would be time wasted. There are better ways of taking them—and it will be done. For the present we will not give chase."

Ordered to do so by Calhoun, the conductor signaled his engineer to proceed to Marked Tree, where the bodies of the slain men were taken from the train.

A search of the body of Shorty revealed nothing of an enlightening nature, and Cal ordered it prepared for burial. Flobert's corpse would be held, pending instructions from his family. Before daylight Cal was off to Oak Donnick, ranger headquarters, fifteen miles up the St. Francis River. He remained at headquarters for the balance of the day, during which he was closeted with various members of the force under his command. Then, after nightfall, he dropped from sight.

Sitting there in the sub-cellar the ranger reviewed the happenings of the past few days. He had hidden in the swamp until his beard had time to grow out, changed his natty uniform for the rags he was now wearing, then slipped into Memphis aboard a fast freight. That night, behind closed doors, the fake trial for vagrancy, and the workhouse sentence was planned, as was every move involved in the subsequent escape.

If Calhoun's suspicions proved correct there would be certain men in the court room during his trial—men who made a business of getting acquainted with crooks. The success of the scheme he had evolved depended upon them being there.

So it had fallen out. The man Ray, and his companion, had taken the bait.

When Calhoun removed the mask from the dead bandit's face in the smoker and recognized him there flashed across his mind a reenactment of the scene he had observed on the river that morning. The Panther slipping to her berth before the wood-yard, and the tall man with the, limp, together with the Redeye, walking off toward the city. The man who shot Flobert was that same tall woodsman Calhoun accepted without question. They had even then been on their way to the Frisco freight yards, their purpose being to reach the crossing before Number Five's time, and rescue Sneaker, just as they had done.

Questioning the officers who had arrested Barbe on the river front, the ranger learned that the Panther was docked that morning at the wood-yard, and that Barbe had been taken near the place.

Cal pondered that, and came to certain conclusions which resulted in his present masquerade. He had long suspected that an organized gang of men were engaged in running crooks through the swamps to safety, and that they maintained a hideout somewhere in the recesses of the wilderness.

Shorty and his partner had come upriver aboard the Panther, and it was almost certain that Barbe had done likewise. That argued the existence of a retreat somewhere below the city—a retreat in which Barbe had been safely hidden since his spectacular escape from the officers at Helena. News of his capture had undoubtedly been taken downriver by the Panther's crew, and his rescue planned.

Suspicion as to the real activities of the stern-wheeler, the Panther, once aroused in the mind of the ranger, it was not difficult for him to visualize her engaging in the business of running wanted men up and down the river—a feeder to the underground railway he felt sure was maintained in the swamp.

For the purpose of capturing Barbe and his limping companion, and to break up the jungle gang, Cal had planned and executed the dodge which had, so far, worked without a hitch.

"I'm just at the beginning of the trail, though," he reflected, "and there'll be hazards in plenty before the end is reached. Sneaker, for instance."

A noise above warned Cal that some one was in the act of raising the trap, and he glanced toward it to find Ray's face framed in the opening.

"I'm bringing you some company," the crook called softly. "Three more that want to disappear from their usual haunts—and do it pronto. You'll have a chance to get acquainted."

The first of those who descended the ladder into the subcellar was a middle-aged man whom one might have mistaken for a fairly prosperous merchant, but whom Cal later learned was one of the cleverest forgers in the country. He gave the ranger an appraising glance, then sat in a chair as far away from him as possible.

The second to descend was of a clearly defined criminal type—a weasel, was what he put Cal in mind of.

The third was a woman. Dressed in man's clothing, her hair cut short, yet unmistakably a woman.

The ranger wondered, but asked no questions. There are many women among the denizens of the underworld, and they, as well as the men, have cause to seek new fields where, theoretically, the past will not rise up against them.

It was the Weasel who opened up conversation.

"Stake me to a match, Bo?" he inquired, approaching Cal and holding out a clawlike hand. "I had to duck quick, and ain't got a one in my clothes."

Cal obliged him.

"You skinning out, too?" the newcomer asked, striking the match with a hard thumbnail.

"Yeah."

"What you done—or is it any of my business?"

"Ain't done nothing," Cal replied. "Just taking a little vacation."

"You are—like hell!" the woman gibed with a laugh. "You made a get-away from the cops this morning. Ray told me all about you before I came down." There was the vibrant tones of youth in her voice, though her eyes were hard.

"Maybe Ray talks too much," Cal grunted, a frown on his face. "He never told me anything about you," he went on, pointedly.

"There ain't anything to tell," the woman explained. "My man is hiding out, and I'm joining him. We're figuring to shake this part of the country for good; and where my man goes I go."

"Sure. Wonder how many more we'll have before time to start?"

"Ray said there were two more in sight, and no telling how many the boys will dig up before the Panther leaves."

So, it was the Panther! Cal betrayed no interest in the information the woman had given. She went on talking.

"The Red Cloud, from upriver in the St. Louis-Cairo trade, docked an hour ago," she volunteered. "Likely enough the Panther will take a bunch off her. Hell, the organization reaches as far north as St. Paul, and south plumb to the Gulf. We, my man and me, want to go out the other way, though—West. Kansas City, then on."

"Maybe I'll go that way, too," Cal speculated aloud. "Ain't made up my mind yet."

"After your—er—vacation—is over?" grinned the Weasel.

The trap opened again; this time four men were added to the group in the subcellar.

Cal made a mental calculation. "Eight times two hundred—one thousand, six hundred dollars! Maybe more.

Some of these fellows look like ready money, and probably paid a bigger fee. Not bad for an afternoon's work!"

The magnitude of the thing was beginning to dawn upon him. Crooks from all points of the compass, picked up by man-catchers in the organization, pretty much as runners for employment bureaus work in the larger centers, and smuggled to a safe retreat in the wilderness. There, as in a bank clearing house, divided in groups and scattered in the various directions of their individual choice. Yes, the thing was assuming gigantic proportions, and it was patent to Calhoun that never before had he been in so delicate a position—had so great a need for caution.

"But," he reflected, an anticipatory glow warming him from within, "what a fine batch of fish to take in one net!"

5

SOME STARTLING INFORMATION

NIGHT, AND A driving rain whipping the surface of the Big River.

Calhoun, crouching in the protection of the pilot house, on the port side, knew only that the Panther's destination was somewhere upstream. No information as to the exact point of debarkation had been given the group in the sub-cellar when Ray sent them scurrying, one by one, down narrow aisles of stacked cordwood to the dock against which the Panther lay. On board they had been told to scatter and remain out of sight. Cal had taken refuge in the crowded cabin until Memphis was far astern, then had climbed to the hurricane deck. He preferred the clean-smelling out-of-doors, rain-drenched though it was, to the ill-conditioned quarters on the boiler deck.

"The hangout must lie somewhere between Memphis and Cairo," he argued. "And that trip from below, bringing wood, was made for a stall. Well, I'm not kicking. I'll be all the closer to headquarters when the big thing breaks."

Speculation as to a probable meeting with Sneaker Barbe, somewhere in the swamp, occupied the ranger's mind. The more he considered that eventuality the more relieved he became about it. For, he argued, Sneaker would undoubtedly lie close, even in the security of the woods, and not venture out where a chance hunter or trapper might recognize him and pass the information along to the authorities.

Sneaker had been much in the limelight of late, and would be in more danger of recognition than the lesser known crooks. He would, in all probability, not mix with the newcomers at once, there being always a chance that an officer might be among a fresh contingent. Sneaker would be foolish not to keep himself hidden until his time came to leave for distant parts.

"He's the only one I'm uneasy about," Cal told himself. "And if we don't meet accidentally, there's a good chance of him not seeing me at all. The woman's information about herself and her 'man' is a good tip. I'm going to ask for a run West. That will take me out of the swamp at least as far as Crowley's Ridge—and then I'll double back to Oak Donnick, get my bunch and take the whole caboodle! Yes, that tip is going to prove a life-saver."

A shrill, ear-piercing yell, coming from out of the darkness on the starboard side of the pilot house, as nearly as Cal could determine the source, brought him to his feet in a bound. He listened. Was it a splash he heard, or merely the beat of the steamer's paddles on the water?

The next moment he darted around the rear of the pilot house—and came face to face with the bearded skipper of the boat. He was leaning against the starboard guardrail, and, Cal thought, his chest heaved as from some recent exertion.

"Well," growled the skipper, "what you prowling around here for?"

"Ain't prowling," Cal replied. "Thought I heard some-body yell, and came around to see what the trouble might be. Guess I was mistaken, though."

A vivid flare of lightning showed the evil eyes of the riverman, set in a rugged, hard-lined visage. There was a sinister grin on his lips.

"Guess you heard somebody yell, right enough!" he declared, chuckling. "Sometimes a sheep in wolf's cloth-ing—a dick, masquerading among his betters—gets caught in the act. He never is caught more than once, though. Except, of course, when somebody fishes his carcass out of the river, somewhere below. Then, chances are, he ain't recognizable—and it's a dead sure cinch he can't give any information about himself. At least, not in this world.

"I'm telling you that for your own information—not to pass on. Ray says you're a *bona fide* dodger. I'm taking his word, and your own looks, for it. But—if you ain't, you'd fare better to jump overboard and take chances with the Mississippi than go on where you're going. Now, get out of sight—and keep your mouth shut!"

Without comment, Calhoun slunk away to his former position on the port side of the hurricane deck. With eyes closed against the glare of intermittent lightning he digested the startling information just vouchsafed him.

6

TOWARD AN UNKNOWN PORT

A MAN HAD but a few moments before gone to his death overside—had probably been dead before his body was swallowed by the river!

Who among the eight persons gathered in the sub-cellar that afternoon had been the victim?

"It was one of our number," the ranger concluded. "The Red Cloud took some men off the Panther, but had none for her in return. Must have been one of those picked up to-day. Might be, though, one of the wood barge crew. Not likely, however, since they would, of necessity, be picked men, men about whom there could be no doubt. Who? I'll know, of course, when we are set ashore and I count noses. It might have been any one of the gang just shipped—even the woman. At any rate, my burly captain, you'll pay for it—and pay high!"

The incident made Calhoun more on his guard even than he had been before. It demonstrated the ruthlessness of those with whom he had to deal, and their vigilance as well. No doubt the spy had been known for what he was, and deliberately permitted to ship—with a watery grave as his immediate destination.

"They don't waste any time getting their work in," Cal

grunted. "The least suspicion warrants sudden death for the suspect. Lucky I took the pains to frame that get-away, instead of just drifting in and trusting to luck. I've just seen the brand of luck I'd probably have had. No questions asked—just killed and tossed overboard!"

The two hundred dollar fee demanded by Ray, and secured by Cal during a brief absence from the cellar shortly after dark, had been divided after this manner:

One hundred had been split, fifty-fifty, with Goff, skipper of the Panther, and the second hundred had been intrusted to him for payment to some one in the swamp—a man spoken of by Ray as Crock Shamblin.

"Shamblin," Cal ruminated, "must be the head works. He gets a hundred to himself. Never heard the name before—but he's doubtless the boss of the particular station of the underground for which I am headed. Eight hundred cold for the batch to-night—and no telling how many like cargoes reach him each week. There is considerable expense attached to operating the thing, of course; splits here and there; but, even so, the profits are bound to be enormous.

"When a big crook, one known to have a whale of a roll, desires their services, he pays high for them. Worth it, too. Yes—the profits are large, and no wonder every possible watch is kept on those who want to hit the crooked trail. Every man who does is a potential 'sale' to the business—"

Cal's meditations were interrupted by the sound of footsteps near at hand, and he fixed his glance on the vague bulk of the after-wall of the pilot house. The rain had ceased, but there was an almost continual play of lightning. A slight figure emerged from behind the pilot house and advanced to the guard-rail, about ten feet away from the ranger. A vivid flash of lightning, the next moment, revealed a white, grief-tortured face just above the rail, and Calhoun caught his breath in astonishment.

"The woman!" he ejaculated softly.

Again came the illuminating lightning, and Cal saw that she had fixed her big, darkly circled eyes upon him—was beckoning to him with a long forefinger.

"What is it?" he demanded, making his way to her side.

"My—my man!" she cried, her voice rising in a wail.

"What's the matter with him? You're on your way to join him, are you not?"

A fresh spasm of sobs shook the frail form, and she gasped:

"They sent him to his death! Got him killed like a dog!"

"When?"

"Oh—it was him that the marshal, Flobert, killed! Art Barrows—him they called Shorty!"

"The Redeye!"

"Yes! My man! He was always good to me! Now he's dead—they sent him to his death!"

"But why didn't they tell you? Why let you come up to join him, when to do that is impossible?" Cal demanded, unbelievingly.

The woman grew calm—but it was the calm of a suddenly born vindictiveness.

"Because, damn them, they were afraid I'd raise a great noise over him being killed like he was—all their fault!" she informed the ranger. "They kept it from me, and now I'm on my way upriver—to what?"

7

COLD-BLOODED CAL

CAL FELT HIS blood go cold. He could conjecture—could, in fact, say almost with certainty what fate would be hers once she became swallowed up in the swamp. He did not voice that.

"How did you learn about Shorty?" he asked.

"I was lying on a bunk in the main cabin," she replied. "It was dark there, and Hez Tucker, the mate, was talking to Goff about it. Tucker asked the captain if it would not be better to act now, instead of later. And Goff replied that he'd think things over. Then they went away."

"They don't know you heard?"

"No. I came up here directly. I'd be afraid for them to know."

Well might she be. Cal took thought of the murder of the spy, but did not divulge what he had learned. In his mind a plan began to grow—a plan involving this woman. He might be able to save her—must do so, in fact—and she might be a very material aid to him. It was worth a trial, but he must proceed cautiously. That the woman was in real distress he did not doubt. He had seen her face in the lightning's flash—and it had been enough to convince him of her sincerity.

"Judging as well as I can in spite of the ugly garments you wear, you are not an unattractive woman," he began, speaking rapidly in order to make good use of the little time he probably would have alone with her.

"Why—why, what do you mean?" she flared, drawing away from the speaker. "What has that got to do with it?"

"Listen," Cal ordered, moving closer, "I take it you want to save your life—possibly you would like to get revenge for Shorty's taking off. Am I right?"

"Yes—on both counts!" came the positive assurance.

"There is a way. It may be hard to do, but if you've got the grit, and the wish, it can be done," Cal told her earnestly. "This is the first part of the scheme:

"You will remain here near me until we land. In that way we will make sure that you do land. They won't have a chance to do you harm, if Goff contemplates it. You will be informed about Shorty, probably right after you are taken ashore. Now, here is the hard part: You will cry a little, as though shocked and grieved. After a bit you will dry your tears, turn to Goff, or Tucker—whoever your informant may be—and say something like this:

" 'Shorty was good to me, but, after all, there's others. I guess I can bear it.' "

Cal paused, watching to see how the girl would react to his words. For a moment she stared at him incredulously, then opened her lips to speak. The ranger forestalled her.

"It'll just be pretense—acting," he hastened to assure her. "You will pull the wool over their eyes by letting them think you have no intention of raising a row, probably giving things away on them, over Shorty's killing. That will make Goff and his crew easy in mind about you—and, after all, you are attractive. There are mighty few attractive women available to such as they. You can pretend, then, to make up to some member of the gang. Tucker, Goff—maybe this fellow Shamblin, who seems to be leader up yonder."

"God! But you're a cold-blooded proposition!"

The woman was staring at Cal as though she could not credit her ears. Her eyes blazed with anger.

"Yes—I am cold-blooded," Cal acknowledged. "But it's only to save your life—give you a chance for your revenge! Don't you see the possibilities, and how necessary it is to act?"

A change came over the face of the woman—or, rather, girl. She could not have been more than twenty. A glimmer of understanding lighted her eyes.

"You mean that I'm to pretend that I did not care so very much for—for Shorty? Then they'll think I'm not dangerous, and allow me to live?"

"Exactly. They, ruthless as they are, would hardly kill you unless they thought it necessary for their own protection."

"It will not be easy—pretending that," she told Cal, her lower lip trembling.

The ranger felt a sharp pang of pity for this woman of the underworld. No one knew better than he how loyal such women can be, and generally are, to the man of their choice. The fact that he is a crook—murderer, even—makes no difference. The girl undoubtedly saw something in the Redeye to love—and she had given him absolute loyalty. No, it would not be easy.

She was speaking again:

"What is the other part of the plan—where my chance for revenge comes in?" she asked.

"That will be made known to you in its proper place," Cal replied. "What is your name?"

"You can call me Mollie. Say," with sudden suspicion quickening her breathing, "who are you? What are you, anyhow?"

Cal realized that his moment of danger, so far as the woman was concerned, had come.

"I am a big gun," he assured her earnestly. "Just what I claim to be, and Ray and all the rest think I am. Only, I'm a lot bigger even than they suspect. I don't ever mix in little things. When I pull anything, it's something big. The only reason I'm trying to help you is because you're a woman—and I can't stand by and see you get a knifeblade across your throat, and be fed to the fishes. If you don't believe me, and don't want to let me help—why, do just as you please. I haven't a thing to gain, and a lot to lose if anybody knows I've taken an interest in you. Think it over, but think quick."

Mollie leaned forward, hand on his coatsleeve. A flash of lightning revealed Cal's face—earnest, grim. She shuddered.

"Cold-blooded as you are, I believe you are telling the truth about helping me because I'm a woman," she decided finally. "I'll do what you say, but you'll have to show me a way to get revenge on Shamblin and the others responsible for Shorty being let in for what he got. Will you?"

"I will," Cal told her—and he meant it.

They were not an instant too soon in reaching their agreement, for just then Goff swung heavily around the corner of the pilot-house.

8

GLIMMERING LIGHTS AHEAD

FEIGNING UNCONSCIOUSNESS OF the skipper's approach, Calhoun slipped his left arm about Mollie's shoulders and drew her to him—while his right hand slipped inside the bosom of his shirt, to grip the butt of his revolver.

The girl gasped, put up a hand as though to shove him away.

"P-s-s-st-t-t-t! Careful!" the ranger warned, under his breath. "Goff!"

At that moment the skipper, who had halted briefly at sight of the two against the rail, slouched forward. Laying a rough hand upon the girl's arm, he leaned forward and peered intently into her face. A flash of lightning showed the three distinctly.

"Well, I'm damned!" exclaimed Goff. "If it ain't the little tiger-cat, Mollie!" Silent laughter shook him—laughter in which Cal's keen ears detected a note of relief. "Thought you had one man, gal—but, hell, a woman just naturally can't stay straight!" He peered into the bearded face of the ranger and chuckled again.

"Damned if I admire her taste, Rawlins—but that's something else there's no accounting for in a female.

They're liable to take up with anything—regardless of looks. Now, get below, both of you. We're about to leave the river, and the passage is narrow. At some places the limbs of the trees whip hell out of the guards, and even brush the pilot-house. Get below!"

Without a word, Calhoun led Mollie to the companion-way, thence to the boilerdeck. At the texas door he paused long enough to whisper:

"You are saved! He knows now that you are not going to grieve greatly over Shorty. Keep it up—fall for me. In that way you will be safe, which you might not be, should you make up to some other fellow. Keep near me from now on."

"I understand!" came an answering whisper. "You can count on me!"

Then they entered the crowded, smoke-filled cabin. Cal found a seat in a corner for his companion, then began searching the gathering with his eyes. He was not long in determining who had gone overside from the hurricane-deck.

"The Weasel!" he ejaculated mentally. "A spy! I'd never have believed it. Well, well, poor devil! They must have been on to him from the start!"

By a process of elimination Cal had ascertained the identity of the skipper's victim. Every other member of that crooked group forming the Ranger's cargo was present. It had to be the Weasel.

It was a silent group—every member preoccupied. Cal sensed the reason. Not one of them knew just what lay ahead, and each of them had urgent need for thoughtful consideration of the immediate future.

Among the number were two men whom Cal had readily recognized from circulars in possession of the rangers. Fillmore and Basket, wanted by the government for counterfeiting. Wanted badly, at that. He wondered how many more "wanted" men he would meet with soon.

Signaling Mollie to remain where she was, he went outside and sought a secluded spot on the port side of the texas. The Panther was then out of the current and heading toward the Arkansas shore, dark and heavily timbered. Presently a surge of water against the boat's bow informed the ranger that she was encountering a current from shore, and he knew that the pilot was about to run inland by way of one of the countless small rivers which empty the waters of the Sunken Lands into the Mississippi.

Cal had estimated the maximum speed of the Panther at not more than ten miles an hour, upstream, and was fairly certain of her present position.

"About fifty miles above Memphis," he calculated. "We might be just off the mouth of Black Bayou—only there's too much current."

He hearkened to the surge of water against the bow, and nodded slowly. "Little Bear River, or I'm away off! Little Bear is wide enough, has depth enough, to clear the Panther for a dozen miles inland. About the only stream, aside from Black Bayou, that would. Besides, Little Bear furnishes a straight water-trail, for small boats, clear to Swan Lake, thence to the St. Francis. It's the logical stream."

With a labored throbbing, indicating considerable strain, the boat's engine forced her against the current and into the narrow confines of a marshy creek, walled in by gigantic trees. After a bit the going became much easier, and the Panther, slowed to not more than five miles an hour, nosing her way inland. A thin shaft of light from her bow lantern faintly disclosed the course.

"It's Little Bear River right enough!" Cal exclaimed. "Sixty miles from Hell Hole, and it's Lovett's Wood-camp we're headed for, I'll bet! Right under my nose, so to speak, and I never once suspected it!"

All important streams leading inland from the Mississippi would be patrolled by the rangers. Cal had given instructions to that effect before leaving headquarters. It is true that he had dispatched a large body of men in the direction of Helena and the Bayou L'Anguile country, being under the impression at the time that the hangout lay below Memphis. But the four men at Hell Hole had been told to have an eye upon the larger streams above. They would do so, but would not penetrate as far toward the Mississippi as Lovett's camp, or within miles of it, for that matter.

To get word inland, to the ears of one of those rangers—a difficult task, and uncertain of accomplishment—was Cal's job now.

An hour later the river widened and cleared the middle of Lost Lake—a marshy body of water about four miles wide—and on the right bank, half a mile ahead, Calhoun made out glimmering lights.

The Panther's destination was at hand.

The pilot, knowing the depth of the lake, held a course toward the shore, running slowly. The lights became clearer, and presently a couple of flares dispelled the darkness and disclosed a dock of rough timbers and logs, and a cluster of cabins in the shadowed background.

"What's the word?" bellowed a voice from shore, as the boat dropped alongside the dock.

"All set, Shamblin!" responded the skipper from the bow. "Everything fine—and a good cargo this trip!"

Cal glanced toward the man who had spoken from shore, just as he walked onto the dock.

The fellow was tall, raw-boned and walked with a limp.

Undoubtedly Crock Shamblin, the leader of this particular gang, and the man who killed Flobert were one and the same!

"It's a cinch now that Sneaker is near at hand!" flashed across Calhoun's mind. "He'll be with Shamblin, and I'm bound to meet him. The question is—when?"

9

FOR LOVE OF A MOLL

THE PANTHER'S LANDING stage was lowered and, obeying a crisp order, the passengers went ashore. Shamblin and two hard-faced men eyed each one closely as the group filed across the wharf toward the cabins beyond.

Calhoun looked around for Mollie, found her and fell in by her side. Both passed inspection, and followed the others over the marshy ground to a large, double log cabin, in the windows of which lights shone.

The room they entered was large, roughly furnished with a table, chairs and several home-made benches. Shamblin came in directly and instructed his guests to be seated.

"We've got a few hours left to sleep in," he said. "In the morning we will consider each separate case, and decide what the next move will be. Goff tells me there was a sneak among you when the Panther left Memphis—but he ain't here now. Got lost somewhere. If there is any here who have suspicions about any other member of this bunch, speak out. It's to everybody's interest to smoke out a sneak, and that as soon as possible. Anything to say?"

No one answered.

"All right," Shamblin went on. "Go out to the first cabin on the left and turn in. Plenty bunks there—clean ones,

I'll add." He turned to Mollie. "As for you, sis, Lovett and his old woman will take care of you to-night. This is their cabin and you'll roost upstairs."

It was a dismissal, and Cal, accompanied by the male contingent, retired to the cabin mentioned.

The ranger, being dog-tired, crawled into the first bunk that came handy and five minutes later was asleep.

Breakfast was served next morning just after daybreak in the double cabin belonging to Lovett-ostensible operator of the woodyard. It was substantial, clean and well cooked. Mollie, Calhoun noted, was not present.

After the meal Shamblin summoned them into the big room in front.

"You, Rawlins—that's the name Goff says you're using now—were first in this bunch. Where do you want to make for?"

"West," Cal replied without hesitation. "I'm acquainted up and down the river, and in the East," he went on to explain. "West is the only safe direction for me."

"Good. We'll be sending a bunch through soon. You'll be among 'em." He consulted a notebook. "You've paid up, all regular, and there won't be any further fee. A few directions now covering your actions until you leave. The rest of you folks listen, too, because what I say now applies to all.

"You can come and go when and where you please, provided you don't please to go toward the Mississippi. The back country, as far as the limit of Lost Lake, is open to you. By eight o'clock each evening every man must be accounted for—else we'll be hunting the missing one. When found, there won't be any argument—no excuses will be taken. We've got to be strict. There's no use telling you that. Understand?"

Cal nodded, as did the others.

"Now," Shamblin continued, "you are all wood-cutters, should anybody happen along this way. We seldom see strangers in this place, but an occasional hunter does happen by. Be prepared to go off to the woods, saws and axes in hand, when called on to do so. Don't talk to anybody you happen to meet that way—any outsider; and not too much to each other. A still tongue—eh? Well, that's what men on the dodge can't get along without. You can go, Rawlins."

"Rawlins" was glad to go. He wanted some time to himself, in order to do some intensive thinking.

Where was Mollie? Had she been informed about Shorty's death? If so, had she been able to act out the bit of fiction he had sketched for her? Cal hoped so, for the more he considered the woman, the deeper became the conviction that she would prove useful to him.

"If she doesn't show up at noon," he resolved, "I'll inquire about her. Goff probably told Shamblin about that little scene he interrupted on the hurricane deck, and Shamblin will not take my inquiry amiss."

He went down to the dock and sat on a bit of piling, apparently studying the construction of the Panther—idly, as though killing time.

Lovett's woodyard was known to him by hearsay, though he had never been in its vicinity before. The place was outside the northernmost limits of the territory patrolled by the rangers. Such woodyards are not uncommon. Their owners are permitted by the government to enter upon

its property and make wood of the down timber. Such
timber is useless for anything but firewood, and to allow
it to lie aground and rot would be a foolish waste. So long
as one holding a permit to work down timber does not cut
standing trees, the government encourages his operations.
Timber grows better for not being choked with fallen logs.

Lovett's place, then, would not be difficult to find by the
rangers—the difficulty being Cal's to surmount. He had
to get word of his location to them. He hoped to be sent
through the swamp immediately, and, if so, the rest would
be comparatively easy. With fifty good men, he would
swoop down on Shamblin and his gang, and make prisoners of all who remained on their feet after the scrimmage
should be over.

In the meantime, what of his position?

He had been led into error because of seeing the Panther
arrive at Memphis from downriver, the day of Shamblin's and Shorty's appearance. Therefore, when he left
the subcellar the previous evening, ostensibly to dig up
his "plant," he had sent a code message to Oak Donnick,
stating that he was about to depart for an unknown point
below Memphis—probably not more than sixty miles
distant. He named the Panther as being the boat he would
leave on.

"The boys will be watching the lower country, like hawks
around a poultry yard," he reflected regretfully. "By the
time they suspect a slip somewhere and trail the Panther
up here, I'll either be on my way West, else past the need
of assistance—out of reach of it, maybe. The thing resolves
into this:

"I've got to locate the hiding place of Sneaker, and any

other crooks who may be with him—and I suspect there will be a good number—and then hinge my plans on their movements. First and foremost, I'm here to get Sneaker and Shamblin—and I'll get them, if there is a way to do it!"

Others came from the big cabin, some down to the wharf, and Cal sot up to seek a more remote location. At that moment he saw a woman leave one of the small cabins on the right of the main one and cross the yard toward him.

"By golly!" he exclaimed. "It's Mollie—and in skirts again."

He sauntered toward her, and they met at the edge of the wharf. She had changed her male attire for a skirt and waist, and Cal was constrained to admit that he had been right: She was attractive.

Mollie gave him a wan smile. "How do you like me—now?" she inquired.

"Better, Mollie—much better," he answered approvingly. "How did you fare last night?"

"Very well. Shamblin assigned that cabin I just left, for my sole use while I'm here. I had a bag, of course, and a few things in it." She looked up at the ranger meaningly. "I think Shamblin is going to prove willing to be 'made up to'," she told him. "And I am equally sure making up to him is going to be a dangerous thing to do. I know his kind—and they rush things. They are as mean as the devil, too, if they're crossed. What about it?"

Cal was thoughtful. "Take the chance," he instructed, after a moment. "I'm not going to do much sleeping from now on, and I'll have an eye on Mr. Shamblin. Don't let him make too quick an impression."

"I acted as you told me, and he seemed to think it genuine. The poor fool!"

"Good girl!" Cal applauded heartily. "To tell the truth, it would be hard for anybody to believe you'd fall for a scarecrow like me—for, honest, Mollie, you are a real, sure enough looker! Go after Shamblin—but do it easy. I'll get a chance to confer with you every once in awhile, and if there is sudden need of me—well, Mollie dear, I'll come to your aid, even though I let the cat out of the bag, hind claws and all, in doing it. Trot along now—and be watchful."

The girl flashed him a grateful look, then walked obediently away.

"Lord!" Cal thought, watching her graceful carriage as she climbed the steps to the main cabin. "I may have unleashed a bit of red-hot hell that will be burning right now! I've got to get busy!"

"Hey, you!"

The hail came front behind, and the ranger turned carelessly to find the skipper of the Panther signaling him from the bow of the boat.

Cal sauntered over. "Well, captain, what's wanted?" he queried.

Goff eyed him keenly for a moment then spoke:

"Shamblin had a talk with me about that gal this morning and, take my advice, don't get too thick with her—else you won't be making that run West, like you're hankering to do. If you're the kind of gun Ray takes you to be—and I'm believing you are—you've got more sense than to take up with a moll. But even if you haven't, don't try to cop this one. Shamblin draws quick and shoots straight. Get it?"

"I've heard you; now you hear me," Cal responded, his

face expressing grim earnestness. "I wouldn't take up with a moll right now if she was the Queen of Sheba, had a million dollars in each hand, and was on her knees begging me to take the money and her along with it! Hadn't been for a skirt, I wouldn't be in this hole now!"

With that he walked away.

10

FACING QUICK ACTION

THE DAY PASSED uneventfully. Calhoun saw Mollie at a distance several times, but made no effort to talk with her. If Shamblin had eyes of desire upon her, it would be well not to give him cause for jealousy.

At noon the Panther departed for another trip to Memphis, and the ranger overheard Goff telling Shamblin that he would have at least ten passengers on the return trip—among them some "big guns."

Supper over, Cal sat on the dock and smoked until dark, then started over to the bunk cabin. He meant to get a few winks of sleep in the early part of the night, in order to be awake and watchful later on. He had not forgotten his promise to Mollie to be on the alert.

Nearing the front of the big cabin, where a path of light streamed through the open door, he was about to pass around the corner when he heard voices. Drawing back into the shadow, he waited.

Two men came from the darkness beyond the cabin and passed into the light. One was a beefy man whom Cal recognized—McKay, absconding banker from Little Rock. He recognized the other, too.

It was Sneaker Barbe.

Cal retreated farther into the shadow, circled the cabin and entered the bunkhouse. It was a narrow escape, for, even in the night, it was a pretty certain thing that Barbe would recognize the ranger who had laid him by the heels for the mail robbery—a man whom he hated venomously.

"I'd like to hear what passes between that precious pair and Shamblin," he mused, stretched in his bunk. "But I don't dare take chances on him seeing me. Well, I know this, at least: Sneaker is here, and he and others are in another, more inaccessible, hideout. That's what I wanted to know. Now, if I can get away to-morrow, I'll have the whole bunch in hand before many days pass—including the contingent due to arrive to-night."

Cal did not sleep. Two hours later he was outside the cabin, seated in a chair by the door. Mollie's cabin was within easy earshot, but no sound came from it.

At three o'clock in the morning the Panther returned, and her cargo was even larger than Goff had stated it would be. Cal counted an even dozen. At breakfast he looked them over, and grinned to himself as he recognized two more men wanted for government offenses. Mills and Barrett, confidence men who had used the mails to defraud.

"This will be the greatest killing made in years!" he thought. "It's got to be done, too—got to be!"

Outdoors, in his favorite seat on the dock, Cal smoked a pipe and thought the situation over. Everything depended upon his getting away by the following morning at latest.

"They've got too big a crowd here," he reflected. "Danger-ous, that. They'll be sending most of them out, and soon. Got to make it away to-morrow morning—that's certain!"

Half an hour later Shamblin came down to the boat, saw Cal meditating on the wharf, and walked over to him.

"Be ready to start through the swamp right after breakfast to-morrow," he instructed. "There's five others going. You'll be taken through to Black River, a point near where the Frisco crosses, and it's up to you from there on."

"Good," Cal observed. "That's far enough."

Shamblin passed on, and Cal's grin of pure pleasure was none the less genuine for the fact that it never showed on his sober face.

"Couldn't have happened better!" he exclaimed inwardly. "Couldn't! I'll be at headquarters within five hours after our conductor leaves us on our own!"

Out of a corner of an eye he caught sight of Mollie standing beside the door of her cabin. He faced about, and the girl, after giving him a quick, furtive nod, slipped inside.

Cal got up and sauntered around back of the cabin, where the brush grew high, and approached a low window. He called the girl's name softly.

"Had to take a chance and see you," she whispered, appearing suddenly in the opening, her face white and disturbed. "Barbe was here last night, and the Panther is going to run him and a bunch South."

"When?" Cal demanded.

"They will leave here at eleven o'clock to-morrow night!"

"No!"

"It's certain!" the girl insisted. "That isn't all. Shamblin, since he killed Flobert, is mighty uneasy in his mind. He knows what will happen if he's caught. Besides, he's made his wad and wants to go out somewhere and spend it. So he's ducking with the rest of them. There won't be a crook left here by day after to-morrow morning. I know all this, because he wants me to go with him—insists on it, in fact. You promised to get me out safely, and to help me get revenge. Well, what are you going to do about it?"

11

MOLLIE IS GAME

THE LOOK OF incredulity faded out of Calhoun's eyes, and his face became a stony mask. He did not speak, simply stared. So long was he silent the girl spoke again.

"Well—don't you understand?"

Cal nodded. "Only too well," he replied. "Wait!" he bade her. "Don't talk. Let me think!"

It required very little mental effort, however, to determine this fact beyond doubt:

If the Panther carried its unholy crew away from Lovett's woodyard the following night Calhoun would not be able to reach Old Donnick, organize his forces and descend upon the place in time to stop them. He would not be able to do anything he had planned to do. Granting that he left the woodyard early the following morning, he would still be a day short of the time he needed. If it were possible for him to depart in the early part of the coming night he could, by using the telegraph at Hell Hole, have a United States River Patrol boat at the mouth of Little Bear in time to intercept the Panther. But—how get away? He could, of course, slip off after dark, but his absence would be discovered early the following morning, correctly interpreted, and the departure of the crooks would be speeded up. He would then lose them.

No. He must stay on—and he must get word to Hell Hole.

"Can you paddle a dugout?" he asked Mollie, coming out of his paralysis.

She gave him a look of astonishment. "Raised on the Mississippi and not be able to?" she asked. Then, "But, of course, you didn't know where, I was raised. Of course I can handle a dugout—as good as any man."

"Are you game to try something which may end in getting you a slug of lead?"

"If I have to, in order to get away from Shamblin—yes!"

"It's dangerous—yet perfectly possible of performance," Cal told her. "You may be discovered, and, in that event, you will lose your life. On the other hand, if you stay here—well, what hope is there for you then? Either you will yield to Shamblin's desire, and go South with him, or you will certainly meet with death. My way promises more than the other."

"You are just planning for my escape," Mollie reminded him, a hard note in her voice. "What about that chance to even the score for Shorty?"

"By obeying my directions to the letter you will get all the revenge you want!" Cal told her, almost fiercely. "But forget all that for the present. Will you go through with what I want you to do?"

The girl looked at him long and earnestly. "I believe you are not what you pretend to be," she said after a moment. "I think you are really a—"

"Hush!" Cal ordered harshly. "Keep your thoughts to

yourself. Suppose some one should hear you? I don't mean to be hard, but we are both in a mighty dangerous situation. Only clear thinking and swift acting can avail us. What will you do?"

"I'll do anything you tell me to!" Mollie declared sincerely. "Now—does that satisfy you?"

Cal breathed a great sigh of relief. "You are a good girl, Mollie," he applauded. "And a game one. At nine o'clock to-night slip out of this window— By the by, what about Shamblin? Will he—"

"He'll stay away from me!" she declared, interrupting. "I made sure of that by telling him if he would not push me for an answer to-night I'd give him my decision in the morning. I—I smiled at him when I said it, and the fool thinks everything is settled!"

"Good! Slip out this window at nine tonight, and make your way back of the cabins to where that little creek enters the lake, about three hundred yards west of where we are. Have you any idea of its location?"

"Yes. I observed it to-day."

"Be there—prepared for a journey. I'll duck now. Don't fail!"

He darted away from the window, stepped around the corner of the cabin—and came face to face with Shamblin.

The crook halted in his tracks, brow lowering, his face setting in ugly lines.

"What in hell are you hanging round here for?" he demanded.

"Hanging around where?" Cal parried, a look of puzzlement in his eyes.

"Around this cabin!" Shamblin blazed. "Trying to talk to my girl—eh?"

"Your girl? Didn't know you had one. Who is she?"

"By God, I'll show you who she is!" Shamblin raged. "And if you have been trying to horn in on my arrangements—I'll show you something else!"

He strode to the cabin door and pounded upon it. There was no answer. Again he pounded, adding a kick or two from his heavy boot.

Silence within.

"Why don't you try the door?" Cal queried. "Maybe nobody's in?"

Shamblin seized the latch string, yanked on it and thrust the door open. He strode inside, leaving Cal leaning in the doorway.

The room was empty.

Making sure that the girl was not inside, Shamblin came out rather shamefacedly. "Reckon I was wrong," he grumbled. "I'd have sworn Mollie was here. Guess not—and that let's you out. Don't pay any attention to what I said. Forget it."

"I will," Cal told him obligingly, adding under his breath, as he turned toward the wharf: "If he'd had the sense to hunt in the brush under that window—I wonder?"

12

THE MESSENGER DEPARTS

NIGHT CAME AT last, black, with a threat of rain. After the "show up" at eight o'clock, in the main cabin Calhoun retired to the bunk house. Now that the guests were on the eve of departure they loosened up, became more congenial. Many of them elected to remain in the big room and play cards, and the ranger had the bunk cabin almost to himself.

He remained there until half past eight, then stole away in the darkness to a point above the end of the dock. A number of dugouts, chained to a tree, floated not more than fifty feet from the bow of the Panther, and it was Calhoun's task to steal one of them without being detected by any one who might be on the boat.

Selecting one which lay farthest away from the dock, he located its lock, held it against the bole of the tree and covered it with a corner of his coat. Then he drew his revolver from his bosom, clubbed it, and tapped it on the lock, the folds of the coat muffling the sound. Many times he repeated the tapping, exerting pressure on the staple of the lock after each time. At length there was a slight click of the mechanism, and the chain was free.

Crawling into the dugout he poled it silently along the

edge of the lake until he reached the creek he had spoken of to Mollie, then he crept ashore.

The girl was there. She had changed again to male attire, as Cal could tell by the vague outline of her visible in the semidarkness.

"Listen," he whispered, "and if I am not clear touch my arm. You will follow Little Bear River clear to Swan Lake—a matter of about forty miles through absolutely unsettled wilderness. Arrived at the lake, you will follow the east shore until you are in the St. Francis River, then proceed down the river to Hell Hole Settlement—a matter of ten miles. It is the first settlement you will reach, so you can't mistake it. You should be there by noon to-morrow. Go directly to the cabin of the United States Rangers and deliver a message which I am now going to give you to the man in charge."

He took a sheet of folded paper from the inside of his hatband and placed it in her hand.

"Put it in your stocking," he bade her. "You are less likely to lose it there. It is in code and nobody other than a ranger could possibly read it—but its loss would be fatal."

"I won't lose it!" came in a whisper.

"Sure you understand what you are to do?"

She repeated her instructions word for word, and Cal patted her shoulder approvingly.

"And me—what of me after I get to Hell Hole?" she asked.

"The message takes care of that," Cal assured her. "Girl, there are men here for whom States, individuals, even the government have standing rewards—thousands in rewards. If you do your part I'll guarantee that you will get a big share of the amount of those rewards. It will certainly be coming to you." He hesitated, then went on: "You meant to go West, didn't you?"

"Yes."

"Well, the West is big and fine—and nobody cares what one has been so long as he runs straight there. A girl who wants to go straight, in the West, can make all her dreams come true. I'd go, Mollie—you are too much of a real woman to be associating with men who are crooked. Too good a girl."

"I—I think I'll go," she said, softly. "Shall I see you again?"

"If you get to Hell Hole in time, yes. If not—well, you'd best be going. I've fixed up a little note to leave in your cabin, in your name, for Shamblin. It will be part of your revenge."

Mollie stepped into the stern of the dugout, then silently held out her hand.

"Will you tell me your name—your real one?" she asked.

"Yes. It's Calhoun—Jack Calhoun. Now Hurry!"

All right, Jack Calhoun, you've played square with me—and I'm going to get to Hell Hole in time! I'm going to save your life, in return for your saving mine! Good-by!"

She dipped her paddle into the water.

Cal stood watching the vague spot on the river which marked her position until it was no longer there, then he stole back to his bunk. What had just been accomplished was only a small part of the big task ahead of him—and he had to think out the details of the rest of the scheme.

That morning he had been eager to set out on the trip West. Now he was just as eager not to—meant, in fact, to remain in camp until the Panther departed, and to be aboard her when she did.

That was the part of the scheme he had not thought out yet.

13

"FIST AND SKULL!"

WHEN CALHOUN ENTERED the breakfast room just after daybreak the next morning the thought-creases were gone from his face. He had perfected his plans. Some time during the night he had thought of an apparently unimportant circumstance. It was this:

His place at table was next to Skaggs, engineer of the Panther.

By morning that circumstance had become anything but trivial. Coupled with the fact that Cal, too, had an expert's knowledge of steam, it meant much. Upon it he based his hope of remaining in camp, and, later, going downriver aboard the boat.

Skaggs, a big, surly man, was at the table when Cal sat down. The ranger did not speak to him, nor did the engineer pay any attention to his table mate. Skaggs was not amiable at any time, and certainly not in the early morning.

Cal drank his first cup of coffee hurriedly, diluting it with lots of milk to cool it.

"Bring me another cup of coffee, will you?" he requested the table attendant.

The man brought it, black and scalding hot, and placed

it beside Cal's plate—next to Skaggs, who was on the ranger's right.

Cal reached over to fork a biscuit from a plate directly in front of the engineer,, his elbow struck the cup, and the steaming fluid was emptied into Skaggs's lap—after blistering the skin of his left hand.

With a roar of rage and pain Skaggs leaped up, kicked his chair away, and fell to cursing the author of the accident with all the fluency born of a lifetime spent upon the river.

"You—why, damn you, I believe you done it on purpose!" he summed up at last.

Cal, who had arisen also, stood silently by until the engineer finished his flow of profanity. Then he spoke, his voice monotonous, but holding a deadly ring.

"Accident or on purpose, Skaggs," he said evenly, "no man can curse me and not fight over it. Apologize or I'm going to punch your head—and hard, damn you!"

"Apologize!" roared Skaggs. "Why, damn your measly hide—"

Shamblin rushed into the room, filled now with men who confidently expected a fight, and attempted to pacify the angry pair. It was beyond him, and he, sensing the fact that should he deprive the spectators of the excitement they expected, it would prove very unpopular indeed, desisted with a shrug.

"If you two are bound to have it, go outdoors and fight all you want to!" he ordered.

There was a rush for the yard, and a ring was formed around Skaggs and Calhoun.

"How you aiming to fight?" snarled Skaggs.

"Any old way!" Cal replied.

"No guns or knives, men!" Shamblin hastily interposed.

"Fist and skull, then!" shouted the engineer. "Nothing barred—standing up or on the ground, and fight till one or the other says he's got a plenty!"

"Suits me," was Cal's laconic answer.

Skaggs rushed, landed a hard blow on Cal's chest—and took one on the jaw in return. From then on the big engineer found it difficult to touch his opponent, who fought all around him, landing stinging blows almost at will. Again and again Skaggs rushed, seeking to break down Cal's defense and grapple with him—for that was the engineer's style of fighting. He had the strength of a grizzly, and Cal, once in the grip of those long, hairy arms, could count the battle lost.

After a bit the ranger became less and less able to keep away from his opponent, and on two occasions Skaggs felt victory within his grasp. He grew confident—his intended victim was tiring rapidly.

Then it happened. Nobody saw just exactly what took place, they only knew that "Rawlins" deliberately gave Skaggs a chance to clutch him in his arms, or seemed to, then, quicker than any eye could follow, Skaggs was down—down heavily, his right arm bent under him, and the ragged figure of the vagrant on top.

Almost instantly Cal was on his feet, But the engineer did not rise. A moan broke from his lips, and his face was dead-white. Cal stooped and turned him over.

"What's wrong with him?" Shamblin demanded, hastening into the circle.

"He's stunned by the fall for one thing," Cal replied

quietly. "For another, his right arm is broken—I heard it snap."

There was absolute silence for the space of a full minute, and Cal, intent upon Shamblin, saw his eyes turn green, while his right hand stole back to his hip.

"Broke his arm, hey? Broke his arm!" the crook spat venomously. "Do you know what you've done—damn you? You've disabled the only man here that knows how to run a steamboat engine!"

Cal's hard eyes were blazing into Shamblin's when he answered:

"It was an accident—that spilling of the coffee," he stated. "In spite of that, Skaggs cursed me—a thing I don't allow anybody to do. You might bear that in mind, Shamblin!"

"He done it on purpose!" cried Skaggs, sitting up, his useless arm limp at his side. "He spilled it on purpose, and broke my arm by a trick! Now the Panther can't make that run to-night!"

"Shut up!" Cal snapped, turning to Skaggs. "If you can't run that dinky little engine with one hand, then you ain't no better engineer than you are a scrapper!"

"What the hell do you know about it?" yelled Skaggs.

"A lot more than you do, thick head!" Cal blazed. "I can take the dinky apart and put it back together again, and with one arm in a sling at that, if I had to!"

"Yes, you can! Like hell you—"

"Shut up, both of you!"

It was Skipper Goff who interrupted. He motioned to Shamblin to hold off, and the latter merely hooked his thumb in his belt, instead of drawing as he seemed on the point of doing.

"Are you just bluffing about knowing steamboating?" Goff demanded of Cal. "Or have you had experience?"

"I run the Ohio and the Upper Mississippi for ten years as engineer!" Cal declared heatedly. "Used to be my trade before—well, before I took up another. Of course, I know engines—if you call that teapot of yours one!"

"Then," said Goff slowly, "the Panther will run to-night!"

"How?" demanded Skaggs.

"Rawlins caused this trouble, and he'll have to see us out of it," Goff replied. "He'll run the Panther south to-night!"

Cal's face flushed hotly and his fists doubled.

"I'll not do it!" he shouted. "I didn't pay good coin to come down here and slave in an engine-room! I'm due to go out this morning—and, by God, I'm going!"

"You're going south on the Panther tonight," Shamblin broke in, his voice calm, but steady. "Shut your trap. Take him to the engine-room, Goff, and find out how much he knows. If he's been stalling, shoot him without wasting more time. If he knows his business—well, he'll do what we want—else he'll get his. Take him away."

"But—but," Cal objected, "I'm too well known south! I was to go out the other way! I'll be grabbed—"

"Come on!" snapped Goff. "We'll talk all that over later!"

Cal, grumbling and protesting, followed the skipper on board.

Ten minutes later Goff realized that the unwilling engineer was, in spite of his pigheadedness, a first-rate mechanic, and he voiced his satisfaction.

"No help for it," he added, summing up. "Though you

may be as game as they make 'em, you ain't got a chance if you don't obey orders. As for getting caught downriver, I'm coming back here with the Panther—have to keep on pretending to deal in wood for awhile, until I can get rid of this boat. I'll land you here, and you can go West in a dugout by yourself."

"I reckon there ain't no help for it," Cal agreed grudgingly—then, glancing out a porthole, his eyes rested upon Shamblin standing in the door of Mollie's deserted cabin. His face was black with rage, and his eyes were glued to a slip of paper he held in his hand.

Cal chuckled silently. He, having written it, knew what that letter contained.

"Shamblin," the letter ran, "you ain't half wise. How come you to think that an old, ugly crook like you could hold a candle to Shorty—even if Shorty is dead? You make me sick. I'd rather be loved by a mud-turtle than you. That's why I'm ducking. And you needn't try to find me, either—I'll have twelve hours lead, and I can paddle a dugout as fast as any man of you. So long, old mud-turtle! If there are degrees in hell, I hope you get what you deserve—the hottest hole in the place."

"Yeah," Cal muttered to himself. "Rave on, Shamblin—you've got a right to!"

14

END OF THE TRAIL

CALHOUN GLANCED AT his watch.

"Twelve o'clock. We ought to be in the Mississippi in half an hour," he calculated.

The Panther's machinery was running smoothly, and the ranger busied himself here and there in the smudgy light of the engine-room. While he worked, or pretended to, he speculated mentally.

Had Mollie won through to Hell Hole in time?

If so, a United States River Patrol boat would be at the mouth of Little Bear even now—awaiting the coming of the Panther. In that event, Cal meant to let himself be captured along with the rest of the crew and passengers. He would lay low, in case the patrol found it necessary to fire on its prey—as it undoubtedly would; then show up when the capture had been made. That would be easy.

But—

If Mollie had failed to reach Hell Hole in time?

It was because of just such a contingency that Cal had contrived the fight with Skaggs, disabled him and got himself taken on in the engine room—that he had, in fine, taken the long chance he now was taking.

There was a possibility that Mollie would not get

through in time—quite a considerable possibility. Therefore it was Calhoun's duty to stick to the Panther and learn the name and destination of the boat she would transfer her gang to. Then, in the darkness, he meant to escape ashore and have that boat intercepted farther downstream. At any rate, he would have a line on where that batch of "wanted" men were and their subsequent destination. With that much to go on, the government could pick them up with comparative ease.

As Cal poked about from place to place in the engine-room, watchful eyes upon the machinery and ears cocked for any irregularity that might arise, he suddenly became conscious that he was not alone. He saw no one, but he had the feeling, nevertheless, that some one was peering at him from a vantage point invisible to himself.

His thoughts leaped at once to Sneaker Barbe. The latter was aboard, he knew. Long before the time for the gang to assemble, Cal had, in cleaning up around the machinery, contrived to accumulate a mask of grease and dirt which had the effect of transforming him from a scarecrow into a super-scarecrow. It also added much to his safety, should Barbe take it into his head to visit the engine-room.

Without betraying the least uneasiness, Cal walked to the port side of the room, thence back into the dark recess where the port drive-shaft connected with the steamer's paddle-wheel. Laying his hands upon the joint, following its revolutions, he loosened a nut in a place where a loose nut would do the most good—from Cal's point of view; then he sauntered unconcernedly back to the front of the room.

Goff, Shamblin and Sneaker Barbe stepped out of the shadows in the fore part of the room, and the skipper spoke:

"You're wanted up in the cabin, Rawlins," he said. "I'll take charge here until you return—if you do."

"What's up?" demanded Cal.

"Maybe nothing—maybe a lot," Shamblin answered. "Anyhow, come on with us. And," he added, "don't try any monkey business."

Cal's eyes dropped to Shamblin's hand. He had his gun out.

"Sure," he replied. "Anything to oblige."

Walking directly in front of Shamblin, he mounted to the boiler-deck and entered the texas. It was occupied by only half a dozen men—all of whom eyed him curiously, not to say hostilely, as he took a seat beside a table above which hung a smoky oil lantern.

"Barbe, here, thinks your mug looks familiar, and wants to ask you a few questions," Shamblin informed the ranger. "And if you are wise, you'll answer without us having to use any rough stuff."

"Sure. Ask anything you want to," Cal agreed amiably, turning to Sneaker, who sat in the chair next him, but withdrawn about three feet. "I ain't got nothing to hide—and the gent may have seen me before. I've been mixing with, er—with gents of his kind for a good many years!"

"Cut that kind of stuff!" Barbe gritted.

Cal was thinking hard. The Panther should now be all but afloat on the Big River. Would he hear the high, shrill siren of a patrol boat signaling the Panther to lay-to? Or had Mollie failed, after all, leaving him absolutely on his own?

"Where'd you come from, feller?" Sneaker was asking.

"About everywhere," Cal replied. "From St. Louis directly to Memphis, however, when I got picked up and vagged."

Sneaker peered at him intently, then spoke to a man near him.

"Get a wet towel," he ordered. "I want a look at that face—without the grease on it."

Cal knew what that meant. His gun nestled inside his shirt, and his right hand stole gradually toward it. Careful as he was, however, Sneaker caught the movement.

"Grab him!" he yelled, reaching for his hip.

Cal was seized from behind and borne backward.

At that instant there came a loud, crashing report from below decks, accompanied by a swaying motion of the boat. Almost instantly the engine was shut off, and from the pilot there came a mad jingling of bells.

The loosened nut had done its work!

The door of the texas crashed open, and Goff stormed in.

"The port drive-shaft has gone to hell!" he raged. "Our wheel is hanging helpless in the river—we can't do nothing but drift ashore, crippled, and maybe a whole day before we can run again! And," he went on, leveling a stubby finger at Calhoun, that devil is the one that done the damage!"

"Kill him! Stand away from him men!" yelped Shamblin, his voice a high streak of rage. "I'm going to shoot the damned sneak—"

Then Cal's ears caught it—a high, shrill note cleaving the air like the wail of a panther!

Mollie had reached Hell Hole in time!

The men in the cabin heard it, too—and froze for an

instant in their various positions. The two who were hold-ing Cal relaxed their grips, so intent were they—and the ranger acted.

Wrenching free, he swung at the hanging lamp with his hat, caught it fairly and plunged the cabin in darkness. Then he lunged toward where he had last seen Crockett Shamblin—and gripped him around the throat.

Shamblin's gun arm swung up—to be caught by Cal and forced down. The blaze from its muzzle lit the cabin instantaneously—it was the last sight ever to greet the outlaw's eyes.

Cal's powerful fingers closed down—and something snapped. It was Shamblin's neck.

"Lights! Lights!" Came a chorus of yells from all sides. Men came pouring into the already crowded texas.

Then a slight jar informed the ranger, who, in the dark-ness, was half out of the texas door, dragging the body of Shamblin with him, that the patrol had laid alongside.

The next moment his amazed eyes rested upon the tall figure of Hub Wheeler—Wheeler himself!

By then the Panther was swarming with rangers and deputies, and the boat was theirs.

The ranger chief peered intently into the face of the scarecrow before him, then ejaculated in utter astonish-ment:

"By the Eternal, if it ain't Calhoun!"

"Yeah!" Cal acknowledged, grinning weakly. Then he glanced down at the corpse he still held. "And this," he added, "was Mr. Crockett Shamblin—leader of the jungle gang, and the man who killed Flobert. He ain't anything now!"

A year later Chief Inspector Calhoun sat in the doorway of the ranger cabin at Hell Hole. The promotion had
come, and Cal no longer feared that he would grow stiff
in a chair. Being chief inspector, his job kept him almost
continually afield, and his activities were vastly increased.
For that he was grateful.

On this day the ranger's mind was taking him back, over
that trail he had followed into the jungle; the subsequent
breaking up of the formidable and far reaching organization operating the Underground Railway; the capture by
Wheeler and his men, that night aboard the Panther, of
men wanted by nearly every State in the Middle West—
and, lastly, the execution of Sneaker Barbe for his share in
the killing of Flobert, and the life sentence Goff received
for dropping the Weasel overboard. All those things were
good to think upon.

The mail came up the river, and a subordinate handed
the inspector a letter bearing a Wyoming postmark.

Cal, wondering who in the world could be writing him
from there, opened the communication and read:

DEAR JACK CALHOUN:

You were right about the West. It is a place where a girl
who runs straight can make her dream come true. Mine
has—he's big, strong, generous; everything, in fact, that I
used, long, long ago, to hope my honest-to-goodness man
would be. I have you to thank for him—and I do.

The best of everything good to you, from

MOLLIE.

ONE GOOD MAN

"If You Do Find 'Em," Snarled Lundsford,
"Better Slip Away Without Lettin' 'Em
Know It—They're Bad Medicine!"

1

WHERE THE JONESBORO, Lake City and Eastern Railroad spans Lake St. Francis, that body of water is a mile wide. The railway trestle describes a long curve, beginning immediately it leaves the west bank, and an eastbound train becomes invisible from Lake City, the village at the head of the trestle, almost at once. There is no town on the eastern bank of the lake. Nothing, for miles, but wilderness.

Lake St. Francis is something of a wilderness in appearance itself. The channel of the river from which it takes its name is but a narrow ribbon, flanked on the east by cypress trees, mud banks, flags and other growths—a paradise for fishermen. A stranger, however, would need a guide to find his way about in the eastern portion.

Just after dark, one September night, two long dugouts glided up the lake, crossing occasional areas of moonlit water, but invisible from the town because of the character of the place. Each craft held two men, and they were silent; even the dip of their paddles in the water made not the slightest ripple. Reaching a tree-clad mudbank a hundred yards below the juncture of railway trestle and shore, both boats found the shadowed side and laid against it. There was no conversation, no smoking—nothing, in fine, that might have betrayed a presence there.

After half an hour's wait, a tall man in the first dugout,

He reached the shadow of the tree before
Calhoun's clubbed gun dropped him

who appeared to be leading the expedition, silently nosed
his boat away, and slipped through the growth to a landing
on the east shore. The second craft followed as noiselessly.

Fifteen minutes later, the night train for Barfield's Point
left Lake City for the eastern terminus. It consisted of two
coaches and a combination express, baggage and mail car,
the latter having two men aboard. The engineer felt his way
carefully over the long trestle, for the unstable foundations
of the piers made caution imperative; until the low ground
of the lake region should be left behind, he would proceed
under close control, a sharp lookout for bad track.

The last coach had barely cleared the approach on the
east side, and the engineer was cautiously giving his cylin-
ders more steam, when a red lantern seemed to leap out of
the night, ahead, describing frantic revolutions, as though
the bearer were in a high state of excitement.

The engine driver applied the air, and the train slid to
a screeching stop; then he stepped to the cab door and
called out:

"What's wrong? Track dropped down?"

That was the bit of roadbed nuisance causing the greater part of trouble on the line.

"No—but you'll drop down, and out, if you don't obey orders, and hustle about it, too!"

The voice came from directly below, and the engineman looked down into the muzzle of a revolver. A second later, a tall man, completely masked, swung up into the cab and another boarded the engine from the fireman's side.

A shrill whistle sounded from the rear, and the tall man swung his gun on the engineer.

"Pull ahead until I tell you to stop—and give her steam!" he ordered.

The engineer, too astonished to use his tongue—for no such thing had ever before been perpetrated on the little road—obeyed.

When the train came to a stop, Morris Brake, the mail messenger, opened the door of the car and looked ahead— to find himself caught by the ankles and brought to the floor with a thud. An instant later two men crawled over his prostrate body into the car. They were armed, and wore masks. One seized the messenger and drew him inside, then closed the door. At that moment the car, cut loose from the rest of the train, began moving rapidly ahead.

"Open your safe!" came the command from one of the bandits, while his mate held the baggage man helpless under his gun.

Brake got to his feet, and turned to the safe. He was a man of high courage, and there was an unusually large sum of money in the safe—used jointly by the mail service and the express company. He manipulated the combination, swung the door open, seized a revolver which lay inside and wheeled—to meet instant death at the hands of the bandit.

The whistle of the locomotive sounded a short blast—evidently a signal to the men in the car. Paying no attention to the dead messenger, the bandit took a grain sack from beneath his coat and scooped the contents of the safe into it, then turned to the door as the train slowed to a stop.

"All right, Bud!" he exclaimed.

The man called Bud swung his clubbed gun, and the baggageman dropped heavily to the floor.

In the engine cab, both the driver and the fireman had been rendered unconscious in a like manner, and, ten minutes after the holdup began, the four thieves were racing to where their boats lay hidden. Racing for Lake St. Francis, to lose themselves in the great swamp to the south—trackless, wild, almost impenetrable save to those in the know.

In the sack carried by the bandit who had slain the mail messenger reposed the sum of ten thousand dollars—funds of the express company and the government.

2

JACK CALHOUN, UNITED States Ranger stationed at Hell Hole, in the Sunken Land region of Arkansas, dropped the boot he was polishing and gave entire attention to the telegraph instrument clicking on a table in his cabin. His call had been sounded.

"Headquarters. Wheeler sending," came the message. "Train number two, J.L.C. and E., held up at east end trestle on Lake St. Francis, last night. Four men, possibly more. Express safe robbed. Mail looted, and messenger killed. Possible aids in identification: Leader a tall, spare man. Two others medium height. Fourth, who shot Brake, short, heavy-set, red hair. All masked. Escaped by boat. Bloodhounds followed trail to lake. Blair, of Craighead, and posse combing lake country north of railway. Lundsford, of Poinsette, and posse of ten just passed here in motor boats to search south. Advise not joining them, but go on your own. Communicate when possible."

"Got it," was Calhoun's reply.

He resumed polishing the boot. The hour was two in the afternoon of the day succeeding the robbery, and the ranger was putting a bit of spare time to good use by burnishing his equipment. He was in no great hurry even now, and for a very good reason.

Wheeler had said that Sheriff Lundsford was on his

was upriver with a big posse. Therefore Calhoun would
wait until they had come and gone, before taking to the
wilderness.

"I'll find out where they are going, and then go an
entirely different way," he was thinking. "Wheeler needn't
advise me not to join the sheriff's gang. Man-hunting in
a motor boat!"

There was scorn in the ranger's voice, and a look of
disgust on his face. His contacts with the sheriff from Poinsette County had been of a character calculated to arouse
just such feelings.

"Lundsford never played a solo hand in his whole term
of office," Cal soliloquized. "Always has to have his posse.
I actually believe he brings his armed gang into the swamp
for his own protection, more than for any other reason. A
good enough office sheriff—but worse than useless on a
trail. No, Wheeler need not have told me to lay off him
and his gang!"

The surface of the boot now shone like new copper, and
Calhoun laid it aside. From a locked cupboard he took a
roll of stiff blue print paper; spreading it out on a table, he
fastened the corners down with thumb tacks and sat down
to consider it.

The thing before the ranger was a map of the Sunken
Land Country. Not the official one, but a comprehensive,
painstaking plat made by Cal himself. On that paper, carefully traced, was the record of the ranger's explorations in
the district. Every creek, slough, bayou, no matter how
small and unimportant; every island, lake and donnick was
there in its proper place. Distances were faithfully recorded.
Little dots here and there showed the exact locations of

the cabins of the natives—and the name of the occupant appeared in tiny letters below each cabin. With the map, Calhoun had the country before him as it really was, and not as it was rather vaguely depicted upon official plats of the region. He had more than once found it of inestimable value.

The scene of the train robbers' operations was sixty miles north of Hell Hole, at the head of Lake St. Francis, which was eighteen miles from end to end, and as many as four miles wide in some places. The ranger considered the lay of the land in and around that portion of the district.

"They would not go north," he reflected. "Two good reasons for not doing so. One, that way lies civilization. Secondly, they'd have a current to buck, after leaving the lake, and consequently make slow progress. No. They'd likely follow the lake down, get into the current of the river as soon as possible, and take advantage of that in their get-away. Blair, of Craighead, is a good man and a fine officer—but he's wasting his time in the territory north. Now, where would they be liable to leave the lake?"

He followed the outline of the big body of water closely, noting the many small streams leading from it to the interior.

"None of those would likely attract them," was his conclusion. "They lead nowhere."

Near the foot of the lake, Big Bayou takes off in a southeasterly course for some fifteen miles, then straightens out due east for five miles and finally angles northeast to Reed Lake. The ranger gave that course very close attention.

Following the line of the bayou, Calhoun's glance wavered and stopped at a point where an arm of the larger stream takes off nearly south and joins Little Bear River. Little Bear has its origin in Swan Lake, and runs a fifty mile course straight to the Mississippi.

"I wouldn't be surprised, now, if that is the route they'll take. It's the logical one. I can't imagine four crooks with ten thousand dollars cash split up among them, lingering in the swamp any longer than they have to. Nothing to spend money for here. The old Murel Route, part of the once used underground system used in running slaves South, would naturally be known to them.

A direct outlet to the Big River—and never a foot upon the ground. Once on the Mississippi, it would be easy to mingle with the roustabouts of a steamboat at a small village or woodyard, and get away north or south with little chance of detection. Moreover, Little Bear traverses a wilderness—cane-brakes, flags, river-grass line its shores. Plenty of cover in case of pursuit. At any rate, I'm going to proceed on the theory that they would seek that particular outlet—and try and grab them there."

He returned the map to its cupboard, and began leisurely gathering his kit for the trip. He was in no hurry. The bandits would be somewhere west of the junction of Beaver Creek and Little Bear, and there was ample time for him to travel down the river to the point where it absorbed the creek, before they could possibly reach it. Lundsford out of the way, he would start.

Two hours later the put-put-put of a pair of motor boats announced the coming of the sheriff and his posse.

"Noise enough to wake a graveyard full of dead people," Cal commented as he went to the landing to meet the party. "Must be a dozen men all told," he estimated, as the two motor boats came to anchor.

"Well, Cal, I guess you've heard the news?" Lundsford called, stepping ashore. "Why ain't you out in the timber?"

"I've heard the news, yes," Calhoun replied. "And I'm getting ready to strike out. What are you holding—a convention of some kind?" he queried, eying the escort.

Lundsford flashed him a hard look.

"I'm out to get those train robbers—and get 'em right!" he exclaimed heatedly. "Stopped at Oak Donnick and consulted with Wheeler—invited him to send some of his men along. What you reckon he said?"

Calhoun shook his head. "Haven't any idea what the chief said," he replied, a glint of humor in his eyes. "There are so many things he might have, you know. Suppose you tell me."

"He put out the same old stuff!" Lundsford declared. " 'One good man,' he said, 'is worth more than a dozen, in such a search. The dozen are, by reason of the noise and confusion of their number, foredoomed to failure. Calhoun is at Hell Hole, and he'll take care of any bandits who come his way!' That's the line of talk he handed me!"

Calhoun grinned. "The chief isn't very strong on the gab," he told Lundsford. "Reckon he must have believed the way he talked, else he wouldn't have so expressed himself."

"Believe it!" the sheriff exploded. "Why, hell, the man is plumb rotten with confidence. Thinks he's got an unbeatable organization, and while I'll admit you boys are doing very well, nobody is unbeatable! Here's something else he handed me. I says to him: 'What could Cal do by himself, if he was to run smack onto the four?'

" 'In the first place, Cal isn't going to run smack onto them,' he replied. 'He's too careful for that. But if he locates them, he'll bring 'em in—dead or alive. One good man, working on the side of the law, is more than a match for half a dozen crooks.'

"Stuck on himself and his bunch? Well, I'll say he is!"

Lundsford's red face and angry eyes testified to his wrought up condition. Calhoun, secretly amused, changed the topic, directing the sheriff's mind back to the business in hand.

"Where you headed for now, sheriff?" he wanted to know.

"To the most likely place in the swamp to catch that gang," Lundsford told him. "Swan Lake. What better place in the whole region for them to hide out? A lake fourteen miles in circumference, and chock full of islands, big and little, and water growths of all kinds, couldn't be beat for a hideout. We're going to comb that lake from end to end—and we're going to bring out our men! Want to come along and see us do it?"

"Well, no," the ranger answered. "Thank you just the same. I'll cover another part of the swamp. Got an idea they might not come down as far as Swan Lake—and I'm going to test it out."

"One man stunt!" Lundsford exclaimed derisively, as he returned to his boat. "Well, take my advice, Cal, and if you do happen onto that gang, slip away without letting 'em know it. They're bad medicine—take it from me! Bad!"

Calhoun watched them depart, then took to the river in his bateau.

It was exactly ten miles from Hell Hole Settlement to

the foot of Swan Lake, and the ranger reached the place at five o'clock—a wilderness of water, studded thickly with trees and small islands, through which the St. Francis traces its course. The distant put-put-put of Lundsford's motor boats advertised the presence of his party in the vicinity.

3

CAL FOLLOWED THE shore line on the east, and found his way to the source of Little Bear River. There he nosed his bateau onto a mudbank and considered his next move.

"If the thieves are not together," he thought, "my chance of picking them up is almost nil. They may have split, of course, but such a thing is unlikely; they would, in all probability, stick together until out of the swamp. That, in case of pursuit and battle. According to my calculations, they should now be somewhere between the junction of Big Bayou and Beaver Creek, and the junction of Beaver and Little Bear. I'll run the river to-night, and ought to get below the mouth of Beaver before they do."

He swung his boat into Little Bear, and plied his paddle with strong, steady, distance-eating strokes. He did not waste any time planning what to do in case he should locate the thieves. To locate them was the paramount thing; after that, he'd consider ways and means of taking them.

Now that he was actually on the old Murel Route to the Mississippi, the conviction became stronger than ever that the bandits would make for that outlet to the river. They would have to travel by boat, since the vast wilderness spreading eastward to the Big River was so crisscrossed by sloughs and bayous, to say nothing of immense areas of treacherous marshland, as to render overland travel practically impossible. Furthermore, so long as they kept to the water, hounds could not trail them.

It was a thousand to one that they were following some stream in the swamp, and Calhoun was guessing at which one. He felt that, given his exhaustive knowledge of the country, his choice was something better than a guess. It was a well-based calculation.

The channel of Little Bear River is not more than one hundred feet at its widest; on each side the wilderness walls it in; having no banks, the stream spreads out through crane-brakes, cypress swamps and flats, sometimes for miles into the timber. The dead water back of the brakes can be navigated by boatmen who know the stream, and it is possible to travel the whole length of the river without ever showing up in the channel. Slow progress, certainly, but safe, since to find a craft in the tangle is virtually impossible. Whisky runners know the ins and outs of such trails well, and make good use of them.

When Calhoun reached the juncture of Beaver Creek and Little Bear he was, according to his calculations, at least six hours ahead of the quarry. He knew the distance they would have to cover to get there, and he knew the maximum speed they would be able to make in their boats. At the outside, he had six hours this advantage.

The hour was nine in the evening, and a late moon was silvering the water, showing up objects in the channel, but intensifying the darkness of the shore lines. Cal continued downstream for half an hour longer, then steered his bateau out of the channel and back of a screen of cane on the left hand side of the river. He took a spool of black sewing thread from his pocket, attached one end to a stalk of cane about three inches above the surface of the water, then crossed in a straight line into the cover on the right hand side, unwinding the thread from the spool at he went. There he secured the free end of the thread to a second stalk of cane, anchored the bateau and spread his blankets in it. That done he untied the thread and fastened it around the thumb of his left hand.

"A boat can't pass without striking the thread," he said to himself as he stretched out, "and I've got a sensitive thumb."

Two minutes later he was sleeping.

Whether it was the jerking of the thread or the rocking of the bateau that awakened him Cal did not know. Dawn was just breaking when he became dimly conscious that the weather had changed during the night, and a wind storm was brewing. He sat up, and at that instant the thread suddenly tightened about his thumb, then released suddenly as the bow of a boat dove it in two.

Calhoun was wide awake on the instant, peering through the opening in his screen at the stretch of water immediately within his vision.

A long dugout, carrying two paddlers, slipped by, followed by another a moment later. It also carried two men. Cal waited, scarcely breathing. There were no more.

"I guessed right!" he exclaimed mentally, a pleased grin on his face. "Now I know where they are, and their probable objective—what?"

"That was a matter demanding most careful consideration. Cal settled back in his bateau, and did some swift thinking. He could easily have picked off the bandits with his rifle, had that been his desire. At least he could have gotten the two in the first boat that way, and probably captured the remaining two. But Calhoun was never a man to shoot unless it became absolutely necessary. It was not his nature to do so. Furthermore, the Government wants its culprits taken alive. An officer who has to kill his man to get him does not last long in the service. He is dropped, and should be. Calhoun kept his gun in its holster, and used his head.

"They are making for the Mississippi," he argued. "Of that I am certain, because there is nowhere else they could be headed. Now, if I follow them until the Big River is reached I will have the aid of the officers of the boat they select to escape on. That, if I have luck. On the other hand, they may give me the slip, since I will necessarily have to remain at least an hour behind them. A boat may be just in the act of clearing when they arrive. If so, good-by. They looked fresh enough this morning, so they probably slept a good part of last night, and will go far to-day. Half the distance, probably. So I've got to-day, to-night and to-morrow in which to think up a scheme that will work." He looked off through the timber to where dry land showed. "A bit of breakfast will help the thinking along," he decided, and struck out for the shore.

While he cooked and ate breakfast he continued to canvas the meager possibilities the situation presented. When he took to the river again the problem had narrowed down to this:

"I'll follow an hour behind, then when the Mississippi is near I'll crowd them as closely as I can with safety," he decided. "I've got to get there right on their heels, that's certain. Morgan's wood yard will probably have a steamer or two taking on fuel, and a steamer is their only chance.

If they get aboard and away before I can stop them I'll follow in a motor boat—commandeer a steam boat if I have to. Anyhow, Wheeler has said that one good man working on the side of the law is more than a match for a dozen crooks—and I'm not going to be the one to make him eat his words!"

The storm, threatening since before daybreak, suddenly broke, and for the next hour the ranger had all he could do to make headway in the terrific wind, to say nothing of the necessity of bailing almost constantly. The rain fell in torrents, and Calhoun soon had evidence that the region about Swan Lake had suffered a deluge. Drift began to show on the river, logs from drifts disturbed by a sudden rise. That, he knew, would constitute a hazard for night traveling.

"If drifting logs delay me, they will also delay the quarry," he argued. With that thought he was content.

The danger of rounding a bend and coming suddenly upon the quartette was ever present—a possibility fraught with disaster for the lone pursuer. Whether or not they would lie in frequent ambush depended upon how safe they felt against pursuit—depended, also, Calhoun's life. He knew that, and took all turns with infinite caution, usually dropping into the cover of the backwater and returning to the current well below the bend. In that way he might easily become the pursued rather than the pursuer, but it was a chance he had to take.

The day wore on, the storm finally abated, but the drifting trees and logs increased in numbers. About five o'clock Cal, coming to a sharp bend, suddenly scented wood smoke, and took cover instantly.

"They've stopped to cook supper," he reasoned. "Want to avoid a night fire. That looks as though they are going to run the river, logs and all, after dark."

Tying up to the tallest tree he could find, the ranger climbed to the top and scanned the shore line below. At length a thin wisp of smoke, whirling above the tree tops, betrayed the location of the camp. It was less than a quarter of a mile distant.

Cal remained in the tree. The river channel was visible to a point several hundred yards beyond the camp's location, and he meant to make sure that the campers were really the men he sought. A hunter might possibly be the builder of that fire, but there was not much likelihood of one being in that particular part of the forest. It was a bit too remote even for hunters.

Half an hour passed, and two dugouts crept out of the cane and headed downstream. Each was manned by two oarsmen—undoubtedly the same party Cal had seen at daybreak.

The ranger descended to his boat, waited three-quarters of an hour, then took up the trail again. Reaching the point where the camp had been, he paddled through the cane and stepped ashore beside the dying embers of a fire. Replenishing it, he boiled a pot of coffee, cooked supper, and fed heartily. While he ate he examined the ground about the fire. Tracks, a few burned matches, cigarette stubs, and the refuse from the meal of which the crooks had partaken was all he found.

After eating, it occurred to him that it might be well to scout among the bushes with which the ground was all but choked in the vicinity of the camp. Painstakingly he covered it and, just before nightfall, had his reward.

In the center of a clump of buckrush he located a small leather bag—such a one as mail messengers use for carrying registered matter. It had been gutted with a knife, and the contents removed.

"That argues that a divvy was made at this point," Cal reflected. "Means, too, that they are going to split right away. Hell—suppose two go down the Mississippi and two go up? The question then will be: Which two shall I take first? The redhead, of course, since he is the man I'm after more than the others. He did the killing."

Then another thought struck him.

"Suppose they mean to split before they reach the Mississippi. There are many small streams branching off from Little Bear, between here and its mouth. Against that, though, is this: They can't get far, by boat, on any of those streams—and the going afoot is bad, gets worse the closer one comes to the Big River. No, I'm still betting they're making for a get-away by steamboat, and that, for safety's sake, they'll stick together."

Concealing the bag under his pack, he set out again. Night had come, and extreme precaution would be necessary until the moon rose, which was due to occur about nine thirty. The storm clouds of the day had dispersed, and the sky was studded with stars. There would be a moon.

The hour passed slowly, and slowly also went Cal's bateau—barely moving at times. At length there was a sudden stir in the forest—as palpable as a gust of wind, but hardly as easily defined. An owl screeched weirdly off in the timber, and was answered from half a dozen leafy hiding places. The plop-plop-plop of a 'coon's feet, splashing through shallow water; the startled leap of a larger animal—a deer, probably—which, disturbed by the ranger, went crashing off into silence; the high-keyed wail of a panther, somewhere close at hand on the left—all told Cal that the moon was up, and that presently it would rise above the tree line and whiten the waters of the river. The denizens of the forest were astir.

4

SOMETHING ELSE WAS astir, too. Cal rounded a bend just as moon thrust itself above the trees and spilled its rays over the river. It revealed a moving object on shore in the bend, a quarter mile away, and glinted upon the polished metal of a rifle barrel. The revelation was kaleidoscopic, passing almost before Cal's eyes had caught and identified the impression.

It was enough, however. The ranger slipped silently into cover, and cast his painter around a cypress tree.

"They've made a night camp," he told himself. "Three sleeping, while one guards. Thanks to whoever it is that hangs out the moon, I'm still alive! Five minutes later—but why speculate? I'm here, and they're there. Question is, does that fact mean anything, or doesn't it?"

He knew the utter impossibility of sneaking up on that camp from the shore. Too much brush, and the exact location of the bit of high ground they occupied unknown. It was really as impossible to gain the camp from the river. The man on guard would shoot him the moment he nosed his bateau into the moonlight. That was certain.

"Yet they are there—and three of them no doubt asleep," the ranger argued. "Now, if I can't take four men, while three are dead to the world, what becomes of the chief's boast about one good man? Hell—"

A big log drifted along in the current just outside the cover Cal was in, and an idea came to him. A possible method of gathering in the whole party—but one entailing immeasurable risk. A hundred-to-one shot it was. But, Cal argued, hundred-to-one shots sometimes win.

He removed his boots and, standing up, stripped to the skin. Then he buckled his gun-belt about his neck, allowing his six-shooter, in its waterproof holster, to swing between his shoulders. To that he attached his hunting knife, and four pairs of handcuffs, then, crouching in the bateau, he glued his eyes to the river.

Logs floated along occasionally, but none were to his liking. After a bit a big cottonwood drifted slowly into view, and Cal slipped overside into the water, making no more splash than a swimming fish would have done. The log came abreast of him and he let it pass, then swam silently until he over took it, and was covered by it from view of the man on shore. At the log's stern he clung with one hand, his face barely above water.

The current carried the floater slowly downriver, Calhoun keeping its bow pointed not too directly toward the spot where he had caught a flash of the guard. Presently the outlines of two dugouts showed indistinctly along shore, and he steered the log closer in.

A movement at the water's edge told him that the guard had seen the object in the water and was examining it. There was no challenge, however, and Cal rightly concluded that the log had been recognized for what it was—a harmless drifter. Treading water, he held it motionless while he eased it gently, inch by inch, now toward the nearest dugout, then he let it drift again.

Another movement on shore, this time accompanied by a low oath, as the guard, concerned for the safety of the bateau which the floater menaced, stepped into the shallow water and prepared to shove it off.

Cal, peering from behind the log's stem, saw him set his boot upon its bow and thrust outward. It eased off a bit, then, manipulated by the ranger, it perversely sloughed about and crept toward the dugout.

Again the guard raised a foot and set it upon the log—this time at the stern, for the bow was almost against the boat.

Cal released his hold, seized the man by the ankle in a powerful grasp, and jerked him down into the water—his attempted cry of alarm cut short by a sudden and complete immersion. The log drifted on, and the ranger, astride the guard, brought all the terrific pressure of his sinewy fingers to bear upon his windpipe. When his captive became limp beneath him, Cal took him in his arms and crept ashore.

When the prisoner finally gasped and opened his eyes, it was to find himself stripped to his underwear, his hands shackled, ankles bound with his own belt, and his captor dressed in the clothing he had worn.

Cal's left hand instantly closed about the prisoner's throat, while his right, armed with a long knife, menaced him.

"Make the slightest unnecessary noise and I'll drive this into your gullet!" he whispered grimly. "When I give you air enough to do so, I want you to answer my questions—truthfully, understand. If you make a mistake, unintentional or otherwise, you are going to die, and die quick! Get it?"

He released the pressure on the guard's windpipe, and the man gurgled and nodded.

"Where is your camp—how far ashore?" Cal demanded.

The answer was wheezed out with difficulty, but it came:

"About three hundred yards inland—straight up from here."

"Were you to be relieved?"

"Yes."

"When?"

"About half an hour from now."

"Who is to relieve you?"

"Bud."

"Bud's asleep, eh—along with the rest?"

"Of course."

"How was he to know when to relieve you?"

"I was to slip up and wake him."

"Sure of that? Remember, any mistake you make will spell the end for you. Sure about it?"

"How you reckon he'd know when to come?" demanded the prisoner. "Think we carry an alarm clock?"

Cal laughed softly. "Good enough," he replied. "Guess an alarm clock would be excess baggage on a trip like this. Where is Bud lying; in what position, with reference to the others?"

"Well, he's the nearest one—the others are beyond him."

"You're just to wake him quietly, tell him to come on, then turn in in his place? That the racket?"

"Yeah." The answer was delayed—came hesitantly.

Cal's knife pricked the tender skin at the base of the prone man's throat.

"Take that blade away!" came in a fierce growl.

"Listen," Cal told him, increasing the pressure until the needlelike point pricked the skin, "I'm going to gag you, roll you into the brush, where you'll be hidden from all but me. If I make a mistake, due to you, I'm going to break for you—and kill you. No matter what happens to me later, I'm going to see to it that you don't benefit. Get that?"

"Yeah," was the surly reply.

"Now—tell me the truth."

"Well, I'm to wake Bud, then come back here until he has a chance to heat some coffee—we've got a bit of fire farther back in the brush, hid by logs. I'm to watch here until he comes down. And now, damn you, take that knife off my gullet!"

Cal took the knife away, and with it cut off the tail of the shirt he wore. Then, before the prisoner realized what was taking place, he stuffed the cloth into his mouth.

"That'll keep you quiet, I reckon," Cal told him, as he lifted the guard and carried him twenty feet down the bank, depositing him where the river grass made an excellent screen. "I'm taking a chance—but you're taking a longer one than I am!"

He returned to the point where the dugouts lay, got into one and paddled across the stream, towing the other and his own bateau. When he returned, he came in his own boat, leaving the others.

"If anything starts that I can't handle," he reflected, "I may be able to get away—and leave them marooned."

He anchored in the shadows near where the prisoner lay, then crept inland toward the camp—almost as noiselessly as a water-moccasin would have crawled. Every few feet he paused, held his breath and listened. At the fourth or fifth pause, he caught the sound of some one snoring lightly—and knew the camp was at hand.

5

WITH HIS SIX-GUN in hand he crept onward, and halted beside a blanketed form on the ground. A moment he hesitated, then reached out and caught the sleeper by a shoulder.

"Bud!" he said gruffly, under his breath. "Bud!"

The sleeper stirred. "Huh?" came drowsily from the blanket.

"Come on! It's your turn!" Cal whispered.

"Hell!" The man called Bud yawned. "All right, Becker. Soon's I git some coffee inside me. All quiet?"

"Sure! Nothin' stirrin'!" Cal answered. "Hurry—I'm dead for sleep!"

He faded away toward the river—breathing heavily from the strain. Reaching the shore, he sought a place to hide, and found it behind a big gum which grew beside the path Bud would have to follow when he came down.

The relief was not long in coming. He reached the shadow of the tree—and did not pass out of it. He dropped without a groan, as Calhoun's clubbed gun crashed against his skull.

To bind and gag Bud required perhaps five minutes, and he was still unconscious when the ranger slipped back toward the camp—and the most dangerous part of the job he had set for himself.

Inch by inch, pausing frequently to listen for the slightest sound which might warn him that his men were awake, he crept upon the camp, until he found himself beside a long figure, tightly rolled in a blanket. Calhoun was not squeamish—besides, his own life hung by a hair. He clubbed his gun.

Suddenly the sleeper stirred, opened his eyes; his jaw dropped in consternation, then snapped shut, and he made a wild scramble to sit up.

Cal swung swiftly; putting power behind the blow, and the blanketed figure dropped back and lay still.

The noise of the scuffle, however, was sufficient to wake the second man, who threw aside his blanket and called out:

"Rhodes! I say, Rhodes, what's going on?"

Then his glance fell upon Calhoun, who crouched ready to leap. His hand flashed down and came up with a gun, as he got to his knees.

Cal's weapon spurted fire, there was an oath of agony from the man on the blanket, and the next instant his shattered right wrist was bound to his left with steel.

The man called Rhodes was stirring, and Cal took the precaution of rendering him harmless with the remaining pair of cuffs. Then he turned to the man he had shot.

"Well, Red," he remarked quietly, "I ought to let you bleed to death, but since the Government prefers to have you die by the rope, I'll patch you up temporarily. Hold out your hands!"

In late afternoon of the day after the storm, Sheriff Lundsford and his bedraggled, disgruntled posse returned to Hell Hole. They were a wornout crew. Cal was still absent, but they made themselves at home in his cabin; fed themselves and, night coming on, occupied the bunks with which the ranger's quarters was plentifully equipped. It was Lundsford's intention to use Hell Hole as a base, and work out of that place until all the surrounding territory had been covered.

"Cal will come moseying in about tomorrow," he told his men. "And maybe he'll have some information of value. A good man, Cal—but awfully stuck on himself, just as Wheeler is. Still, he does have good luck getting his man when he starts out for him; no doubt about that. These grandstanders generally do have luck—else they'd soon cease to be in position to grandstand!"

Having thus delivered himself, Lundsford turned in. Shortly after daylight he awoke, stretched himself, wincing at the soreness in his limbs, and looked out the window at the head of the bunk. He sat up suddenly—then, a minute later, though only partly dressed, was streaking it for the landing.

Three craft—two dugouts and a bateau, were there ahead of him. In the bow of the first dugout to land sat a short, redheaded man, his right arm in a sling; manning the stern paddle was a tall, spare man, his head enveloped in a bloody bandage. The second canoe held two men, one of whom had seemingly rammed his head into something solid, for he, too, displayed a blood-stained bandage.

In the bateau, watchful as a hawk, sat Calhoun.

Lundsford's eyes dropped to the feet of the prisoners, and noted that each man was secured by a pair of handcuffs about his ankles.

"Make yourself useful, Lundsford," Cal called out,

tossing a bunch of keys ashore. "They've been on a forced march, and are too tired to run!"

Members of the posse now came upon the scene. Cal made no answer to their inquiries until the last prisoner was ashore and stretching his legs leisurely, then he spoke:

"I ran onto them in a night camp," he stated, "and brought 'em in. That's all."

The crowd fell silent. Then Lunsford spoke:

"I know you done just that, Cal," he said dazedly, "because they're here! And now you've fetched 'em this far, I'll just relieve you of them and take 'em along with me."

Cal eyed the sheriff for a long moment.

"Ever observe the conduct of buzzards, Lundsford?" he asked. "They hang around until some other bird makes a kill, then try to hog it. Some birds, though, won't stand for it. I'm that kind of bird."

He turned to his prisoners.

"Get over to my cabin, men," he ordered.

In silence they obeyed, leaving Lundsford more disgruntled than ever, wondering just what the ranger had meant by his reference to buzzards, and whether or not it called for a reply.

Inside, Cal replaced the handcuffs on the prisoners, then made his report to Wheeler.

"Calhoun sending. Found the train bandits in a night camp on Little Bear, a day's journey from the Mississippi. Brought them to Hell Hole this morning. Had to bung three of them up, and they should have medical attention soon. The loot is in my possession. Am holding them here, pending your arrival."

He signed off, then cocked an ear for the chief's reply.
After a moment it came—a laconic:

"O.K."

THE LAND OF LIMPING LAW

*Deep In The Jungleland Of The Bayou
Country, Inspector Calhoun Brought A
Swift Justice After A Fleeing Crime*

1

"YOU KNOW NOTHING,
SAW NOTHING!"

NONA LEMAIRE, CROUCHING in the bow of old Pierre Lemaire's dugout, her slim body protected against the driving rain by the folds of a voluminous gray blanket, saw a long, black log revealed by a flash of lightning. It was drifting down Bayou L'Anguile, and, because the bayou was rising rapidly that night, lay far over against the levee where it crossed Hickory Flats.

The little French girl was a product of the Sunken. Lands—that portion embraced by the district called L'Anguile Bottoms—and a drifting log was not in itself a thing of interest to her. This particular one, however, caught her eye.

"See, papa, it ees what you call ze foxfire!" she cried, pointing away through the night to where she had last seen the drifter. "It glows like wet matches!"

Old Pierre, hastening toward Hulet's Point, where he intended to take refuge with his daughter until the spring rise should subside, glanced over his shoulder grumblingly.

"Chut! You have eyes for ever'ting but ze bayou ahead!" he chided. "How you know we not bump into somet'ing, when you not look?"

Nona clapped her small hands and laughed.

"It look so ver' funny, papa!" she cried. "Like beeg alligator wit' lantern on hee's tail! Look! You see heem?"

"I see, certainly. Now do you keep doze eye on bayou ahead!"

Nona turned her attention to the course they were running, and the log drifted on through the black curtain.

For fifteen minutes thereafter, while Pierre paddled laboriously against the current, Nona was silent. Then she broke into speech again.

"Will ze new levee hol', papa?" she wanted to know.

"How I know?" demanded her sire. "Eet have not been test. How I say eef eet will hol'? Eengineer for gove'ment say she hol' tight, an' all doze new settler' een Hickory Flats be safe from flood. Dat what heem say, but how I know eef heem say trut'? Be please to hush, chatterbox, an' keep doze eye out for drifter!"

Thus admonished, Nona turned her attention to the bayou ahead, visioning it in the yellow flare of intermittent lightning. But Nona had many thoughts crowding each other in her active brain, and her tongue would clatter.

*The two men on the levee were deafened as logs—
bayou, the whole universe suddenly leaped upward*

"When you las' see dat eengineer, M'sieu Marcee, papa?"
she asked presently.

"Las' week," was the reply. "He come up bayou when
water she begin go on raise. I t'ink he no so sure 'bout levee
will hol' L'Anguile. M'sieu Marcee go up to M'sieu Hulet's
point, an' mos' prob'ly ees there now."

"Oh! Then we see heem!" exclaimed the girl. "We lak
heem ver' much—eh, papa?"

The old man merely grunted, and plied his paddle.

Meantime the long, black log drifted down the bayou,
bumping occasionally against the mud of the levee. It
no longer shone in the light of what Nona had termed
foxfire—fungus of phosphorescent character common to
swamp countries. It now looked like any other log afloat
on the muddy tide.

But it was not like other logs. An hour after the Frenchman and his daughter encountered it two other pairs of
eyes saw the log and idly watched its progress.

Levee Patrolman Frank McArthur, and his partner, Joe

Bland, trudging along the top of the embankment, anxious eyes scanning the soft earth for sign of hole or gap, paused with their backs to the slanting downpour, while McArthur tried vainly to light his pipe. They saw the log.

There was nothing about it, not even a light, to hold their attention. Just a log—one among many that were then or soon would be afloat on the bayou. It drifted by them, bumping against the soft bank at intervals—held there by force of the spreading water—and neither gave it a second thought.

Then, when the drifter had put perhaps a quarter mile between itself and the patrolmen, and McArthur had given up the attempt to light a smoke, the levee, bayou, the whole universe, seemed suddenly to leap upward, to rock and pitch, then to break up in huge segments. At the same time a terrific explosion deafened the two men on the levee.

Floundering in the mud where the concussion had thrown them, they were rendered speechless by the shock. McArthur, struggling at length into an upright position, had just time to shout an amazed ejaculation when the mud bank crumbled beneath his feet—and his voice was lost in a watery gurgle. The bayou engulfed him.

Bland, his right arm dangling uselessly at his side, broken at wrist and elbow, was swept into the water at the same time. As he went down the heavens were momentarily alight, and where the levee had lain like a huge, brown, glistening snake, extending southward across Hickory Flats, was now a boiling tumult of muddy water, trees and logs. The levee, as far as he could see, was as though it had never been.

Far up the bayou, almost within sight of the lights of

Hulet's Point, Nona Lemaire, clutching the gunwales of the dugout, which leaped and tossed on the disturbed water like a bit of bark, raised terror stricken eyes to her father. So startling and so violent had been the explosion it was several moments before she could speak.

"Wha—what was it, papa?" she gasped. "What made eet go off lak that? Boom! Eet soun'lak ten million gun, all shoot at one tarn! Oh, papa, somet'ing awful has happen! I feel—"

Old Pierre's face was white as though death had taken him. It was several moments before his palsied tongue could be brought to obey his will. When he spoke it was to utter a command.

"Hush, you!" he cried fiercely. "You know not'ing! You saw not'ing! Dat log—you no see heem! Un'erstan'? You see not'ing, an' you know not'ing! *Mon Dieu!* Dis night mak me feel lak I weesh I'm dead! I no can b'leeve—but I no can help b'leeve! But you, chatterbox, min' w'at I tell you: You know not'ing, an' you no see not'ing at all!"

Nona, who had never seen her happy-tempered father in so violent a state of emotion, was subdued by his fierceness, Meekly bowing her head, she turned her eyes again ahead.

"Lights, papa," she said softly. "Eet is M'sieu' Hulet's point at las'!"

2

LIMPING OR RUNNING FREE

NATHAN HULET SHOOK his massive head from side to side until his black spadebeard swished with the motion. He spoke sadly, and with resignation.

"It is hopeless! I call to mind what the circuit rider, Mr. Markham, said when he stopped at The Point two years ago. Says he:

" 'Brother Hulet, the trouble hereabouts is this: Crime runs on nimble feet, while the law, like an ancient cripple, only limps along. So far as I can see, there is little chance of early remedy for that condition. Lack of funds to carry the law into the remote sections, together with political manipulation, dooms this part of the wilderness to remain in its present primitive social state for a long time to come. One day all will be different, but that day seems far distant.'

"And ever since that remark," Hulet went on, "I've thought of this section of the swamp as a land of limping law. The outrage of the other night—the wrecking of the levee, and the consequent destruction of the improvements of the settlers in Hickory Flats, is conclusive.

"It serves notice on the government, and all others concerned, that the time is not yet ripe for settling and reclaiming the swamp. A land of limping law it now is, and a land of limping law it seems likely to continue to be—world without end!"

Hubbard Wheeler, chief of rangers for the Arkansas swamp lands, remained silent and thoughtful for a moment after the wealthy hide dealer, who had bestowed his own name on the settlement in the heart of the wilderness, ceased speaking.

"It may be as well to remember that the explosion is, by some persons, attributed to an accidental discharge of dynamite probably left in the levee at the time it was built," he reminded Hulet, after a bit. "Dynamite in large quantities was used during construction, and a box might have been neglected and allowed to become buried in the fill. Lightning, striking a box of detonators—which may have been buried along with the explosive—could have caused the damage."

Hulet looked at the speaker, in evident surprise.

"Do you believe that?" he asked.

"It doesn't matter what I believe," Wheeler told him. "The point is that many in the district do believe the destruction to have been the result of an accident. They, many of them, resent the government undertaking to trace the cause; say that it is only an attempt to stir up trouble, and fix blame upon somebody for a thing which came about in a wholly unavoidable manner. Suppose you tell me what you believe?"

"Well," Hulet hesitated, "I can't say just what I do believe—only this: It was not an accident. That supposition about dynamite being accidentally buried in the embankment, accidentally discharged— Pshaw! That's bosh!"

"You think, then, that it was the work of natives who

resent the settling of Hickory Flats by 'outsiders'—home-steaders—and who determined to let the water in on them, thus driving them out?"

"I know of at least a dozen natives who lost their squatter rights, so called, in Hickory Flats when the government removed everybody from the district before starting to reclaim it. I have heard, right here in my store, nearly every one of those losers threaten to ruin the government's project over the Flats.

"No idle boasters, those fellows, but resentful, law-resisting men who would stop at nothing in order to get revenge. I'm telling you this, and you will, of course, make what use you want of it."

"McArthur, the patrolman, evidently saw something illuminating, or, at least, startling, just before the bank crumbled and he went to his death in the water," Wheeler conjectured. "Bland says he heard him give voice to a shout of astonishment, and that he turned toward the point where he, Bland, was; attempted to impart something, but was precipitated into the torrent before he could give utterance. Got any idea about what that thing seen by the dead patrolman might have been?"

"Not one," Hulet told him. "Frankly, I think McArthur saw nothing. He was quite naturally excited. What he meant to impart was the fact that the levee was going out. Bland, when found half dead and clinging to a log, by a rescue party to the Flats, was certainly not in a very clear mental state.

"His recollections may be discounted. What could McArthur have seen? Not the man or men who set the stuff off. They would not have been anywhere in the vicinity when the explosion took place. Of that I think there can be no doubt. What, then, was there for McArthur to see?"

Wheeler shook his head slowly. "That is something I do not know," he answered. "But," he added, "I mean to find out."

"Hope you find out—not what McArthur saw, but who the guilty parties are," Hulet remarked, while Wheeler's eyes were on a tall figure making its way through the mud and water from the river bank. The approaching man was Chet Marcy, government engineer.

"You say Pierre Lemaire and his daughter were on the bayou when the explosion occurred?" Wheeler queried.

"Yes. They got here shortly afterward. Many of the swamp folks had come in to the Point that day. The water was threatening the west bottoms—that part across the bayou from Hickory Flats."

"Know much about the Frenchman?"

"Surely. Bought hides from him for the last fifteen years. He's square—at least, I know nothing against him. He is one who lost a squatter right in the Flats. Resented it, of course. But, then, all of them did. Pierre's all right, so far as I know."

Marcy came in, his hip boots wet and muddy.

"Well, Captain Wheeler," he greeted, "I'm glad to see you. I take it you are here to investigate matters?"

The ranger chief studied the tall, clear-eyed, capable looking young man for a moment before answering.

"Sorry to see you in such a plight, Marcy," he returned. "The work of long, hard years gone for nothing. Too bad. Yes, I'm here to investigate—or, rather, to look things over before the real investigator gets on the job. He'll be along presently, if he keeps his appointment—and he invariably does."

"Who?" The query came from Hulet.

"Inspector Jack Calhoun," Wheeler replied, again looking toward the bayou. "He's coming now—he and his men. You folks are going to enter upon a new regime, beginning now."

There was a change in Wheeler. His long body was militarily erect, and there was a gleam in his eyes.

"What's doing?" Marcy asked, looking off to where a dozen bateau were slipping in toward the Point.

"This," Wheeler answered. "The law is coming into the L'Anguile country—whether it is limping in or running free. The point is, it is coming—is here, in fact. And," he paused, giving emphasis to his words, "it is here to stay!"

At that moment Inspector Jack Calhoun, tall, immaculate in spite of mud and water, entered the store—entered quietly, and stood at attention before his chief. In the background could be seen twenty more men, as like him as one brown Leghorn egg is like another.

"I report my detail ready for duty," Calhoun stated. "The country above Marked Tree flooded in spots, but all quiet."

"Good," Wheeler commented. "You are in charge. You know your instructions. Report to me when possible."

3

BEWARE OF THE SILENT

INSPECTOR CALHOUN, IN going over the ground around Hulet's Point, locating quarters for his men, found a land made desolate by flooding waters. But—and there was food for thought—it was only the land which wore the look of desolation; the occupants of the land seemed unperturbed—snugly complacent, even.

Why?

The question puzzled Cal, but he had not then time in which to analyze it. That would come later.

"The Sunken Lands are pretty much divided by the Kansas City, Ft. Scott and Memphis Railway," had been Wheeler's words before setting out for Hulet's Point. "The northern portion, under our present operations, has a semblance of social regeneration. The southern portion, except for the reclamation work in the vicinity of Hulet's, is in a state of nature.

"No respect for law, and no attempt on the part of State and county authorities to inculcate it. It's a do-as-you-please country. Orders are, since the destruction of the levee, to establish law in the lower country. I have all I can do here, so that big, important task is up to you, Calhoun.

"Work out your problem, and the district's salvation, in

your own way. Catching and punishing the criminals who blew up the government levee is the first step. Get sufficient men together, picked to suit yourself, and follow me down as soon as possible."

Cal had done that, and now was wholly on his own responsibility. His word would be law in the lower country from that time on—provided he could enforce his mandates. He was fairly certain he could.

Yet there was much to be considered. Each step had to be thoughtfully planned. A miscalculation, resulting in noticeable error, would be a confession of weakness, inability to handle the situation. Cal's long experience with the natives informed him that they would, one and all, be alert to catch him in error; would rejoice if they should do so.

Bayou L'Anguile rises far up in Craighead County. It is a drain for the lowlands, and is, at its source and for many miles thereafter, properly a bayou—that is to say, it is sluggish and without banks.

Later, however, when it crosses into Poinsette County, it takes off the waters of many creeks, cuts for itself a deeper channel, becomes swifter of current, and is, therefore, not a bayou, but, properly speaking, a small river. The designation "bayou" is not lost with the change in character. Bayou L'Anguile it was in the beginning and so it remains to-day.

In that stretch of country traversed by L'Anguile after it enters Poinsette on its way to the Mississippi above Helena, there could be found, in the late nineties, as fair a sample of what is meant by the term "jungles" as America boasted. Virgin forests of the finest growth of hardwood covered its trackless acres, and it was crossed and recrossed by countless sloughs, creeks, and bayous.

It was a boatman's country, with never a sign of agricultural improvements in the whole of its million acres. The inhabitants lived by the trap and the gun. They lived primitively, as befitted men who maintained life as they did.

Few of the natives could read or write; moreover, few ever desired to do so, and, to make the cycle of illiteracy complete, few wished, or even could be brought to permit their' offspring to learn their A-B-Cs.

Schools, in the L'Anguile country, were not to be found. Couples married without troubling to get a license. They merely appeared before their nearest "preachin' man"—all communities had at least one, and some even were really ordained—and were later dismissed as man and wife. Be it said, there was no such thing as divorce and remarriage there.

Few cases of infidelity, on the part of husband or wife, were known, and, on the whole, family life in the lower country was, in the nineties, on a far more solid foundation than was later to be the case. Civilization, when it finally came to the Bayou L'Anguile country, brought its little defects in its train.

As may be inferred from the name, Bayou L'Anguile, many French, and persons of French extraction, dwelt along the borders of the stream. They were, for the most part, from the lower Louisiana district. A few French-Canadians were also there, but they were in the minority.

Of Indians—Delawares and Osages—there was what might be termed a double handful; half-breeds, too, of course. Then there were many families of what may be called, for lack of a more definite designation, simon-pure American natives of the hinterlands.

The latter were, by far, the most troublesome—the least apt to accept the tenets of the law.

Hulet's Point, consisting of, perhaps, two score cabins set high on piling, was the only settlement of any consequence within a radius of twenty miles, the Point itself being the hub. Nathan Hulet conducted a general store there, but his main business in life was the buying of hides from the native trappers.

He had grown wealthy in the fur business, and had prospects of becoming wealthier still. There were other small stores, mostly dealing in traps, nets, hardware, and such commodities at the Point; but Hulet was by far the big man of the place. A bachelor, he lived alone in the rear of his store.

Near the bank of the bayou stood a cabin, in which Chet Marcy, the engineer, had his quarters, and thence Calhoun repaired after a cursory survey of the Point.

"Make yourself at home," Marcy bade the inspector. "Plenty room for several of us, and I'll confess I'd like company. I—the fact is, inspector, I'm jumpy as hell. Don't know why, exactly, but the truth remains that I have lately become almost afraid to be alone.

"Of course I've been threatened, time and again, since undertaking the maintenance of the levee; even been shot at from cover two or three times. That did no more than disturb me at the time.

"Since the levee was blown up, though, I have been a victim of a tormenting feeling which I am unable to analyze—an indefinable dread which pertains, not to me alone, but seems to embrace the whole district. I can't get rid of it, or explain it. I only know that it is present, and damnably disquieting."

"I'll make my headquarters here for the present," Cal told him. "It's handy. As for that feeling you tell of, I'm thinking it is quite a natural one. The country hereabouts is seething with rebellion, though very little of the condition shows on the surface. You sense it, and are disturbed by it. We'll cheer you up—and, in the meantime, do you mind being questioned rather exhaustively?"

"Not a bit, old man," Marcy assured him willingly. "Set up your pump, and start it going. I'm anxious to talk, if only for sake of talking."

"How many miles of the levee went out after the explosion?"

"Six. The break begins just below the Point, and extends downstream fully six miles."

"Do much damage to the homesteaders in the Flats?"

"Destroyed their planted fields, washed away some of their buildings, drowned a lot of cattle, sheep, and hogs— played the devil, truly."

"Many of 'em leave the country after that?"

"Several families—disgusted."

"Humph. There can always be found the weak brothers who can't stand reverses. Others will replace them. How many families are left over there?"

"I'd say perhaps seventy-five or eighty."

"Any natives mixed with them?"

"Not a family. They refuse to have any 'truck' with the outlanders."

"Tell me, are the natives in general very bitter toward those homesteaders? I mean, do they go about talking of what they mean to do to get rid of them, or just how do they demean themselves?"

The engineer's brow grew thoughtful. "Some make a lot of threatening talk," he said finally. "Others do not. Frankly, I believe it is the silent ones who really contemplate taking drastic action to rid the section of the undesirables—the active evidence of encroaching civilization.

"The talkers are not, I think, very strong on doing. Knowing that they really have no notion of taking the violent action they proclaim is in their minds, they feel safe in talking loudly and wickedly. I would look for the doers among the silent."

Calhoun nodded. "Always," he remarked succinctly. "I've heard mention of a man named Pierre Lemaire—a French trapper—and his daughter. Nona, I believe, is her name. Rumor has it that they were on the bayou, at or near the point of first destruction, the night it occurred. Know much about Pierre?"

Marcy's rather sallow face took on a sudden tinge of dark red, and he debated his answer for a full minute.

"I do know Pierre Lemaire—and his daughter," he said firmly. "I know them both to be honest, peaceable folk—incapable of doing a fellow man injury. I know them, and like them. Pierre, I am aware, talked a great deal about what he would do in revenge for being turned out of his unlawful squatter holdings in the Flats. That sort of thing ceased from him, however, when I pointed out that it might be dangerous. He cannot have destroyed the levee, or have had prior knowledge of it."

"I'd like to see Pierre and his girl," Cal told him. "Must do so, in fact, at the earliest possible moment—"

"That moment is now!" Marcy exclaimed, rising. "Pierre and Nona have just landed, and they will undoubtedly come directly here."

4

A PARTY OF SQUATTERS

CAL GOT TO his feet as a white-haired, black-eyed little man stepped inside the engineer's cabin a few minutes later. He was accompanied by a slim girl nearing twenty—a girl with beauty enough to make her noticeable anywhere, and certainly to raise her into a class to herself in her present environment.

"Welcome, Mr. Lemaire," Marcy greeted cordially. "Miss Nona, the place is yours. I must present Inspector Calhoun, of the Rangers. He is to quarter with me for a spell."

Lemaire bowed gravely, shook hands, and sat. Nona gave Cal a long, searching look out of a pair of black eyes, which made the inspector think of big, swamp-grown muscadines, then her red lips parted in a quick smile.

"M. Calhou' belong to gove'ment," she said lightly. "All mens that belong to gove'ment are fine mens—except," she flashed a swift glance to where Marcy stood, "except—but it ees not what you call polite to mention names, ees it not?"

"Miss Nona has a quarrel with me, inspector," said Marcy with a laugh. "She was to have had lessons in English, of my teaching, during the past two weeks, and extending—well, I hope, for a long time. This levee matter, though, has crowded even such pleasant occupation into the background—"

"He has not even been near to our cabin!" Nona cried.

"I'll remedy that neglect—"

"You were both on the river when the explosion occurred?" Cal broke in with businesslike tones, addressing the father.

There was silence for a moment.

"Yes, m'sieu," said Pierre Lemaire.

"Did you see anything unusual going forward just prior to the explosion? Any person or persons on the bayou?"

"No, m'sieu."

"Any notion as to how the thing was done?"

There was a scarcely perceptible hesitation, then Lemaire spoke in complete denial.

"Not'ing, m'sieu."

"Papa," Nona spoke excitedly. "Remember the foxfire—"

The old Frenchman's face clouded suddenly, like the abrupt appearance of a thunder head in a sky of summer blue.

"Quiet, chatterbox!" he admonished harshly. Then his white teeth showed in a quick smile, and the cloud was gone. "I have promise to show ze little one where ze foxfire grows—ze fungus that glows," he explained. "Like all children, she weesh to see right now. You will pardon her, m'sieu? And what more is there eet ees your weesh to know?"

He turned suavely to Cal, to find the latter studying him from under slightly lowered brows—his gray eyes glinting between slitted lids.

Jack Calhoun was not one to ask idle questions or make

aimless comments. He contented himself with a long, thoughtful examination of the Frenchman's face, and said nothing. He sensed that Nona Lemaire had been on the verge of saying something her parent desired left unsaid. That was clear.

But he knew very well that to let Pierre know that he had caught the significance of the interruption would only put him on his guard, and make it harder later on to get him or the girl to speak freely.

"You are well acquainted with all the residents of the district, I take it, Mr. Lemaire?" Cal queried after a bit.

"Yes, *m'sieu*. I have ver' wide acquaintance wit' mos' ever'body 'round here."

"I shall ask you to speak out freely, if you have suspicions which point to any man or group of men. So far, there is absolutely nothing to work on except the known enmity existing in the minds of those persons who were forced out of the Flats, against the present occupants. There may be other reasons which might have actuated the move against the government, of course, but, if so, none have even been hinted at. Perhaps you have a theory to advance?"

"None, *m'sieu*. I know nobody dat would blow up ze levee. Dere ees many dat feel ver' sore 'bout losing claim in Hick'ry Flat, but not one, I fink, dat would do so much awfulness. No, *m'sieu*, not one!"

Cal was about to make some comment when his glance was attracted by a body of men in motion out of doors. Some fifteen or twenty natives were moving toward the engineer's cabin. He quietly called Marcy's attention to them.

"Humph!" ejaculated the latter. "All men who formerly

lived in the Flats. They look businesslike, and are evidently coming here! I wonder!"

The party of natives came on until they were about twenty feet from the door of the cabin, then Calhoun stepped out upon the door log.

"What do you want, men?" he asked. Looking over their heads, he could see half a dozen of his rangers unobtrusively in the background.

A lank, gray-bearded native stepped out from the crowd.

"Air you-all Inspector Calhoun?" he inquired.

"Yes. Who are you?"

"My name is Davis—called Bobcat Davis," was the answer. "I used to live over in th' Flats. All of we'uns here present did. I ain't pertendin' that we air exactly happy over losing out over thar, or that we-all has any love for them as is settin' on our ground—"

"Fuddermo'," broke in a squat man who stood at Bobcat's elbow, "we-all ain't none sorry for whut happen' to 'em a week ago. Tell him that, Bobcat—"

"You-all shet yore trap, Mooneye!" Bobcat spoke sharply. "I war done app'inted to do th' talkin' for all of us, an' I aims to do it!" Turning to Calhoun, he resumed: "It air jest as Mooneye Briggs done said. We ain't none regretful about th' blowing' up of th' levee—"

"Then what are you here for?" Cal demanded. "Get to the point."

"Well, it has done been norated about that we'uns which lived over in th' Flats, leastwise some of us, blowed up th' levee. That's whut we got together an' come to see you about. It's thisaway: I ain't denyin' that had th' levee been a State levee, or a county levee, we would 'a' blowed hell outa it long time ago.

"Never would 'a' stood for it bein' built in th' fust place. But it air a gove'mint levee—an' none of us is damn fools enough to projeck with th' gove'mint in no such manner. Thar ain't a one of us here present which had a hand in th' skullduggery which war afoot that night a week ago."

Cal was thoughtful as he contemplated the now silent men. They seemed ill at ease, and the ranger sensed the fact that all were laboring under a strain. He believed he knew the cause of their perturbation.

"So, believing that the government, in the effort to catch and punish the guilty, might carelessly gather in a lot of likely suspects and make them suffer, whether or not they were guilty, you decided to come to me and put yourselves before me in your proper light," he told them.

"I'm glad you did. Now, bear this in mind: No innocent man shall get into trouble over the wrecking of the levee. Each of you who has a clear conscience may go right along about his business, certain of the fact that he will not be harmed or interfered with in the least. Government will find and punish the guilty—if, indeed, the thing was not really an accident—but not an innocent person shall suffer. Go back to your homes, and your—"

5

THE KILLING OF INJUN PETE

CAL CEASED SPEAKING, his glance traveling above the crowd and resting upon a man who staggered into the clearing before Hulet's store coming from the fringe of timber on the north. He stumbled, fell to his knees, struggled up and staggered weakly toward the engineer's cabin. Leaping down from the door-log, the inspector hastened to his aid.

Murdock and Shane, two rangers, reached the afflicted man and were supporting him when Cal arrived. The swampers gathered about, blank of expression, while Pierre Lemaire, his face white as chalk, clutched an arm of his daughter.

The man supported by the rangers was already on the threshold of death. His muddy clothing was soaked with blood which came from a wound in his throat. He had barely voice enough to gasp out a few disjointed words.

"Shot—in my—cabin—las' night," came in a throaty gurgle. "Man—outside. Don't know—who—unless it— war— Unless—"

He made a valiant effort to finish the sentence, while Calhoun held an ear close to catch the slightest murmur. The effort was of no avail. The wounded man went limp,

his eyes closed and his jaw dropped. It looked as though
death had come. A few seconds later he rallied slightly.

"Damanite! Damanite!" he gasped. "Th' levee— All
gone! He needn't be afear'd, now! He needn't be af—"

With a final gasp the limp body collapsed. Death was
only an instant away.

"Who is this man?" Calhoun demanded, turning to
Bobcat Davis.

"Injun Pete," the latter informed him. "Half-breed
Osage, that lived two mile north of here. Trapper—when
he wa'n't too drunk."

"He's dead," said Murdock briefly, straightening from
making an examination. "Shot through the throat."

"Did he live alone?" Cal asked.

"Yeah."

"Know of any enemies?"

"Naw. Nobody would of kilt him, less'n he started th'
thing hisself. These Injuns, an' half-breeds, sticks together,
an' nobody don't bother 'em, savin' they has to."

The rest of the crowd nodded agreement with their
spokesman.

"Take him into Hulet's store," Cal ordered. "I understand Hulet does the undertaking for the settlement."

"He don't do none of it hisself," Bobcat corrected. "He
sells th' boxes for th' corp, an' has a room to dress 'em up
in—if so be they's any dressin' up to be did. Pete won't be."

"I want you, Bobcat, and another of your party—choose
him yourself—to go with me to Pete's cabin. I want to go
now. Murdock," he said to the big ranger, "you will come
along too. Shane, you are in charge here. Let's get going."

He turned to Marcy, an invitation to him on his tongue.

But the engineer had his back toward the group, while he stared after Pierre Lemaire, who, gripping Nona's arm, was hurrying toward the bayou and his bateau.

Reaching the boat, he thrust the girl into the bow, leaped into the stern, seized a paddle, and sent the craft shooting down the current, looking not even once back toward the party on shore. He paddled with all the speed of one who had but a single desire, and that to put a great distance between himself and the spot he had just quitted.

Marcy turned slowly and stared at Cal. There was a look of complete mystification in his eyes as he shook his head negatively in answer to the glance of inquiry the ranger directed to him.

Cal, thoroughly nonplused, turned to the task immediately in hand.

Led by Bobcat Davis and Mooneye Briggs, Calhoun, Murduck and Marcy set out through the timber for Injun Pete's cabin. Cal was silent during the trip, his mind busy.

What was back of the Indian's slaying? Had it a direct connection with the blowing up of the levee?

It seemed so. The dying man had spoken of dynamite, and his words, in all likelihood, referred to the wrecking of the embankment. He had said that some one needn't be afraid. Who was that some one?

The more Cal thought of the situation in the swamp, the harder it was to believe that the natives had acted in retaliation for the taking away of their holdings in the Flats. Cal knew the native, through and through.

He knew that no one of them would, single-handed, tackle the government. He knew also that they were individually of a suspicious turn of mind. They did not trust each other. Therefore it was unlikely that a number of them would get together and destroy the levee.

More than all else, the natives were, in their new homes, as well located as they had been in the flats. They had, in reality, lost nothing that they could not easily regain in another locality. They had done so.

Why, then, having little or nothing to gain, should they run the tremendous risk involved in destroying government property? The natives of the Sunken Lands feared neither State nor county—but they unquestionably feared the United States Government.

"Some man, or party of men, with a great deal to gain by the act, did the wrecking," was the conclusion Cal reached, simultaneously with the arrival of the party at Pete's lonely cabin. He had suspected as much before coming to Hulet's Point. Now the tentative suspicion had become concrete conviction.

He must look for those who would profit financially by the removal of the homesteaders from Hickory Flats.

Raising the latch string, Cal entered the cabin alone. It was in a state of filthy disorder, not to mention the fearsome blood splotches which lay on the floor in all directions, and even stained the walls. Evidently Pete had struggled long and hard before finally becoming sufficiently aroused from his stupor to make his way out of doors and to the Point.

The furnishings were crude, home-made articles, the cooking having been done on a wide, stick-and-mud fireplace. On a table before the hearth was a half empty jug, the contents a cheap grade of whisky. One glass beside the jug argued that the Indian had been drinking alone. Bits of coarse food on a plate further testified that he had not been companioned.

A chair with the back toward the east wall indicated the place where the drinker was sitting when the fatal shot was fired, and a hole between the logs where the clay had fallen out fixed the position of the killer, outside.

Cal went out and stood beside the hole, then examined the ground beneath it. There had been tracks—but he who made them had carefully obliterated them with a side scraping of his boot sole. Just a smear of disturbed earth below the hole, and immediately back of that spot the grass grew high.

The inspector returned to the interior of the cabin, his companions waiting silently in a group outside. With minute care he searched every nook and cranny of the single room. The floor was fully three feet from the ground, since the cabin stood on stilts, and light showed through the cracks between the rude puncheons.

At length the ranger came to a place in the floor where no light showed. He fell to work prying up the boards at that point, and uncovered a small shallow cubby-hole attached to the underside between the joists.

In the hidden space were three sticks of dynamite, a coil of fuse, half a dozen detonators, all carefully wrapped together—and nothing else.

Cal stared hard at his find, then, taking out a pencil, he made a faint mark upon the wrapping of each stick of the explosive. Replacing the flooring over the dynamite, he went to the door and called to his fellows to come in.

"I find nothing of consequence," he stated when the group stood within, eyes scanning the place. "Not a thing to indicate the identity of the killer. He came up to the east wall, thrust a rifle or revolver through a hole and shot the half-breed down. Left him for dead, no doubt. That is all—at present. We may as well return."

6

THE MACHINE OF LAW STARTS

"WHUT DID YOU-ALL expect to find?" queried Mooneye, when they were on the back track.

"A clew," Cal replied. "Usually there is one; sometimes many. I failed back yonder, however."

"You-all mean to say you can look around a place wharat somebody has been kilt, and Agger out who done it?" came the amazed demand.

"Sometimes," Cal told him good-humoredly. "You see, in this case, the killer was not inside the cabin with his victim. He crept up and shot from outside. There are no tracks—he wiped those out. Hence my failure to find anything pointing his way."

"Reckon, then, he ain't goin' to be ketched?" Bobcat wanted to know.

"I reckon he is going to be," Cal answered shortly. "Sooner or later, he'll answer for his crime. Be sure of that."

The two natives shook their heads in unbelief, then fell silent.

Night was falling when the party reentered the square before Hulet's store. The proprietor was standing on the gallery before the door, and a blanketed figure squatted on the floor near by. When Cal approached, Hulet hailed him.

"Inspector," he called, "there's an Indian here who says he can tell you something about Pete."

The figure in the blanket straightened from its reclining position, and became a tall buck of the Osage tribe.

"It's Charlie Redoak," Mooneye volunteered.

"You know something about Pete?" Cal queried.

The Indian spoke after a long stare at his questioner.

"Pete go away two weeks ago," he said. "Stay gone till last night. Then come to my cabin, send me to Hulet's for jug. I get 'em jug, tak 'em to Pete, then go back to cabin. I drink maybe two times out of jug. No more."

"Did you see him after that?"

"No see him."

"Got any idea who shot him?"

"No."

"Are you sure that Pete went away two weeks ago, a week before the levee was wrecked? Think hard. Are you sure that he went, and that he did not get back until last night?"

"Sure."

"Where did he go?"

"I no know. Maybe to settlement up the bayou, twen'y miles, called Little Neck. Many Osage there. Pete went there lots of times. I no know nothing else."

Questioning elicited nothing further. The Indian, having heard of Pete's death, had come to the store and, later, volunteered his information to Hulet. The storekeeper had prevailed upon him to wait and repeat it to Calhoun.

The inspector watched the blanketed figure fade away southward in the twilight, then his mind went back to that cache of dynamite, and Pete's dying words.

"If Pete went away before the levee was destroyed, and

stayed away until last night, then he could have had nothing to do with the job. That's flat. But—he had dynamite,
and dynamite is not easy for Indians and natives to come
by. No. Whatever Charlie Redoak may say about his tribes-
man's perambulations during the past two weeks, he knew
something about the thing I am interested in. He was,
somehow, someway, mixed up in it—and I'll bet a dollar
he was killed because of such connection."

Summoning Murdock, he drew him aside and gave him
whispered instructions, then returned to Marcy's cabin for
supper.

"WELL, WHAT DO you make of things?" asked the question
after he and Calhoun had eaten supper, and were sitting
in the cabin.

The inspector filled a pipe, carefully packing the tobacco
in the bowl, applied a match and took several deep inhala-
tions before replying.

"The natives, as a whole and acting in concert, did not
destroy the levee," he asserted. "I never thought they did,
in the first place. I know them pretty well, and am able
to form a fairly accurate idea of what they will do under
almost any given circumstances. I do not say, mind you,
that a native did not do the job. I am saying, though, that
if one did he was not acting for his fellows.

"I noticed when I first arrived here," Cal went on, "that
every man, woman and child around the Point seemed
tickled over something. At first that attitude puzzled me,
but I think I understand it now. They are all glad that the
levee was wrecked. They figure that civilization is, if not
vanquished entirely, halted for a long period.

"Queer, but by following the line of thought of the average native back to its inspiration, I believe I have struck the real clews to the reason for dynamiting the embankment."

Marcy glanced up quickly and fixed the speaker with his eyes. Cal, without betraying that he noticed it, marked a worried expression on the engineer's face—a look of concern.

"Mind telling me what you have in mind about that?" Marcy asked.

"Not just now," Cal refused. "When I'm certain of my grounds, I'll let you in on it. In the meantime, this neck of the woods is due to get the most thorough shaking up it has ever had. I'm establishing, first thing to-morrow, a sort of curfew. All stores in the district will be closed at six o'clock in the evening.

"Any man, woman or child, caught off his premises after nightfall, unless with an excuse which I approve, will be taken into custody and punished. Drunkenness, fighting, thieving—all those things must come to an immediate end. This district will be policed so thoroughly even the wild animals will have to move easy not to be observed."

"Don't you think you are tackling something a bit too big for you to handle?" asked the engineer.

Cal grinned. "Ask the natives north of Marked Tree whether the job was too big for the rangers there. They'll set you right about what our organization can or cannot do when it takes hold. Better yet, keep an eye on developments here. They will be convincing, I assure you."

"Make anything of the death of Pete?" Marcy queried, dismissing the matter of Cal's plans for policing the district.

"Quite a bit—yes. Pete blew up the levee, I believe."

There was no doubting the genuineness of Marcy's

surprise at that quiet statement. He came to his feet, eyes wide with astonishment.

"Why—why, man you are dead wrong!" he exclaimed. "Pete! The idea is preposterous! That shiftless drunkard—why, it mattered not one whit to him whether a levee was built across Hickory Flats or not! He never lived there, and had no interest in it!"

Cal looked at the excited speaker calmly until he ceased.

"Pete, acting under directions from some one, maybe several persons, set off the dynamite in the levee," he reasserted positively. "I will venture the prediction that I will find dynamite, or other evidence, in or around Pete's cabin to-morrow. I had not time to make a thorough search this afternoon. To-morrow I am going to pull the shack to pieces, if necessary, and examine every board in it—every possible place of concealment. Pete did it, and I'm going to establish that fact. Then I'm going to get the men who backed him."

During the latter speech Cal had raised his voice to a pitch much higher than was his custom, as though desiring to emphasize his remarks. The look in his eyes would have notified Marcy, had he been observing the inspector carefully, that he was listening intently. A moment, and his face relaxed in a slight smile. He got up and sauntered to the door, swung it open and stood on the threshold.

Almost immediately Shane appeared in the darkness below the sill. He spoke in low tones, then disappeared. Cal returned to his chair.

"Was somebody listening?" Marcy demanded.

"Wouldn't be at all surprised," Cal replied.

"Who—"

"My man was unable to recognize him. Guess I'll go to bed, if you'll point out the bunk you want me to occupy."

"Of course. Any time you get ready, just turn into the handiest bunk you see. Mine is over in the corner."

Cal started unlacing his boots.

"I'm not going to be able to sleep," Marcy said uneasily, eyes upon the inspector's preparations. "Think I'll take a pull on the bayou. Visit the guards on the lower end of the gap, maybe, before I get-back. Make yourself at home, old chap, and if I'm not here at daylight, you'll be able to throw some breakfast together, I know."

"Sure," Cal agreed yawningly. "Hop out and get your nerves under control. I'll do very well alone."

Marcy promptly withdrew, and a few minutes later was on the bayou headed downstream.

7

BOBCAT COMES ALONG

CAL CEASED UNDRESSING. He sat in his chair for ten or fifteen minutes after the departure of the engineer, then relaced his boots, got up leisurely and stepped out into the night, going toward the landing.

Ranger Ball sat on a stump where the boats were anchored. He got up at Cal's approach.

"Anybody on the bayou from here?" the inspector asked.

"Marcy just went down," was the answer. "No one else has left the landing since I came on at nightfall."

"I'm going downstream," Cal informed the watcher. "Don't know when I'll get back. Shane and Murdock will act in my stead, until I return. Report anything suspicious—above all, departures and arrivals by boat—to one or the other."

"Right!" Ball answered.

Cal got into his bateau unhurriedly, and dropped silently down the bayou. The destruction of the levee had let the rising water out over the flats, thus diverting the flood from the west bank to the eastern district. The cabins of the natives in the interior to the west were on dry ground, while the homesteaders in the Flats yet were flooded. Cal caught the glimmer of lights on the east, signifying that many settlers were sticking with their claims.

"Marcy is as easily read as newsprint," Cal reflected. "If he covered up better I'd think him mixed up in this thing, too. As it is—well, he'd lots better have been frank with me. It would have paid him to be."

Far down the bayou a light glimmered on the west bank, and Cal went ashore when he reached it. The cabin was that of Bobcat Davis, who answered a summons guardedly, but without delay.

"Air you-all wantin' of me, inspector?" he asked, stepping outside and closing the door.

"I want you to guide me to Pierre Lemaire's," Cal told him. "I also want you to forget that you did so, just as soon as you do it. Think you can?"

"I'm absolutely shore of it!" the native declared. "Wait tell I git my hat an' gun."

Bobcat returned almost at once, head covered, and bearing his long-barreled rifle.

"We kin go downshore a matter of a quarter, then strike off west along a trail for near about a mile to Pierre's place," Cal was informed. "Course we can drap down in yore boat—"

"We'll walk," Cal decided.

"You realize, don't you, Bobcat, that in asking this service of you I am, in a manner of speaking, taking you into my confidence?" the inspector remarked, as they trudged down the bank.

"Shorely," the native replied, evidently pleased. "I knowed you-all war too dang cagey to be mistook right in th' beginnin', an' think us fellers that lived over in th' Flats done th' damanitin'. Why, we-all bein' th' ones hurt most, wouldn't dast do it. S'picion would naturally p'int to us, an' fur that reason, if fur no other, we-all would be bound to behave. I told the fellers that, an' so we went to see you about it."

"Glad you did," Cal approved. "Now, suppose you tell me anything you may have in mind that might shed light on who really did the work."

Bobcat was silent for a space, then: "Dang it all, Mr. Calhoun!" he exclaimed. "I ain't th' man to git nobody in trouble, an', besides, I ain't rightly got no suspicions about nobody. Still—now, looky here, supposin' you-all owned the only high ground in th' whole L'Anguile country, an' it lay down th' stream on th' west bank.

"Say you-all war tryin' to git a plantation started thar. Along comes th' gove'ment an' builds a levee on th' east bank, reclaimin' a lot of lowlands an' settlin' homestidders on it, an' only jest promises you that later on a levee will be built for your perfection on th' west bank.

"Say th' rise spread over your high ground, stid of into th' Flats lak it used to, an' you found yore plantation—say four hundred acres of it, half cleared—under water. Wouldn't you-all feel kind of like blowin' hell out of th' dang levee an' lettin' th' water go on whar it ought to go?"

"Who owns such a plantation, in these parts?" Cal asked.

"Jasper Wondell. It air eight miles downstream, an' th' levee done ruin it."

"Humph. Jasper Wondell. Never heard of him before. Seems that he has cause for objecting to the levee, for a fact. Still, the reclamation work is bound to be of inestimable benefit to him in the end. Much obliged for the tip, Bobcat. I'll look Mr. Wondell up."

"We turns here," the native directed, a moment later, and struck off along a trail faint in the moonlight.

"Suppose we step lightly, and make as little noise as possible," Cal requested. "I'm paying a sort of stealthy call on Pierre. Won't feel a bit bad if he is not aware of it at all."

Thereafter there was no noise made in the progress into the deep timber. Cal was thoughtful, considering the bit of information vouchsafed him by the native. Jasper Wondell. Who would have a more urgent reason for wishing the levee destroyed than he?

"Wondell's entrance gives a different turn to affairs than I expected," he soliloquized. "Still, Pete could have been working in his interests as well as those of some one else. Damn it, why have I heard no mention of this Wondell person before? Why didn't Marcy, or Hulet, speak of him? Both are bound to know his position regarding the plantation. Yet neither so much as rung him into the thing. Queer, to say the least."

Presently Bobcat began speaking again, in undertones:

"Mr. Inspector, did you you-all hear whut happen' to th' engineer, Marcy, whilst th' levee war bein' built?" he asked.

"Suppose you tell me," Cal requested noncommittally.

"Well, he war in charge of th' whole thing, at fust. Then, all of a sudden, he was took off an' another engineer-man, named Sholes, put over him. I don't rightly know why, but Marcy was shorely down in th' mouth about it afterward. Politics, maybe, caused his takin' off. Leastways, he said as much. I'm not sayin' anything ag'in' Marcy, but them's th' facts."

Cal saw the point instantly—and it showed considerable shrewdness on the native's part. Marcy, disgruntled, might have wished ill to the work of his successor. Hardly a palatable thought, that, but one which nevertheless demanded consideration.

"Thank you again, Bobcat," said Cal. "You are telling me real news—and I won't forget it."

He would not commit himself as to Marcy. The truth was, the engineer had at least a suspicion as to the perpetrator of the levee outrage. The inspector had suspected that from the start. Marcy had acted queerly, and no mistake about it.

For instance, Cal knew very well that since the sudden departure of Pierre Lemaire that afternoon, the engineer had been on needles and pins for an opportunity to slip away to the Frenchman's place. The inspector had known Marcy's objective, the moment he voiced a desire to go out on the bayou. That he had stalled about visiting the guards on the lower end of the levee-break was patent, and therefore Cal had permitted him to depart, then followed at his leisure.

"There are altogether too many likely suspects in this case," was the inspector's thought, as he slipped silently along in Bobcat's wake. "I've got to narrow things down—"

Cal came up against Bobcat's back, the native having stopped suddenly in the trail ahead.

"S-sh-h-h!" came a whispered warning. Cal bent his head in a listening attitude. "Somebody walkin' along th' trail ahead!" whispered the guide.

"I hear 'em," Cal told him. "Slip aside into the brush!"

Both men immediately and silently disappeared.

8

AN IMPORTANT ARREST

THE WALKERS CAME on, and a low rumble of voices soon became distinct conversation.

"I tell you, Nona, Pierre knows all about the thing," Marcy was saying. "His actions show it!"

"He had not'ing to do wiz it!" declared the girl. "Papa is not ze kin' to do such awfulness! And," her voice rose vehemently, "you nevaire should 'ave come an' called me out to-night! M. Calhou' ees no fool—he ees, on ze contraire, ver' wise an' smart. He maybe will know where at you 'ave come, and I already t'ink he suspect papa 'ave a han' in t'ings! No, nevaire you should 'ave come!"

"I'm sorry, Nona, that you don't approve," the engineer told her, as the two came to a halt not more than ten feet from Calhoun. "But my love for you is so great I can't bear the thought of ill befalling your father. I know he did not shoot the levee, but I am equally sure he knows who did. That is why I wanted to urge you—do urge you now—to prevail upon him to tell Calhoun all he knows. That is the only way. Do you think you can get him to do so, dear?"

There was a short silence. Then:

"Ah, M. Marcee, you do dis for me—for Nona—and zat make up for much!" the girl said softly. "But I do not t'ink I can get papa to say zat which he not know about. He knows not'ing, I tell you. No, not wan t'ing!"

"You are wrong, Nona," Marcy contradicted. "Pierre's actions to-day, when Pete came into the clearing, showed great fright. Others besides myself noticed it. Besides, there are other things I could mention that implicate Pierre. I do not think he had a hand in the actual destruction, but I do believe that he knows who did. I am aware that he has been under cover, along with—"

B-o-o-o-m-m-m-!

Startlingly near at hand, a gun shot broke the stillness, echoing and reechoing through the timber walls. Calhoun caught his breath, and laid a restraining hand upon Bobcat's arm. He waited.

"Run, queek!" cried Nona, an instant later. "Somet'ing 'ave go wrong at our cabin! I feel eet—run, queek!"

With a startled exclamation, Marcy ran back along the trail, the girl, with flying feet, crowding close behind.

"Quick!" Cal ordered, darting out of concealment. "Right after them!"

There was a light in the cabin when they reached the door log, and they were just in time to hear a piercing scream from the lips of the girl as she collapsed across the body of a man upon the floor.

It was the body of Pierre Lemaire. He was dead—shot through the heart.

Cal stepped inside, eyes fixed upon the ghastly face of the engineer. After a long, significant look, he bent and lifted the swooning girl, laid her upon a bed, then swiftly examined the corpse.

"Died instantly," was his decision. "Davis, see what you can do to revive Miss Lemaire. Stop!"

The order was directed to Marcy, who suddenly came to himself and started toward the bed upon which the girl was lying.

"I said for Bobcat to minister to the young woman." Cal said evenly. "You've got a lot of explaining to do, Marcy—and until then, you are under arrest!"

"Arrest! Good God, inspector, for what?" cried the engineer, starting back, wide eyes staring in unbelief.

"I'll tell you that later," Cal snapped. "For the present, sit down on that chair against the back wall—and don't move out of it until I say the word!"

Silently Marcy dragged his feet across the floor and sank into the chair indicated, burying his face in his hands.

While Bobcat labored roughly, but effectively, with Nona, Cal left the cabin and searched the ground about it. There were plenty of holes where a killer could have thrust a gun. He could not identify any one as the particular one used. Night time defeated all effort at tracking the assassin, and Cal returned to the cabin.

Nona Lemaire, restored to consciousness, was huddled by Marcy's chair, clasped in his arms. The engineer shot Cal a baleful glance when he came in.

"Surely I am not forbidden to offer what consolation I may to this poor child?" he said coldly.

Cal eyed him with equal coldness. "Don't forget that you are under arrest," he retorted. "And that prisoners are apt to get into trouble when they get impudent. Bobcat," he went on, "I shall want you to go to the Point, notify Ranger Murdock of what has occurred here, and tell him to send down half a dozen men. Let Hulet know. He'll have to prepare Mr. Lemaire for burial. Also"—here he turned his eyes upon Marcy—"you may say that I have made an important arrest—Chet Marcy."

"Oh, for what you arres' heem?" demanded Nona, leaping to her feet and confronting Cal.

"For enticing you out of the cabin, for one thing," Cal told her coolly, "so an assassin might creep up and kill Pierre Lemaire. There are other counts—but I mention only one."

"And I say, onlee little w'ile ago, zat you are wise, and smart!" wailed the girl. "I take all dat back! I now say you wan beeg, dam' fool! M. Marcee love me ver' much—he 'ave say so! How, zen, you theenk he help keel my father?"

Cal merely turned his back.

"Off with you, Bobcat," he ordered.

9

TO GET THEM TO TALK

"IS THERE ANOTHER room where we may talk?" the inspector asked when Bobcat had gone.

Nona arose. "Dere is ze kitchen," she replied, leading the way into a lean-to at the back of the room.

"Shall I take the chair along with me?" Marcy asked sarcastically, getting up also. "Or will another do as well?"

"As you please."

The engineer walked into the kitchen, and Cal followed, closing the door.

"Now," he began, going at once to the point, "it is time for both of you to put your cards on the table. Marcy, you have been holding out on me from the first, and you, Miss Lemaire, have information, whether you consider it as such or not, which you should give me at once.

"I will say, now, that while it is favorable to my purpose for it to be generally known that Marcy has been arrested for complicity in the act committed here tonight, and, furthermore, in connection with the shooting of the levee, I might have found another and not quite so harsh a way of effecting my purpose. You brought it on yourself, Marcy. You deceived me as to your destination to-night—or, rather, you thought you were misleading me. Why?"

"I don't feel like answering your questions," the engineer said haughtily. "You have illy used me—heartlessly so. At a time, too, when any humane man would have held off—"

"A surgeon is sometimes apparently heartless," Calhoun broke in quietly. "He has to be to effect a cure. You laid yourself open to grave suspicion, Marcy. You slipped off down here, pretending that you were going elsewhere, called Miss Lemaire from her home and, while she was gone, her father was killed. That looks very much like complicity. I want to know what you were about to say against Pierre Lemaire when the gunshot sounded. Will you tell?"

Cal waited silently for an answer.

"Tell heem, M. Marcee," Nona urged. "I am not afraid for heem to know."

"I was about to say that Pierre Lemaire has long been a silent partner in the hide buying business with Hulet," the engineer explained. "While pretending to be a trapper, and a poor man, he was, in reality, fairly wealthy—part owner, in fact, of Hulet's store and his other interests.

"That, in itself, is not sufficient grounds to suspect Pierre of underhandedness, since he would have a right to keep his business to himself. But—and here's the rub—why should he be under cover? His interests and Hulet's are identical—do you get the significance of that, inspector?"

Cal nodded. "I do. I have not overlooked Hulet's interests here in the swamp, and now that I know Lemaire's connection, I am not surprised that you looked on him with suspicion. Pierre, however, did not blow up the levee. Neither did Hulet.

"You, I presume, were afraid to let me know how you felt

about Pierre, thinking I would go off half cocked, and make trouble for him. In acting as you have, you laid yourself wide open for suspicion. For instance, there is the matter of your removal as chief of construction before the levee was completed. You might have resented that."

"I did," Marcy acknowledged. "But not to the extent of destroying the dam."

"So much for you," Cal said. "Now, Miss Lemaire, what about the foxfire? You were about to say something while at Mr. Marcy's cabin this afternoon, when your father interrupted. What was that?"

"Oh, eet was not'ing at all!" Nona exclaimed. "Papa, I know not for why, tol' me nevaire to mention ze foxfire dat I see on ze log. I forgot, and he remember me. Dat ees all."

"When did you see the foxfire on the log?" Cal asked.

"We come up ze bayou dat night before ze levee she blow all up. Dere comes wan beeg log float down against ze levee. W'en she pass me, I see foxfire glow on heem end— lak beeg alligator wiz lantern on hees tail. I mention so to papa; he look and see, zen he say: 'Keep doze eye on bayou. Nevaire min' log wiz foxfire.' Dat, *m'sieu*, ees all."

Cal was gazing directly into the big black eyes of the girl. On his face was an expression of intent interest. Marcy also watched Nona. Evidently he had heard nothing of the log.

"I am sure that is not all," Cal said after a moment. "Had it been, your father would not have objected to your telling of it. Think, please. How long was it after you saw the log that you heard the explosion?"

The girl's face grew thoughtful. "Maybe half, t'ree-quarter hour," she said finally. "Jus' before we see ze lights at M. Hulet's Point. I am talk to papa when, *boom!* Jus' lak dat:

B-o-om-m-m! Ever't'ing go tumbling. Water, she jump up, zen she fall and swing from side to side: Ze bateau, she almos' sink. I ver' much scared. Papa, he hurry for landin'.'"

"Still there is nothing about your seeing the log with foxfire on it which could possibly account for your father's avoidance of the subject. Did he tell you, after the explosion, not to say anything about the log?"

"He say: 'Shut up, chatterbox! You see not'ing! You know not'ing! Min' dat—you nevaire see not'ing!' Dat, *m'sieu,* ees all."

Cal consumed a full minute in thought. "Tell me, Miss Lemaire, how did the foxfire look? Describe it to me."

"Well—she look lak some blue fire. She dance lil bit, zen she sparkle—"

"Ah—it sparkled!" Cal interrupted, his tones denoting sudden enlightenment. "You are sure it sparkled?"

"Oh, *m'sieu,* yes! It sparkled!"

Cal gave Marcy a significant glance, and the engineer nodded uderstandingly. "I see your drift, inspector. I ought to have known that your action to-night, harsh though it was, had a deep purpose underlying it."

"Yes. I had to make you talk, and I had to make Miss Lemaire talk. The best reason of all, though, is this Bobcat has borne the news of your arrest to the Point. That, after all, is what I desired most. Kindly continue to act like a prisoner," he went on, a glint of humor in his eyes. "Draw on your imagination. Believe me, it may help."

Nona Lemaire's excitement over her lover's treatment at Cal's hands had absorbed her to the extent of giving her something else to think of besides the death of Pierre. Suddenly the awful fact thrust itself anew into her consciousness, and Cal departed from the cabin, leaving Marcy to do what a lover could to assuage her grief.

"It 'sparkled,' huh?" Cal queried himself, sitting on a log beside the path over which Murdock's men would come. "The foxfire sparkled? Well, I'll be damned! So simple as that!"

10

WHO LOSES THOUSANDS?

RANGER MURDOCK ARRIVED in haste an hour later, finding Cal still sitting on the log outside the cabin, smoking his pipe. He reported, and Cal, nodding with satisfaction, got up and entered the house.

Nona had succeeded in subduing her grief, and when the inspector told her that it would be necessary to make a careful search of Pierre's effects, she nodded permission and returned to the kitchen, followed by Marcy.

Murdock and Calhoun began a systematic investigation of the room in which the dead trapper lay.

"I'll go through this cupboard where Pierre seems to have kept his business papers, letters and other documents. You can search the kitchen and the loft, Murdock," said Cal, after the rest of the room had been gone over, and nothing important found. Murdock went into the kitchen, and the inspector sat down before a shallow wall cupboard, containing many pigeonholes, and began taking out the contents.

Letter after letter was read. They were business communications, mostly, and were in Hulet's handwriting, signed by him. They established Pierre's business connection with the merchant beyond question. Cal summoned Marcy into the room.

"When, and how, did you learn that Pierre was a partner of Hulet's?" he asked.

"When I asked Mr. Lemaire, two weeks ago, for permission to pay attention to his daughter," was the reply. "He told me then that Nona would receive a substantial dowry from him, and that she would come into considerable property at his death. I was greatly surprised, and asked why he had kept his financial condition a secret."

"Did he explain?"

"Yes. He said he believed he could live on better terms with his neighbors if they thought him only a poor man like themselves. He loved the wilderness, liked his occupation of trapping, and preferred to live simply. A better reason, which he did not touch upon, but which I believe to have been at the bottom of his reticence concerning his wealth, is the fact that he feared robbery, should it be thought he possessed money. Pierre was not a very brave man—and this country is about as lawless as one could find."

Cal nodded. "That last reason is probably the real one," he agreed, "Do you read French?"

"No. Nona, however, is able to do so fairly well, although Pierre always spoke in the English tongue, even with her, and took little or no pains to instruct her in French. Shall I call her?"

An interruption came from outside. The party from Hulet's Point had arrived. Bobcat Davis, Mooneye Briggs, several other natives, including two sympathetic women, came into the room. They were followed by half a dozen rangers.

"I couldn't raise Hulet, Mr. Calhoun," Bobcat reported. "He wasn't in the store, or in his room. So I left word for him with one of your men."

"Very good, Bobcat. You were speedy. I am going to leave some of my men here to bring the corpse of Pierre Lemaire to the Point," he went on, addressing them all. "I hope the ladies who just came will remain and assist. As for the rest, including Bobcat, Marcy, and Miss Lemaire, you will all go to the Point with me. Come, Murdock."

Cal left the room and waited on the trail until the rest of the party were in readiness.

"What's afoot, inspector?" Marcy asked when he came out.

Cal's face wore a grim look, and he gave an evasive answer. All set out for the Point. Arriving there, Cal called Nona into Marcy's cabin, alone, and when he returned to those who waited outside, his face was a cold, hard mask.

Murdock hastened to his side, coming from the direction of Hulet's store, and spoke in an undertone.

"All right, folks," Cal told them, "come with me."

He led the way directly to Hulet's, and pounded on the front door. It swung open, disclosing Ranger Shane, who stood aside while Cal and his party filed in.

The light of a swinging lamp in the rear of the big room revealed two rangers, one on either side of a third man, all of them sitting.

The third man was Nathan Hulet.

"Find seats, all of you," Cal bade them. "I'm going to reconstruct this case for you—beginning some time before the destruction of the levee, and bringing it up to date. Only by doing so, showing each step, both of the criminal involved and of myself and my men, can the thing be made clear."

There was deep silence, attention centering upon Hulet. The latter sat with closed eyes, paying no attention to any one. He lounged comfortably on his chair, as though nothing out of the ordinary was taking place.

"Hulet," said Cal, when all were seated, "the law has limped along rather speedily, this time, perhaps you will admit. No? Well, it doesn't matter. The fact remains that it has done so.

"This man," he continued, addressing the awed crowd, "is under arrest for the murder of Injun Pete, Pierre Lemaire, Patrolman McArthur—and for instigating the destruction of the levee.

"Hulet came to this part of the wilderness for the purpose of making a fortune in buying and reselling furs. For years he has had the trade of the district, with no competition worthy of the name. His profits amounted to many thousands of dollars yearly—ten' or twelve, at a conservative estimate. He had, gentlemen, a business with great future possibilities. Then, all of a sudden, he found that business in a fair way to cease altogether.

"I remarked when I arrived at the Point the seeming joy of all who dwelt hereabouts in the destruction of the levee. The source of that attitude was not far to seek.

"It is this: Bobcat Davis makes probably five hundred dollars a year out of the hides he traps. He would be sorry to lose that money. The coming of the settlers to Hickory Flats meant that others would soon come, other districts would be reclaimed and put to agricultural purposes—and agriculture is the arch enemy of wild animal life. When the levee went out, Bobcat rejoiced. Civilization had received a serious set-back—maybe would not attain damaging proportions for many years to come. Bobcat liked that.

"Now, as Bobcat felt, so did all the other trappers in the district feel. They saw that the wrecking of the levee was a protection for their individual four or five hundred a year. Yes, they were happy.

"I was able to get the viewpoint of the individual native, who desired to cling to his meager profits from the hides he trapped, and by looking farther—back of the native—I found my eyes upon one who, had the natives' attitude toward the advance of civilization, only multiplied several thousandfold.

"Hulet stood to lose thousands, where the individual native lost only hundreds. Hulet was the one man who would profit greatly by the destruction of the levee.

"The fact that he would so profit did not mean that one bit of guilt attached to him. It merely furnished a likely suspect—a man to be watched. He was watched, folks— so well watched that his fall was inevitable. Here is how it all happened."

11

LINKS IN THE CHAIN

THE INSPECTOR PAUSED for a moment, evidently marshaling his thoughts in proper sequence. Then he resumed: "When the levee reached a state of completion—or at some time before or shortly after, which is unimportant—Nathan Hulet proposed a plan to his partner, Pierre Lemaire, whereby the embankment could be destroyed, with little or no danger to the perpetrators of the deed. To Hulet's surprise, Pierre objected strongly; he would have none of it.

"Hulet dismissed the subject, in so far as his partner was concerned, and began laying plans on his own. He sought for and found a tool to do his will. That tool was Injun Pete, shiftless drunkard, who could be bought with cheap whisky.

"Hulet chose a time when the bayou was on the rise. He knew that his work could best be done at that time. Two weeks ago, one week before the shooting of the levee, Pete, the tool, left this district and remained away, so far as was known, until last night—night before last it now is, since it is nearly one o'clock in the morning. Pete's absence was calculated to prevent suspicion attaching to him.

"But Pete did not stay away all that time. On the night

the embankment was destroyed he returned. He was across the bayou at a point below this place. What was he doing there?

"First, he loaded a hollow log with dynamite—a log previously selected by him. The dynamite was supplied by Hulet. He rolled it into the bayou. The fuse intended to discharge the explosive was attached to the top of the log, having been timed to do its work perhaps an hour later.

"Having placed the log in the bayou—where it would stay close to the levee, since the spreading water would hold it there and allow it to drift slowly down—Pete lit the fuse. He probably used a lighted cigar, since the wind was high and a match could not have lived. After that he sped up the levee, thence back into hiding.

"Nona Lemaire and her father were on the bayou almost opposite the point where Pete rolled the log in. Nona thought the light on the log was foxfire—but Pierre knew differently. Foxfire does not sparkle. The light Pierre saw did. It was the spluttering of the fuse as it burned down and into its waterproof casing. Pierre knew what that log held—what, in fine, was afoot. He cautioned Nona to say nothing about having seen it, and hastened to the Point.

"The levee was blown before they reached here.

"What passed between Pierre and Hulet during the days immediately following is something that will never be known, unless Hulet tells. It is easy to imagine, however, that Pierre was greatly incensed; may even have threatened exposure. He made no such exposure, however.

"Night before last, Charlie Redoak came to the store after a jug of whisky for Injun Pete, and Hulet learned that his tool had returned. That return was a bad move on Pete's part.

"Hulet probably planned the half-breed's death at the time he bought him for the job of destruction. At any rate, Pete was shot and left for dead on the night of his return. He recovered sufficiently to reach the Point, but died before he could name the one whom he believed fired the shot.

"Immediately after Pete's death I searched his cabin, finding, in a cubby-hole attached to the floor on the underside, three sticks of dynamite, some detonators, and a coil of fuse. Now dynamite is not easily come by in this part of the country. Hulet has a permit to sell it—the only one who has.

"The settlers in the Flats use a good deal of it in blowing up stumps, trees, and breaking up drifts in creeks. Hulet sold a deal of it to them. Pete, of course, might have bought the dynamite outside the district, else have stolen it. I thought not, however. I was, in fact, fairly certain of the source of the dynamite.

"Why, you may ask, did Pete keep some of the explosive, instead of using it all in the log? Dynamite is useful in killing fish—and fish are worth money in the settlements. Pete probably figured that he would not need all the stuff just to cause a breach in the levee so the water could get through and destroy it.

"He held out some. That, at least, seems probable. I discovered the dynamite, but did not remove it. Instead, I replaced the flooring above the cache—replaced it clumsily, so that any one who searched after me would be bound to notice the place. Some one did search it. Hulet did."

For the first time since the party came into the store Hulet's eyes opened. He sat up a bit straighter, gave Cal a long glance in which a slight trace of uneasiness was perceptible, then the lids came down again, and the storekeeper slouched in his chair as before.

"Ranger Shane will tell you about that—he and Murdock," Cal informed them, and Shane spoke:

"Instructed earlier in the afternoon to watch Hulet, I saw him leave his store after dark last night. He made his way to the back of Marcy's cabin, stopped there in the darkness and listened. I signaled, in a manner understood by my chief, what was happening. Presently Hulet left the cabin and struck off north through the timber. Murdock picked him up then."

Shane ceased speaking, and Murdock took up the recital.

"I followed Hulet to Pete's cabin, saw him search it, then followed him back to the store. Shane watched at the front, and I took up a position where the back door was under my eyes. Hulet lit a lamp and apparently settled down for the night."

"Now," Cal resumed, "when Ranger Shane signaled that a listener was outside, I remarked loudly to Marcy that I thought it likely Pete left something incriminating behind him, pointing to the author of his destruction, and that I meant to make a thorough search of the cabin the following day.

"Hulet, hearing me say that, set off at once for Pete's place. Pete might have scribbled something on a bit of paper, after being shot, naming his killer. Other evidence, too, might be there. Hulet could not afford to chance what that cabin might hold. He had rid himself of his tool—

but the tool might yet arise as his accuser. He searched the cabin, saw the loose boards which I had relaid so clumsily, and unearthed the dynamite.

"That gave him a start. Should it be known that Pete possessed the explosive, Hulet might be brought into the investigation, since he alone could legally sell the stuff hereabouts. So Hulet recovered the three sticks, fuse, and detonators, went back to his store and returned them to the case from which they were originally taken.

"Why not? He had dynamite in stock, and those three sticks would cause no comment. His store was the safest place for them. Bring out that case, Shane."

The ranger brought forward a case in which perhaps a dozen sticks of the explosive lay. Cal looked them over, withdrew three sticks and placed them on the counter under the light.

"The store would have been a safe place for them—only for this: I marked the sticks found in Pete's cabin. Here they are. Hulet thought no one had seen them. He slipped there."

The storekeeper shifted in his chair, eyes hatefully on Calhoun. He moistened his lips with his tongue, and spoke.

"All you say is interesting, inspector," he remarked with a credible nonchalance. "It sounds very much like a story in a yellowback. I'll have my say later—when you are through romancing."

"Quite right, Hulet. As you say, you will have your innings. But to get back.

"Already there is sufficient evidence against Hulet to hold him prisoner. There is, however, more to come. Hulet was not through with his fiendish work yet. He had only seemingly settled down in his room. The country had suddenly become flooded with rangers, bent on probing the levee case. Pierre Lemaire, none too courageous, might weaken.

"Hulet figured he probably would, and that what he had to say would turn suspicion his way. He decided to kill Pierre. I will go further and say that he probably meant to kill another—Nona Lemaire. By a fortunate circumstance, the daughter was not in the cabin when the killer arrived, and he could not wait for her return, since he knew instantly that his shot, fired at Pierre, had attracted attention and that several persons were racing toward the cabin.

"Hulet ran away and hid in the forest. Murdock will tell you what Hulet did, after seeming to settle down for the night. How he and Shane lost him—just long enough to enable him to slay Lemaire."

"We, Ranger Shane and myself, watched the front and back of the store, with our eyes on the windows on the sides as well, after Hulet returned from Pete's cabin," Murdock stated. "The hours passed; the light in the back room continued to burn behind drawn shades.

"Finally Bobcat Davis came up with news of what had happened at Lemaire's. He attempted to rouse Hulet, but could get no response. Shane and I entered the store, searched, and found no sign of the storekeeper. He had, in spite of our watchfulness, got out of the building. After a bit we found the means he used."

Murdock walked to a spot near where Hulet sat, and raised a trapdoor in the floor.

"He had but to drop through this trap and slip into the brush which grows close to the wall of the building on the south side. He did so. Shane set out immediately to notify Inspector Calhoun of what had happened, and I waited inside the store for Hulet's return.

"He came shortly before the return of the party from Lemaire's—and I took him in charge when he climbed through the trap."

Murdock drew a revolver of large caliber from his hip pocket and placed it on the counter.

"Hulet's," he said succinctly. "One shell discharged. He did not have time to clean it."

12

THE FRENCHMAN'S DAUGHTER

THERE WAS SILENCE in the room—then an angry rumble from the two natives of the group. Cal turned to them rebukingly.

"Hear the rest, men—and remember that there will be no violence. Hulet killed Pierre to make sure he would not one day accuse him. But he killed him too late. Pierre did accuse him. I am going to offer proof."

Cal drew a folded paper out of his pocket and beckoned to Nona. The girl came to his side, and received the paper from him.

Hulet, eyes staring, sat forward now, a look of wonderment on his face.

"It is a letter," Cal said, indicating the paper Nona held. "Pierre suspected that Hulet might do him in, and wrote down certain things, in French, in a letter addressed to his daughter. She will read it to you."

The girl choked, brushed the tears from her eyes, then read in a low, but distinct voice:

"Dear Daughter:

"I am uneasy concerning the future. Nathan Hulet made known certain plans to me relative to destroying the levee.

That was several months ago, and I refused to have anything to do with it. Now the levee has been wrecked, and by the method Hulet mentioned. I am certain he had it done.

"So long as I live I shall see to it that no innocent person suffers for the crime. The future, however, is uncertain. Should I be killed mysteriously, you will hand this letter to the inspector of the rangers. Should I die a natural death, and some one other than Hulet is arrested for the crime, you will make this letter known.

"What you thought to be foxfire, that night, was in reality the sputtering of the fuse which exploded a dynamite log against the levee. That was the method Hulet proposed that we use. Do not fail to follow my instructions, if the need arises.

"Your father,

"Pierre Lemaire."

Profound silence prevailed after the reading of the letter. Hulet seemed to have lost interest in the proceedings again. He slumped in his chair, eyes closed and face expressionless.

"That letter," Cal said, breaking the silence, "was not needed to fasten the guilt upon Hulet. His arrest had occurred before Miss Lemaine made me acquainted with the contents. It is, however, a final link in the chain—a chain which I believe is now complete."

He addressed Hulet.

"What have you to say?" he asked. "You have informed us that you would have your say later. You may have it now."

For a moment it seemed that the storekeeper had not

heard, then he straightened up, fixed his glance upon Cal, and spoke.

"What have I to say? I have much—but it will not be said here. You are a very clever man, inspector—but not so clever as others!"

With astonishing agility Hulet leaped to his feet, swung his left fist to Shane's jaw, the ranger being in a chair beside him, and toppled him backward. His right hand shot beneath his vest and came into view clutching a derringer. At that moment he had gained the edge of the trap, evidently intending to leap down and run for it. He swung his derringer upon the inspector, a fiendish, jeering laugh upon his lips.

Cal's gun crackled spitefully. Hulet's form tensed, his eyes opened to their widest, and into them came a look of astonishment, hatred, defeat.

A MOMENT LATER he swayed upon the rim of the trap, then plunged through it to the ground below.

Nona Lemaire shrieked and sought refuge in Marcy's arms.

Murdock leaped through the trap on the instant. After a brief stop below he reappeared, raising himself to the floor.

"Hulet is dead," he announced simply.

A month later Calhoun sought Marcy in his cabin, where he and his bride had gone to live until matters in regard to Pierre's estate could be untangled and settled. In his hand the inspector carried a long, white envelope.

"Marcy," he said, after greetings were over, "I owe you something for putting you through that night when Pierre was killed. As it turned out, I need not have done it. I didn't expect things to break quite so quickly. I am going to pay my debt. Here."

Marcy opened the envelope. It contained his appointment as chief of construction in the rebuilding of the levee.

"Don't thank me," Cal remonstrated, when Marcy attempted to express his gratitude. "Thank my chief, Hub Wheeler. It was his influence that got it, not mine."

"Ah, M'sieu' Calhou'!" Nona cried, running to his side. "I say, firs' tarn I saw you, dat you ver' wise an' ver' smart! I say so now—an'," she flashed merry eyes toward her husband, "an' add dees to eet!" And she gave the inspector a tight hug—along with a kiss full upon his lips.

www.ingramcontent.com/pod-product-compliance
Lightning Source LLC
Chambersburg PA
CBHW031201020726
47499CB00002B/447